The Harbour Series

Book 1

Kat —
Enjoy Alex & Ella's
steamy love story :)
Happy Reading
XO Christy Pastore
8/5/17

Christy Pastore

Disclaimer. This is a work of fiction. Names, characters, places, brands, media, and incidents are either a product of the author's imagination or are used fictitiously; any resemblance to actual persons living or dead, business establishments, events or locations is entirely coincidental.

The author acknowledges the trademarked status and trademark owners of various products referenced in this work of fiction. Any trademarks, service marks, product names or named features are assumed to be the property of their respective owners, and are used only for reference. There is no implied endorsement.

*Warning:* Please note this novel contains explicit sexual content and crude language and is intended for mature audiences. Parental/reader discretion is advised.


First Edition, 2017



Cover photographed and designed by Sara Eirew of Sara Eirew Photography
www.saraeirew.com/
Editing provided by Missy Borucki
www.missyborucki.com
Proofreading provided by Robin Bateman of Robin's Red Pen
www.robinsredpen.com
Book formatting provided by Stacey Blake of Champagne Formats
www./champagneformats.com

Publication Date: January 24th, 2017
ISBN: 978-0-9907099-7-8
Bound to Me (The Harbour Series, #1)

We set the rules. . .

Well, I set the rules. . . he agreed.

I left before we could break them, or so I thought I had. . .

Ella Connolly is looking forward to starting a new adventure in her life. After putting her party girl, headline-grabbing tabloid exploits behind her, she has become a responsible and successful entrepreneur. Moving across the pond to Manhattan, she's determined to make the dream for her boutique to become an international retail brand come true.

While in the States, her overprotective brother insists she have a full-time security detail. This complicates Ella's plans in more ways than one.

Alex Robertsen's life is in shambles. After losing the woman he loves to his brother, he's been on a steady diet of booze and easy women in an effort to make himself numb. Things needed to change.

Change is good.

Good, that is, until Alex finds himself thrust into an all too familiar situation.

He's obligated by a professional oath to protect Ella at all costs.

She's vowed to not let distractions, even the ruggedly handsome ones, keep her from her goals.

But old habits die hard. . .

We'd broken the rules. . . more than once.

We were bound to. . . and we agreed it was worth the risk.

He left before it shattered us both. . . or so we thought.

# Dedication

For my girl, Jennifer Smith Vaughn, a long time ago you asked me a very important question.
The answer was yes, I did have the courage to leave the shore.
Thank you for the push and encouragement to try new adventures.

“Be brave and fearless. Know that even if you do make a wrong decision, you’re making it for a good reason.”

—Adele

# Prologue

## Alex

*Year—Classified*
*Location—Also Classified*
*Final Mission for Elite Eight—Covert American Intelligence and Counter-Terrorism Unit.*
*Commanding Officer, Lieutenant Alex Robertsen.*

Blood was everywhere and I felt it seeping into my mouth as I lay face down on the cold concrete floor. Two feet from me, a man lay with his throat slashed and two holes to the chest. No doubt that was Rebecca's handy work. Fucker probably mouthed off about her female assets.

*"Horton, get back, get back!"*

My ears registered the sound of Sully's voice echoing through the gunfire.

*"Coming up on your six, Sully! Watch out!"*

Shots continued to strike out from automatic assault rifles, by my count two people were shooting while the others reloaded their guns. Good, thank fucking God. Seems as if we're all alive.

*"Rebecca, cover us back there!"*

I rolled onto my side, pulled my bandana from my pocket and wiped the blood from my face. The hairs on my arms stood straight up at the sound of a hailstorm of pops and flashes. Vibrations from the explosion rang in my ears like metal dragging across glass. Lifting my head, my eyes flicked to the ceiling and to the walls, faint light poured in through the west wall window. Dust and debris clouded my vision, but I could see the outline of three figures at various points along the wall of the warehouse. Sully, Horton and Rebecca all accounted for. Where was Sasha?

*"Zero, this is Delta team, do you read me?"* The message rang loud and clear through my earpiece.

Aside from twinges of pain in my arm and chest, I felt fine, probably just a cracked rib or two. I'd been shot before, but there was no physical sign of trauma. I eased up and there it was, a burning ache. I felt my shoulder and sure enough my shirt was soaked with blood. *Shit!* I had been cut, but definitely *not* shot. I don't know how I did it, but I managed to use my bandana as a makeshift compress.

Still no answer from Zero. Rebecca, Elite Eight's Chief Communication Officer and field operative, tried three more attempts to get command on the line. Through squinted eyes, I identified three large barrels in front of me and to my left. Aware of the bullets whizzing above, I managed to stay low and crouch behind them.

Seconds later, glass popped and shattered. The explosion rocked me back about four feet, slamming me into an iron bar. Bits of debris rained down from the ceiling, and I narrowly escaped getting knocked the fuck out by a goddamn two by four. I shook it off, and then pulled my handgun from my vest. Plaster fell, giving way to live wires sparking each time they hit the ground. Black smoke billowed outside, dancing with a raging fireball. *Fucking terrorist scumbags.*

"Everybody okay?" Horton called out.

I took this as my opportunity to let them know I was alive. "Robo here," I shouted back. My eyes fully focused once more, allowed me to survey our surroundings.

"Nice to see you're awake, Sleeping Beauty! We missed you."

"Fuck you, Sully! I'm touched by your concern. You good?"

"Yeah, just another day in paradise," he yelled, before firing off four rounds. "Whoo! Take that mother-fuckers!"

I craned my neck, and in the dusty light not more than five feet away lay Sasha Bloom, Elite Eight's Intelligence Analyst. Without concern for my own life or the pain in my chest, I ran to her. Dark liquid oozed across the floor in a stream, and that is when I saw the jagged metal lodged in her leg. My heart crumbled, under a hammer of pain. I knew this wasn't good. I ripped the bottom of her right pant leg and made a tourniquet and used the remaining cloth to apply pressure to the wound.

Kneeling beside her, I grabbed her hand. "Sasha, hey, baby. Can you hear me?"

"Alex," she whispered weakly. "One leg hurts and the other is now cold."

I chuckled. "Sorry about that, but I needed it." I pointed to my injury to keep her mind off her own pain.

"It's okay, but I thought tough guys like you didn't get hurt?"

"Oh that's just a scratch, baby," I joked, and got a clearer look at her wound. It was gushing blood, the metal sliced right through her femoral artery.

*Fuck!* If we didn't get out of here soon, she would die on the floor in this dirty warehouse. And I couldn't allow that to happen. I loved her too much. Plus, we had plans after this mission, a date on the rooftop bar at the The Hilton Molino Stucky. Her choice. She called Venice the most romantic place in the world. The view of the lagoon from the terrace was something Sasha loved, and she had told me all about it on more than one occasion.

"Rebecca," I yelled, over my shoulder. "Get command on the line! Tell them Bloom is hurt and we need an extraction plan, now!"

*"Fire, fire, fire."*

The window above us shattered. Instinctively, I covered Sasha's body with my own. I wouldn't let it end this way.

Not here.

Not now.

Not ever.

"It's okay." Her breathing was shallow, and she swallowed a few times before speaking again. "I love you." Her head lolled from side to side, as her eyes rolled back in her head.

I cupped her face in my hands. "Look at me, Sasha. Stay with me," I begged. My throat was dry and tight. "You're going to be fine. I'm going to get you out of here."

"It's okay, Alex." Her words came out soft and comforting. As if I was the mortally injured one and hanging on for my life. Her pulse was weak, and I knew the blood coming from her nose was a sign of internal bleeding. I was losing her. *Fuck!*

"Baby, please don't leave me," I pleaded, aware of the desperation in my voice. "Trust me. I'll get us out of here."

An explosion rocked the building sending more glass and metal down from the ceiling. I held Sasha in my arms, protecting us both from the flying debris. I don't know how long we stayed like that, but I heard machine gun fire followed by another explosion. Through the haze of smoky fog, the chopper came into view.

"Babe, the cavalry's here," I said relieved, looking down at Sasha. Her eyes were glassy, wet from tears that never came. "Sasha, no . . . *no*," I whispered, pulling her closer and burying my face in her hair.

Numbness settled around me. I'd failed her and it was my fault that she was dead.

# Chapter One

## Alex

*Eight Years Later*

*What in the hell was I doing?* Sitting at a bar downing my fourth scotch and soda was certainly not what I *should* be doing. I should have stayed on that beach, by myself. This place was infiltrated by one Millennial too many for my taste. Listening to the girl next to me jump from talking about politics in Greece to animal testing in the cosmetics industry then segueing into a debate about whether or not her flat iron was causing global warming was making my ears bleed. I'm pretty sure I just bumped into "the girl you wished you never started a conversation with at a party" from those *Saturday Night Live* skits.

Part of me wanted to join in the conversation and poke holes in all her insane theories, the other part of me wanted to take her to the bathroom and shove my dick in her mouth to shut her up. Or maybe shove her panties in her mouth, while I fucked the silly out of her.

After tossing back the last drop of my drink, I stared down at the picture on my phone of my brother, his girlfriend, and their new baby girl, Leandra Evelynn Parsons Everett. One big beautiful family and at one point I thought it would be mine. I didn't need another goddamn reason to have this date permanently etched in my brain. Now I had two: the anniversary of a death and now the anniversary of a birth. Both tied to my own life with significant meaning. Reminders of what I once had, and lost. Of course, I was thrilled for Vince and Amanda on the birth of their baby, but that baby could have been mine.

*Fuck it, I need another drink.*

Fucking and drinking the pain away, this was what my life had become over the last few months. The ache never went away, not completely anyway. It wasn't the booze I needed, no it was the dulling sensation the alcohol provided. Numbness was like a long lost friend, and I welcomed it with open arms. Tapping my empty glass, the bartender poured me another and then slid it in front of me.

I'd been down this road before. Things weren't all bad, *this* time around.

On the upside, I was getting laid on a regular basis. I did enjoy the blowjob from the coat check girl at the restaurant last night. If she fucked as well as she sucked dick, I should take it upon myself to find her.

No matter how many women warmed my bed, or the number of scotches or beers I consumed nightly, I still hurt the following morning. A combination of guilt and remorse, but mostly the physical effects from the alcohol and the havoc it wreaked on my body. I needed a better evening activity, one that didn't make me feel like I'd been hit by a tank.

Silly girl gave me a small smile eyeing me up and down, as I stood leaning on the bar. For a split second I entertained the idea of taking her back to my hotel suite, but then she turned to her friend and opened her mouth again and that was enough to send me, my dick and my ears on our merry way. I tossed back my drink, and signaled for the bill.

As I slapped my second fifty of the night on the bar, the bartender said he'd bring my change.

"Keep it," I called after him.

"Thanks, man," he tossed over his shoulder. "Come back anytime."

Nodding, I dropped my money clip back into my jacket pocket and headed for the door. The bouncer asked if I needed a cab, I told him my hotel was just a few blocks away.

"Have a nice evening," he said after taking a long drag off his cigarette.

A friendly bartender, a considerate bouncer—this was definitely not your mother's Manhattan. Where were all the *"Hey, I'm walking here"* New Yorkers? Four days in the city and I had yet to be accosted by a man selling fake Rolex watches or even cursed at by an overworked cab driver. Pissed off or friendly, either way I'd take Manhattan any day.

As I walked more briskly, trying to keep in pace with other pedestrians, the scent of burning rubber and various spices from food carts whipped around me. Nothing smelled this bad, not even in Detroit, okay maybe Detroit, but definitely not Grand Rapids.

"There *you* are! I've been looking for you all night."

I craned my neck to find myself coming face to face with a model-esque, leggy blonde. When I say leggy, I mean she was all legs because her dress was a good eight inches from the top of her knees and she stood at least five-foot-ten. And because I was a red-blooded man, I thought about how much I'd love having those killer stems tangled around my body. Damn, she was insanely beautiful and her light flowery scent curled around me masking the unpleasantness that hung in the night air. Her golden blonde hair, that looked like perfectly spun silk, hung down to her waist. Then my eyes moved to her lips—cherry red. The kind of red that suggested she was a little bit of a badass underneath that girly pink dress, and probably wouldn't mind getting her lipstick smeared. Or maybe that was my wishful thinking.

She tugged on my jacket, and whispered, "Play along, okay?" Her eyes shifted left and I followed her gaze. That is when I saw a guy who looked like he might be sick any moment leaning against a heavy green wooden door.

"Is your friend okay?"

"He is *not* my friend."

"He looks like a zombie."

"Will you help me put him in a cab?"

I studied her, fixated on that sexy pout, and those long lashes fluttering innocently around her penetrating blue eyes. She flashed a smile at me and I knew I was a goner.

"I've been missing you all night too, *baby*." I wrapped my arm around her shoulders and pulled her close as we walked towards the guy that was *not* her friend.

"Thank you," she whispered.

After we put zombie boy in a cab, my new blonde friend pulled me into the bar next door.

"I require a very large drink after that horrible experience."

"Well, if I'm going to buy you a drink I need to know why?"

She laughed shaking her head. "I met him a few days ago,

and he seemed incredibly nice, but it was a terrible date. He came back from the bathroom with white powder under his nose, and then downed two gin and tonics in less than twenty minutes. When he fell out of his chair, I knew it was time to go."

"Sorry to hear that. The drugs and booze must have had some effect on him. What's *your* poison?" I asked dodging through the crowd like Frogger trying to find an unoccupied space at the bar.

"Thanks. I'll text him later to make sure he arrived home safely. Vodka and soda, but I need to check the brands first. I need to make sure they have the ones I prefer."

I rolled my eyes. Here we go, just what I needed another high-maintenance girl. *Just my fucking luck.*

She laughed. "I saw that. It's not what you think. I am not being pretentious; I have issues with gluten. No wheat for me."

"Oh." My shoulders tensed. "Sorry."

I shouldn't have been so quick to judge, recognizing my own standards. This place didn't exactly have any of my preferred scotch brands. It was certainly a far cry from the comforts of the Skyline Club.

Pointing to the bottle of Ciroc, she shrugged. "It's not too awful, just annoying at times."

I gave her a smile and motioned to the bartender, "Scotch and soda for me, and for the lady, Ciroc vodka and soda, with a twist of lime. She has a gluten allergy. I suggest that you take the proper precautions."

"You're quite assertive."

I shrugged. "Comes with the job."

"Oh," she said casually. My eyes traveled up her legs once again, as I waited for her to ask the question, but it never came.

"Aren't you going to ask me about my job?" I replied

handing her the glass that I hoped contained the correct vodka. I didn't want her to be sick.

She moved through the crowded bar with ease, yelling over her shoulder, "No, I don't even want to know your name."

Perplexed by her answer, I felt the need to inquire further. "And why not?"

We found a table that was mildly clean, just a few water rings and a dirty glass. Being a gentleman, I pulled out a chair for her and took the seat to her left.

Taking a sip of her drink, she replied, "I don't want to be myself tonight. Haven't you ever wanted to be someone else, even if it's just for an evening?"

*This girl.* Who was she? The fact that she wanted to hide her real identity from me gave me a fucking hard-on. Like some perverted weirdo, I was oddly fascinated by the opportunity of role-playing. The red straw passed between those luscious lips, and I wondered if she liked games or if she was really hiding something. *Shit.* I could be sitting next to a serial killer. This pretty young thing could have poisoned zombie boy and I just helped get rid of the body.

Serial killer theory aside, I understood what she was talking about. Today of all days, I wanted to be someone else. The memory of Sasha's death weighed heavily on my mind. More recently, my affair with Amanda had left my life in complete disarray. When she decided to make a life with Vince, and I found out the baby girl she was carrying wasn't mine, I started to unravel. My business was crumbling as quickly as my relationship with my brother. Unable to concentrate on my clients and their cases, I had to get away from the toxicity infiltrating my life so I could refocus and move forward. Coming to New York was the fresh start I needed. At the moment, escaping reality sounded pretty fucking great.

"I guess I can entertain the idea. If that's how you want to play it tonight." I smirked, before taking a drink.

"That is exactly how I want to play it. Tonight we reveal no real names, jobs, or anything remotely close to our genuine existence."

I nodded and my new blonde friend held up her drink offering a toast to our momentary departure from reality. The words sounded like something you'd say before getting black out drunk or dropping acid. *Bottoms up.*

"Tell me how you see this scenario playing out?" she asked, licking a bit of lime juice off her finger.

What I wanted to say was, *"If my chances are good I'll have you back in my hotel suite with those legs coiled around me, driving you to your third or fourth orgasm."* Instead I offered, "With any luck, I see the two of us having fun getting good and drunk."

With a wink, she replied, "The moment I saw you, I knew you were a good time guy."

Three drinks and two shots later, the bar was nearly empty and all I'd learned about her, is that her name is *not* Kate, she is *not* a member of the British Royal family, and she did *not* go to college for Art History. What I have learned about her true identity, is that she's allergic to gluten, loved her tequila, she had an infectious laugh and as much as she tried to hide it, the more drinks she consumed, the more pronounced her English accent became. Her words were smooth and soft, like being covered by a warm blanket.

"Threat and risqué . . . access . . . *assessments*." Her words came out a little broken, slurring slightly at the end. "Have you assessed tonight's threats, *not* William?"

We opted that my fake name be William for the evening. She thought it would be "terribly hilarious" to see how people reacted when we introduced ourselves as Will and Kate. Little did she know that William was my middle name.

Smirking, I replied, "Risk Assessment. Yes, and I've observed that you are much in need of a bottle of water."

Leaning over her glass, her eyes twinkled. "Can you ask them if they have sparkling water, please? By the way, the tap water here is positively dreadful."

I nodded and headed to the bar, returning with a bottle of Perrier and a straw. Again, I watched as her sinfully sweet lips wrapped around the straw and every ounce of blood in my body went straight to my dick. Never in all my life have I wanted to fuck someone as badly as I wanted to fuck her.

"Come on, let's get out of here," she said sliding off her chair.

"Where are we going?" I asked, placing my hand on the small of her back and leading her out the door.

"You've been looking at me all night as if you were undressing me in your mind."

I laughed. "Didn't realize that I was that transparent."

"That's quite all right. I think I'd quite fancy a shag with you."

When we stepped outside, her teeth began to chatter. I pulled my jacket off and put it around her shoulders. Times like these I wished I'd had access to a town car. I should work on that arrangement.

"You should wait inside while I hail us a cab."

"No." She shook her head in protest looping her arm with mine. "I want to wait with you."

"My hotel or yours?"

"Yours."

Six blocks later, we arrived at The York Hotel. I'd booked one of the guest suites, on a private floor with a balcony, for the week. The place would do while my house in the Hamptons was being renovated. I would be buying a place here in the city soon, preferably something with office space in case I needed to work late. Tomorrow, I had a few locations I was going to be checking out, after the meeting with my new client.

I opened the door to the place I had called home the past four days and "not Kate" slipped off her heels and dropped her handbag into a chair in the sitting room.

"Would you like another drink?" I asked motioning to the bar.

She took off my jacket, and tossed it over a barstool. "No, where's the powder room?"

"Through that door to your left."

She didn't look back when she walked away, I watched every inch of her saunter down the hallway towards the master suite. I flipped on a few lights, scanned my emails from my phone, and then grabbed a bottle of sparkling water from the fridge. When I turned back she was standing there wearing one of my dress shirts and I damn near fell over my own two feet. It was the sexiest fucking thing I'd ever seen in my entire life.

"Kiss me," she whispered.

I moved a step closer, my hands reached to hold both sides of her face. Her blue eyes met mine. I studied her red lips for a moment. Her teeth grazed her bottom lip in anticipation. I ached to kiss her. I didn't know what I was waiting for. My lips traced the outline of hers. Her hands moved underneath my t-shirt, and her fingertips skimmed across my abs. As if that was the signal I needed, I pressed my lips against hers. At first it was tender, and she melted against my body. Her mouth opened, and my tongue slid across hers slowly. Her hands smoothed up and down my back, the kisses came faster, firmer. Wanting more I pulled her closer, deepening the kiss. All too soon, our lips separated, I was panting and she was gasping.

"*Kiss* . . . kiss me again." Her words came out breathy.

She didn't have to ask twice and I did the thing I'd thought about all evening, I picked her up and those sexy as hell legs locked around my waist. *Fuck yes.*

My hands on her ass, her tongue sliding against mine, her hands in my hair—it was a miracle I was able to get us to the bed. I desperately wanted to ask her for her name but I'd agreed to the rules for the evening.

*The rules.*

"Can you do me one favor?" I asked, easing her down onto the bed.

"Maybe."

"Can you not shout out the name William when I give you the most earth shattering orgasm you've ever had?"

"Sure," she laughed. "Would it be okay if I just yelled out God?"

"For tonight, I'll play by the rules, but tomorrow morning I might need to know your name. I have a feeling you'll definitely want to know mine."

"We'll see about that," she teased, pulling me closer for another kiss.

I smirked. "Trust me, sweetheart. You might have yelled out *God* a time or two before, but you'll definitely want to separate those memories from the ones associated with me."

# Chapter Two

## Alex

I woke up around four in the morning and "not Kate" was *not* beside me. My hands reached for her side only to find the sheets completely cool.

"Ughh," I sighed rubbing my eyes, bringing more focus in the darkness. There was no sign of her anywhere, except for the pillow on the bed. Her scent lingered and I took a deep breath, getting my fill of vanilla and sweet orange. How could I convince housekeeping to never wash this pillowcase?

I checked the bathroom, the living room and sure enough her purse was gone. My shirt, the one she'd worn, was draped over the back of the chair. It smelled like her, it was goddamn intoxicating. Housekeeping can have the pillowcase, I've got my shirt.

I should have checked her purse for her wallet and looked at her driver's license or a credit card at least. *Okay, that's not creepy at all.* My tired legs barely carried me back to bed. I should never have agreed to her silly game. But if I hadn't, I would have missed out on the most incredible sex of my life. *I sound like a fucking girl.*

With a groan, I turned on my side and tried to go back to sleep. I mumbled into my pillow, "I am so fucked."

After a hot shower, breakfast and a quick read of the morning paper, I was ready to get this new day started. Once again my eyes drifted to the unmade bed. Images of a naked blonde swirled in my mind. I'd give anything to see her again. I'd give anything to be deep inside her again.

Why did she leave? It wasn't the sex, because it was phenomenal. She initiated the last two go arounds. Smiling confidently, I straightened my tie in the mirror.

I grabbed my wallet and keys and walked down the hall towards the door, but not without looking back at the bed for the millionth time. Opening the door, I hung the "Do Not Disturb" sign on the handle. I'd call for clean towels when I returned from my meeting. Even though I had my shirt, I wanted to have one more night with that intoxicating scent in bed with me.

By the time my third meeting rolled around, every tall blonde I passed caused my heart rate to pick up just a bit each time in hopes it was her.

Focus needed now. New client. New job.

I studied the name on the folder: Ella Connolly. A few weeks ago, I received a call from Dean Winters, head of security for actor, Ronan Connolly. In a story of how small the world was, Liam Frost had given my name to Ronan. Apparently they were old friends and Dean asked if I would be interested in looking out for Ella while she was in the city. Liam was married to Ashleigh, the same Ashleigh who happened to be Emily Greene's best friend, and Emily was acquainted with my pal Ethan Carlson. It was all very six degrees of separation.

Opening the folder, my eyes scanned over the details. I barely remembered reading any of this information, but then again I'd shoved this in a drawer and didn't pull it out again until this morning. That could have something to do with it.

No up to date photo. The basics told me that Ella was twenty-seven, owned a clothing boutique and was looking to expand here and that was the reason for her visit. Dean had mentioned that she was recognized by the UK paparazzi on occasion. At one time it used to be an issue, but that seemed to have cooled over the last year.

I hadn't worked personal security detail for a while. In a long while actually, but I was a professional. I'd always been a protector. It was the way I was wired, from looking out for the guys in my squad to keeping an eye on my younger sister, Amy. Background checks were a regular routine where her dating life was concerned. Luckily, I've never had to severely injure any of her suitors. Slipping into this role was as easy as riding a bike.

For the past several years, my company, Robertsen Security, had dealt with private clients exclusively. Working for my brother's company, and with local and state law enforcement was a good cover. In actuality, my company provided advanced special operations, services that no one else could or *would* do. My team was good. We took our jobs very seriously, one wrong step, any miscalculation and people could die. No errors permitted. This is what I trained my guys to do, and I was held to the same high standards. My system was simple: Assess each situation with a keen eye and sharp mental awareness. If a situation becomes intense, remove the threat by physical force. Each of my men was taught to study the probability, the impact, and the effect of every known risk on the project. The "project" being a person, a human life—a life that they would be inseparably connected with and trusted to protect at all costs.

Checking my phone again, I looked up the address where I'd be meeting Dean. My email instructed me to go to The Avondale Conference Room on the 17th floor. The lobby of the building was relatively quiet. The only stirrings were a few staff mingling around the reception desk, a postal carrier shoving mail into boxes, and a young couple talking over coffee near the fireplace. I stood near the elevators and waited as a young redhead with three white poodles exited. She was bobbing her head up and down obviously enjoying the tune coming through her headphones. She flashed a flirtatious smile my way, and I nearly tripped over one of the tiny pups who seemed to want to get back on the elevator with me.

Turning to press the numeric keypad, my eyes shifted to the screen of rotating ads. While watching the ads, I tapped my fingers on the wall under the melodic spell of the sound of "Suicide Blonde" piping through the speakers. I smirked, and I thought about *her* again, and the way she smiled the moment I saw her on sidewalk last night.

The elevator came to a stop on the fifth floor, and a group of "Ladies Who Lunch" stepped in carrying their Louis Vuitton and Prada bags. I hated that I was so familiar with designer handbags; it only reminded me of Amanda's expensive shopping trips. Gabbing away, they stepped off at The Palm Court for, no doubt, what would entail several martinis and tiny garden salads.

No judgement, those particular women were regulars

in my parents' world. Country Club luncheons, extravagant summer parties at the family lake house, and fundraising dinners in the grandest hotels. It was all a day in the life of the Robertsen family.

The car came to a halt, and I quickly popped a breath mint. Stepping out, I took a moment to straighten my tie in the hallway mirror.

The room was immediately on the left, and the door was propped open. I recognized Mr. Winters from our initial meeting a few weeks ago. He stood as he saw me approaching.

"Come on in, Alex."

"Good to see you again, Mr. Winters."

"No need for formalities, Dean is just fine," he said, shaking my hand with a firm grip. "This is Ronan Connolly." He nodded towards the man in the suit.

"Mr. Connolly," I stated, holding out my hand for another shake.

"Alex, it's a pleasure to meet you." He gestured to the leather chair on my left. "And please, call me Ronan."

"Thank you for meeting us, you've been briefed on the job, I assume?" Ronan asked.

I nodded, and held up the folder. "Dean tells me that you're in need of personal security for your sister, Ella."

"Yes, you can never be too careful with the safety of family."

I nodded in agreement. "Of course."

"Your job is just a precaution while she's in the city. What I'd like more specifically is for you to escort my sister around the city during her activities, day and night. There's no need for twenty-four-hour protection, unless the situation surrounding Miss Prescott elevates."

Dean slid a black and white photo of a man with dark hair

exiting the Warwick Hotel and Residences on 53rd. I'd been briefed on the situation regarding Ronan's girlfriend, Holliday Prescott. It was a highly sensitive and private matter.

I studied the photo, taking in all of the details and burning everything to memory.

"If you see this man, alert us immediately," Dean instructed, holding my gaze.

"I will."

"My sister has just arrived," Ronan announced looking up from his phone.

I stood, buttoning my jacket and then adjusted my cuffs. Before I could utter a word, my eyes landed upon the sexiest set of legs I'd ever seen.

*Wait one damn minute.*

I knew those legs. How fucking gloriously predictable. If ever there was a sign of good luck, this was it.

A grin spread across my face. *This will be fun.*

"Hello, Miss *Ella*," I greeted her with a nod.

Her blue eyes popped wide, but she played her part effortlessly. "Hello."

"Funny, you remind me of girl I know, her name's Kate though."

"So you're the one." She straightened her posture, sliding her hair over her shoulder. "The one my brother hired as my babysitter while I'm in the city."

Jesus Christ. Now I was playing out various naughty baby-sitter fantasy scenarios in my head. I had to think about something, anything else other than the fact that I had literally and figuratively *fucked* the client.

# Chapter Three

## Ella

*Well, you've gone and done it now, Ella.* My eyes travelled up his lethally hot body leaving me stunned. The smile on his face broadening as my eyes connected with his brilliant hazel ones that had the most beautiful thick eyelashes I'd ever seen on a man. His suit was ink black, and finely tailored. It was impressive to know that American men actually took pride in their appearance.

Seeing him again took my breath away. Before I'd snuck out of his hotel suite, I took a picture of him with my phone. He looked so peaceful and a part of me felt bad for leaving without saying goodbye, but I thought it would be better that way. No one could have prepared me for this strange encounter.

For a moment I was rendered speechless. I wanted to hold out my hand, and feel his touch again. He didn't offer, and neither did I. Warmth climbed up my thighs and settled right where I didn't need it to, just being near him again.

Wildly raunchy thoughts swirled in my head, like champagne bubbles making me loopy and tingly at the sight of "not Will"—whose name I just learned was *Alex*—standing in front of me. He stood tall and confident at just over six feet, and even at my height of five foot nine, I felt small compared to him. My legs felt wobbly, but that was partly because of the sex marathon I'd had just a few hours ago—with *him*.

The amazing, incredible, out of this world fantastic sex left me craving more, but I had other priorities. Mainly, my boutique, my brand—my business was my focus. Not men, especially not a ruggedly handsome man like Alex. Or one who had the stamina to drive me to five mind-blowing orgasms. He'd made a promise and delivered. If there was an award for world's best orgasm, it would go to Alex. I thought multiple orgasms were a myth, but I was proven wrong four times over.

"Ella arrived in the city earlier this morning," Ronan announced, before taking his seat at the table. I barely registered the rest of what my brother said after he introduced me to Alex.

My shoulders tensed, as I looked to Alex studying his expression. His lips twisted into a sexy smirk. I kissed the hell out of those lips the night before. I could still feel the scratches on my cheek from his silky dark, barely there stubble. He leaned back in his chair and the rich amber color in his hazel eyes glowed warmly. It made me feel all melty inside, like gooey chocolate sliding over a warm slice of cake.

"Is that so," he remarked, as his mouth curved into a slow, heart-stopping smile.

*Stop smiling at me, you handsome devil.*

"How are you finding the city, Ella? Have you had a chance to visit any local establishments?"

Clearly he was trying to rattle me, and something told me he was going to enjoy watching me squirm knowing my little secret. Thinking fast I answered, "I've not seen too much yet, maybe you'd like to take me to lunch and give me a tour?"

The smirk on his face turned to a full grin. "It would be my pleasure." The sound of promise in his voice made me wet and needy.

"Alex," my brother said, as he rose to his feet. "You're officially on the clock. If you'll excuse me, I'm required to be on set in an hour. Thank you and welcome to the family."

I rolled my eyes at my brother's comment of family. It was annoying and cute all at the same time. By nature, Ronan was a protector, and family took care of family. This is why I was required to have a babysitter . . . *bodyguard* while I was here. Now the insanely handsome man I thought I'd never see again was about to be thrust into my life full-time.

My brother kissed me on the cheek, and said, "Go on about your day, and if you need anything call Holliday. My schedule is late tonight."

"I'm sure Alex can assist me with anything I need," I tossed over my shoulder. "There's no reason to bother your girlfriend."

"Very well, I'll ring you later. Have a wonderful day." I watched as my brother and Dean strode off, feeling the heat spread across my cheeks knowing I was alone once more with Alex.

He stood there looking at me intently, and all I could think about was that incredible kiss that led to phenomenal sex. I've had lovers who have rocked my world, but they all paled in comparison to the way Alex moved through—dare I say—my soul. I'm completely snookered . . . or a more American expression—I'm fucked.

# Chapter Four

## Alex

*Get your head in the game, Alex.* Jesus, I couldn't think straight. Not when she was staring at me with those beautiful eyes. They were as blue as the waters on Lake Michigan. Again, I gawked at her legs, noting the skirt she wore was the same vibrant shade as her eyes. Not Kate—*she's* the person I was supposed to look out for at all costs. My dick and my brain were in an epic battle of disagreement at the moment.

"You're looking at me in that same way you did last night," I remarked.

"Honestly, can you blame me?" she asked. Her voice was a bit shaky.

I stepped closer to her, but she took a step back, stumbling into the wall. Her perfume drifted over my nose registering my dick to life. *Fucking Christ.*

"Ella, I don't bite." At the realization of the double meaning, I cleared my throat and spoke again. "I mean . . . I'm here to keep you safe."

Pushing off the wall, she smoothed her palms down her skirt, and tossed her golden hair over her shoulder.

"Listen, *Alex*. . . on second thought, what is your last name. We should keep our relationship completely professional."

"How do you propose we do that?" I laughed, looking at my watch. "We had sex less than eleven hours ago. I can still hear your moans and breathy whimpers in my fucking head."

Her eyes went wild, and she shifted on her heel. Silence curled around us, and I began counting the seconds it took her to formulate any kind of rational answer. Thirty-three seconds later, her reply came and it wasn't what I wanted or expected to hear.

"You . . . you could quit," she offered.

Cocking a brow, I strode towards her. My foot tapped the door, shutting the rest of the world out. This time she didn't move a muscle.

"Now you're looking at *me* the way you did last night."

Beneath the delicate skin of her neck, her pulse thrummed. Her teeth grazed over her beautiful bottom lip, slicked with that cherry red color. Her sweet scent swirled around me, reminding me of how fucking good it felt to have her pinned underneath me—naked and wet.

Inhaling, I leaned in closer. "Can *you* blame me?"

She laughed and said, "You are a bit of a joker, aren't you?"

I smirked, tracing my finger under her chin. "If I remember correctly, it's you who likes to play games."

Dropping to the nearest chair, Ella sighed. Her hands covered her beautiful face. "Oh, Alex." The words came out muffled under laughter. "You have seen me *naked*." The last word left her lips in a whisper.

I sat in the chair across from her, leaning back enjoying her immensely.

"Yes, and a lot more."

She pretended to be shocked, and the faintest bit of pink tinged her cheeks. "Naughty, but I'm being serious. I am quite sure this has broken some kind of ethical rule."

"Nonsense, now we're just better acquainted," I offered spreading my arms wide. But I was kidding myself, because I wanted to be more than just familiar with this stunning creature. And suddenly I found myself back in the same place. This, however, was slightly different than my situation with Amanda, but still it was hard to ignore the signs.

Ella started tapping her finger in an even rhythm against the top of the table. I stood up from the chair, and proceeded towards the door.

"Come on, Ella," I urged straightening my jacket.

She blinked up at me. "What?"

I jerked my thumb towards the hallway. "You mentioned something about me taking you to lunch."

"Oh, yes," she laughed, and hopped up from the chair. "I'm famished. I could go for a burger and fries, minus the bun of course."

"I know just the place."

Taking her hand in mine, I led Ella towards the elevators. I shouldn't have been so casual with her, but goddamnit, I couldn't help it. I wanted to touch her.

Client. She was the client.

*Technically, her brother is the client. She's the project. Nice try.*

Mentally I kicked myself, I needed to stop thinking with my dick and get my head on straight. I could do this.

Standing at the elevator, I released the hold I had on her hand to press the button. As I stared at the cool metal doors, I watched Ella's reflection as she bopped back and forth on her heels. *Fuck.* She was entirely too cute for her own good.

*Cute?*

Since when did I use the word cute to describe women? Puppies are cute. Babies are cute. Women are sexy.

*I'm losing it.*

The doors opened revealing a couple kissing. We stepped into the car, and the hot and heavy pair was unfazed by our presence, keeping their mouths locked on one another. Not daring to look at Ella, I pressed the button for the lobby. I couldn't allow my emotions to interfere with my ability to keep her safe. Despite the fact that we'd known each other intimately, while she was under my protection, things with her had to be as professional as possible.

# Chapter *Five*

## *Ella*

The duo snogging didn't bother to make room for us, leaving me no choice but to stand on the same side of the lift with Alex. With our arms brushed against one another, heat spread across my skin like a raging wildfire. The two of us snuggled close in a compact space. My hand still tingled from his touch. It was impossible to concentrate on anything other than him. He was here. Right next to me, looking gorgeous and smelling perfectly divine. All sense I had retreated from my brain as I stood there fantasizing about pushing him up against the wall and allowing him to shag . . . *fuck* the hell out of me.

*Shut up, Ella, you dirty bird.*

When the car reached the fifth floor, and the couple playing slap and tickle walked out, I stifled a moan of relief. Unsure if I was comforted due to the fact that they left or that

I had Alex all to myself. I glanced at him, trying to get a sense of his thoughts. His mouth was pressed into a hard line, and his eyes remained forward, fixed on the numeric panel.

The lift came to a halt at the lobby and Alex stepped out, his head turned left and back to the right. The unrehearsed movement was fluid. He motioned for me to walk in front of him, but I had no clue where we were going.

"You lead the way."

"All right, but keep your pace with mine," he instructed. His voice was firm not angry.

I nodded, and did as I was instructed, keeping my stride with his as we passed through the spacious lobby. Something had changed his demeanor during the ride in the lift . . . *elevator*. Mentally I noted that I needed to brush up on my American English. If I intended to do business here, I should at least make the effort to know the proper terms.

Once outside, his hand reached inside his jacket pocket, pulling out his sunglasses. As we approached the valet stand, he put them on, shielding me from seeing his gorgeous eyes that reminded me of glowing golden sunlight sifting through deep green leaves.

*Snap out of it, Ella. He's your bodyguard.*

Straightening my shoulders, I hauled my handbag higher onto my shoulder. I vowed to lock all my scandalous thoughts away.

"Oh, it's a traditional English pub!" I couldn't contain my smile as my eyes took in the ambiance of the bar. Colorful knitted scarves were draped over trophies and surrounded bronzed plaques. Rugby balls and footballs . . . *soccer* balls sat perched on high shelves with black and white team pictures in between.

"This place is adorably fantastic."

"I thought you might like a taste of home."

"Where would you like to sit?"

He pointed to the corner and said, "Why don't we sit at that high-top table near the bar."

I slid into the chair, and began studying the menu. God, I wanted a pint of beer, but since I couldn't have wheat of any kind I settled for a mineral water.

"Are you going to have a pint?"

"No." He shook his head. "I don't drink on the job."

This was beyond odd, less than an hour ago we were laughing about our situation and now he was acting as if we hadn't had our tongues all over each other. Well *not* all over. I didn't have the pleasure of having his cock in my mouth.

"What's going on with you?"

A single brow rose, as he eyed me over the menu. "What do you mean?"

"You're behaving strangely."

"I'm trying to be professional and do my job."

My eyes narrowed, and I stared at him wondering what was with the hot and cold routine. After a few moments of uncomfortable silence, a waitress approached our table with two glasses of water, told us her name was Meg, and then took our orders.

"I'll have the cheeseburger cooked medium rare, with bacon slices, no roll and American fries."

Alex opted for a large chicken salad with ranch dressing on the side.

"Could I have a bottle of sparkling water, please?" I asked.

She smiled. "Certainly, I'll bring that right away."

Shifting her body, she turned to face Alex, shoving her

barely covered tits in his face. "How about you, handsome, can I bring you something from the tap?"

"Not today, water will be just fine," he said, holding up his glass.

"Sure thing, honey, if you need anything you just ask."

Even though she was flirting with him, he was uninterested. Does she have no shame? I could be his girlfriend. Meg returned with my sparkling water, giving Alex a toothy smile and a view of *her* goods.

I rested my chin on my hand, studying my lunch companion—my bodyguard. *Bodyguard*, and what a body this man had. Illicit thoughts of our night surfaced again. God, I would give anything to have another go around with him. I liked every inch of him—broad shoulders, long legs and those sexy taut arms with thick corded muscles, but his back, inked with a badass tattoo of two snakes coiled together, was my favorite—okay, *second favorite* of his physical attributes. Alex was built, but not too big—his body was taut, well sculpted. *No bulging beefcakes for this chick.*

For a moment, I envisioned the two of us tangled together in soft sheets. His defined muscles flexing as he fucked me into the mattress, driving me to another earthshattering orgasm.

*Have some class.*

This was a mistake. I should have pulled Ronan aside, and told him that I had familiar relations with Alex, but knowing my brother he might have flown off the handle. The handsome man sitting across from me did nothing wrong, and I wasn't about to let him lose his job. Maybe a chat would lighten the mood.

"How did you find this place?"

"My brother and I used to hangout here. His office is

around the corner."

"Oh, so you're from New York."

"No, I moved here from Michigan. But we'd come to the city for business several times a year." At the sound of laughter, his eyes darted towards the door. A couple of college coeds entered the bar.

"Michigan, yes, the state that's surrounded by the Great Lakes."

His eyebrows rose. Certain it was because I'd impressed him with my knowledge.

He leaned forward, and I kept talking, throwing out random facts about I knew about America. I told him about the time I went to South Beach with a school mate and the strip club we stumbled into. He laughed before taking a sip of his water.

"The owner wanted us to participate in Amateur Night." I smiled at the memory. "I wonder what Sasha is up to these days? I should call her."

His eyes popped out of his head, and his hands gripped the sides of the table.

"What is it? Is it me? Am I chatting too much?" I asked, feeling nervous knots zipping around my stomach.

"Christ, Ella, *no*," he said, scrubbing his hand over his stubble covered chin. *So sexy.*

"Well, something is clearly on your mind. What's the matter?"

He leaned across the table, his hazel eyes fixed on mine. My pulse thrummed as I waited for Alex to speak. He rolled up to his feet and took a step towards me.

"The matter *is*," he hissed, as his warm breath fanned over my neck. "I can't seem to think of anything other than the fact that I'd like to drag you back to my hotel room and fuck your brains out."

*Oh, now we are getting somewhere.*

"Well, I wouldn't object to the notion," I admitted. Yes, I said it out loud. Keeping my prurient thoughts locked up didn't last long.

He lifted an eyebrow. "I *can't* do that Ella."

"And why not?"

Shoving his hands into his pockets, he expelled a deep breath. He stared at me for a moment, before answering, "I can't, because you are my responsibility and bad things happen when I let my dick interfere with my job."

If his dick was involved, then he'd probably had a relationship with someone he was protecting. And bad things? What the hell did he mean by that statement? I doubted there was anything *dreadful* about Alex. He kept others safe, and that told me that he cared about people. Could he hurt someone? Obviously, yes, if necessary, he's a bodyguard—it's in his job description. I wondered why someone like Alex would choose this line of work. Had he been in a fight before? Maybe he'd lost control once? My mind spun with questions. For a man I told the evening before I didn't care to know anything about him, I'd formed a laundry list of questions, that I now *wanted* answers to.

"I'm not sure that I understand."

"No, I suppose you wouldn't," he answered, and tucked a strand of hair behind my ear. "I'll be back; I need some air."

He turned and strode off towards the doors. I sat at the table confused. Heat spread across my cheeks, and down my neck. Clutching the bottle of water, I chugged it hoping to calm my nerves.

Five minutes later Alex returned and Meg brought out our food. Leaning over him, on purpose no less, to give him another glimpse of her tits, she refilled his glass. I admired her effort. She was pretty confident. As well she should be, her tits were magnificent.

"Why don't we talk about how this whole bodyguard thing is going to work," I said, before dipping a fry into some ketchup. "I guess you're my Kevin Costner."

He huffed out a laugh. "Hardly, your brother said that I was to look out for you while you're here in the city. When you go out, I'll be there. Consider me your shadow."

"Maybe this won't be as dreadful as I thought."

Alex looked at me and I smiled, before stuffing four fries into my mouth, not caring if he thought I was a pig. Even though food is sometimes my enemy, I loved to eat. You won't find me ordering a small garden salad and then trying to steal food from your plate.

"Enjoying the burger?"

"Hmm, uh huh," I managed to mumble in between bites. "How is your salad?"

"It mostly tastes like rabbit food." A smile tugged the corners of his mouth.

Deep rumbling laughter rang out behind me. I turned my head to see what the ruckus was all about. A few guys with pints of dark lager ambled into the bar.

*Where did they come from?*

"There must be a party in the upstairs dining area," I remarked.

"There sure is, lovie," someone said in a gravelly voice behind me.

Alex placed his fork into the salad bowl, and wiped his mouth with a cloth napkin.

"Hello, Ella, it's been a while."

I froze at the sight of the man standing before me. He was

correct, it had been a long time since I'd seen him. The hairs on my arms stood on end, and something heavy settled over me. Even though he'd grown a beard, and his dark hair had grey streaks around the temples, he looked exactly the same.

"Charlie, what are you doing in Manhattan? Did you follow me here?"

Alex stood and pushed his stool back. "Ella, is this guy someone who will give you trouble?"

"I see you got yourself a new bloke," he replied, ignoring my questions. "Hey, mate, the name's Charlie and you are?"

"I haven't decided, yet." He stepped closer to Charlie, and I swore I could feel the primal energy bristling off his body. "If the lady says there's no trouble," he added, running his finger against the wooden tabletop, "then you can call me mate. On the other hand, if the lady says we've got a problem, you'll probably refer to me as the guy who told you to leave Miss Connolly alone and mind your own fucking business."

"Funny you mention minding one's own business, *mate*." Charlie eyed Alex over the rim of his pint glass. "This one here ruined my life. Because of her, I had to move to this bloody country."

"You could have moved to Canada or better yet, Antarctica."

"Cheeky as ever, aren't you?" he asked, before slamming back the rest of his drink. Charlie let out a loud burp that made my throat crawl with disgust. "I had to move here because I'm not allowed to sell my pictures in the UK. I'm not allowed to sell celebrity photos to the tabloids and smut rags. Now I take respectable images at political and sporting events. I attend tennis matches, and mundane conferences, instead of red carpet events and ritzy parties. All thanks to Ella here."

"Are you quite finished?" I asked, my voice cracking with

anger.

He chuckled. "Too bad I don't have my camera on me. I'd love to get a picture of you in that dress." He stepped back to gawk at my legs, and I tugged at the hem of skirt trying to pull it lower.

"You look good, lovie, but I don't need to see your arse. I have a mental picture of your sweet body right up here." His thick fingers tapped the side of his head, and he licked his lips.

My stomach lurched, and I'd lost my appetite. Pushing my plate to the middle of the table, I watched him wipe his wet mouth on the back of his sleeve.

"Time to move along, *mate*, before you get yourself into trouble," Alex said, as he sidestepped to directly stand in front of Charlie.

"No trouble," he said lumbering backwards. "See you around, Ella."

"God, I hope not," I mumbled under my breath.

Alex turned to face me. "Are you okay?"

"Yes," I answered, and rose to my feet. "Could we pay our bill and leave?"

"Sure," he said, before motioning to Meg. "This one is on me."

Meg sauntered over to our table, and brushed her arm against Alex's. She had two checks in her hand. Alex took both of them, and a small frown appeared on her face. I spotted handwriting on the back of one of the tickets. Upon closer inspection, ten digits came into focus. I laughed, certain that it was her phone number scrawled across the paper.

Alex handed her his credit card and she walked back to the computer by the bar. After a few moments she came back with a pen in hand.

"Excuse me, Meg," I said, taking a step forward. "You've

been quite obvious with your flirting today."

Alex cocked an eyebrow.

"Here's a bit of friendly advice," I said, taking another step forward.

Meg's eyes widened as she shifted on her heel.

"In the future, I'd advise you *not* to shove your tits in a man's face, *especially* when he's in the company of another woman." I took the pen from Alex, and flipped the ticket over crossing out her number.

Her mouth gaped. "I'm so . . . sorry. I didn't mean anything by it."

"Of course you did, otherwise you wouldn't have done it."

Blotches of red splashed across her neck, and spread down across her chest. She picked up the tickets and stomped off towards to bar.

"You didn't have to embarrass her like that."

"Are you serious? She embarrassed herself *and* disrespected me." I slid my bag onto my shoulder. "Put yourself in my shoes, love, and tell me how you would have liked it."

"Okay, you have a point," he agreed, and nodded towards the door.

For a moment I'd forgotten about Charlie and his band of goons. However, when my eyes focused on the exit, I realized we'd have to walk right past them to leave. I took Alex's hand in mine, and he led us towards the doors. Someone from Charlie's group whistled, and called out my name. Alex kept focused on the exit and gripped my hand tighter.

Once outside, he turned to face me. "I don't like that guy."

"No kidding. He's a wanker," I replied, stating the obvious as we walked towards the end of the block.

"There's history between the two of you, and I don't get a good vibe. There was something about the tone of his words that makes me think he has violent tendencies. He's a threat."

I shook my head. "Charlie, he's a lot of bloody things, but he's not dangerous."

"I don't trust him. What's the history with you two? He mentioned something about photos and having to move. What kind of trouble did you give him?"

I stopped midstride, feeling the anger brewing inside me. "Of course you think I'm the one who'd caused the issue." I folded my arms against my chest.

Alex turned to face me. "Sorry, that wasn't what I meant. He said you gave him trouble, what happened?"

At his words, my shoulders relaxed, and my arms fell to my sides.

"That is a long story."

"Well, you better start talking, Ella, because if I'm going to keep you safe I need to know all the details."

"Bloody hell."

"In fact, I'm going to stay at your hotel with you."

"Absolutely not. That is *not* part of the deal," I argued.

As we strode into the garage where Alex's car was parked, his mobile rang. I was grateful for the interruption, as it gave me time to clear my head. The thought of Alex staying in my suite with me had me sexually aroused. How would I be able to handle that situation, without wanting to tear his clothes off every second? No, I cannot allow that to happen. When I was settled in for the evening that would be the end of his duties, and he would accept it.

"Yes, I see," Alex said, glancing at his watch. "I'll be there in about two hours." He ended the call and shoved the phone inside the pocket of his jacket. "Let's go, you're coming with me."

"No, I need to scout the retail spaces that my father sent

me."

"Do you have appointments?" he asked, walking at a brisk pace.

"No," I answered, trying to match my speed with his.

"So, nothing solid?"

"No, but—"

"That settles it then," he interrupted, coming to a stop at the bumper of his Range Rover. "Today, you'll come with me, then tomorrow, you'll set up your appointments and I'll make sure you arrive at all of them—on time."

He smiled at me, and I swore I heard the sound of my panties being ripped off my body, followed shortly after by the action of him tossing them onto the floor.

Sidestepping me, he clicked the button and opened the passenger door. I climbed in, and settled into the leather seat as the door closed. My head fell back and I blew out a breath. Trapped in a car with Alex for two hours? This should prove to be quite interesting.

# Chapter *Six*

## *Alex*

"Where are we going anyway?" Ella asked, before applying more of that sultry red color to her gorgeous mouth. Then she smacked her lips together, making a popping sound. For some odd reason, I found that to be so damn sexy. It should have annoyed me, but Ella could chew rocks with her mouth open and I'd still want to kiss her.

"We're driving out to my house in the Hamptons. I'm having it renovated."

"You're going to live two hours away from the city? That doesn't make sense to me."

I laughed. "I like being near the water."

"Oh," she said, shoving her lipstick into her handbag. "Why not live in a high-rise overlooking the Hudson River or the bay?"

"It's not the same."

"Any particular reason?"

"You know," I said, flicking my turn signal to change lanes. "Less than twenty-four hours ago, you wanted to know nothing about me. I find it interesting you now have all these questions."

She huffed out a laugh, before popping a piece of gum into her mouth. "Would you like a stick of gum?"

"No, thanks, I prefer breath mints," I replied, patting the pocket of my jacket. The sound of Altoids crashed against the metal case.

She rolled her eyes, and shoved the pack of gum into her handbag. "So, are you going to tell me why you like living by the water?"

"Sure, it offers a quiet and peaceful feeling. I like the sound of water lapping against the shore, and I enjoy running on the beach. Then there's the view—you can't beat it. There's nothing like a sunset over the water. Endless colors, where the sky meets the horizon."

I gave Ella the safe version, even though I felt compelled to tell her the hard truth. Water doesn't remind me of war or death. It reminds me of calm and peace. I spent four months traveling around the Cook Islands, Fiji, Bora Bora, and Tahiti, eventually ending up in Hawaii. My therapist said I needed to find some kind of way to accept Sasha's death and realize it wasn't my fault. Laid back island life seemed the best way to grieve and let go.

Maybe Ella would think I was crazy. Although, something told me she'd be able to handle it. But, in keeping things light and professional, that information didn't fit under the umbrella of discussion topics.

Besides my former squad and, of course, Ethan, I'd never

really talked about my past to anyone. I'd had my will drafted at least half a dozen times, and it changed after every mission. I'd been allowed to tell my father and brother about the two years I'd spent working Special Ops for Elite Eight. Later, I disclosed some information to Ethan, but mostly I shared tidbits of my time with Sasha.

On a few occasions, I'd tried to open up to Amanda, but pillow talk wasn't her strong suit. Maybe deep down, I knew she wouldn't care to hear the ugliness. At the time of our affair, Amanda's world was filled with gloom. Adding to it wasn't something I'd wanted to do.

Gloom . . . *lagoon*. Venice, the trip we'd never made.

"Sounds heavenly—some kind of warm, inviting place." The sound of Ella's soft voice broke through my thoughts. Place, *yes*, and that reminder brings up an unfinished matter.

"Speaking of places, I'm going to upgrade to a two bedroom suite at The York."

She threw her hands up. "No, Alex, I'm not staying with you. It's completely unnecessary. My brother is being overprotective."

"Oh yeah? Tell me about that? There has to be a reason for Ronan to want to make sure that you're safe while you're here."

"I am certain this has something to do with his own personal experiences and being famous. Trust me, no one gives a fuck that I'm Ronan Connolly's little sister."

The quick defensive tone in her voice told me she was hiding something.

*I know. I'm a regular Sherlock Holmes.*

"If there's a potential threat, I need to know. Is it that guy we ran into at the bar? Charlie?" His asshole remark about having a mental picture of her body, made me want to crack his head against the wooden tabletop. I took my eyes off the road to study her reaction to his name. Ella closed her eyes and blew out a deep breath.

"No, I had no idea he was even here. I told you, Ronan is just being *ov-er-pro-tec-tive*, like an annoying older brother." She shifted in her seat, crossing her left leg up and over her right knee. Her skirt bunched higher, revealing more of her creamy skin. The sound of a loud sports car zipping by us drew my attention back to the black pavement. "Don't you have any siblings *you* look out for?"

I ran my hand along the steering wheel, and took a deep breath. "Yes, my little sister. And my older brother . . . *well*, not so much anymore."

*Shit.* I shouldn't have said that. Maybe she wouldn't pry. The sounds of "Rebel Yell" by Billy Idol filled the cab, and Ella started singing along and swaying to the beat.

"I simply adore this song," she yelled over the music.

"Yeah, I can see that."

I turned and studied those lips of hers as she belted out every word, and wanted nothing more than to seal my mouth over hers and kiss her deeply. Shaking my head, I forced the idea out of my mind.

The chorus of the song blasted through the speakers of my Range Rover . . . and the words—more, midnight, hour, and the phrase "she cried" all screamed through my brain. I was back to picturing Ella naked in my bed, moaning and begging me to fuck her harder. I looked at my watch, only another hour and seventeen minutes to until we reached my house. But really, who was counting?

# Chapter Seven

## Ella

An hour and twenty-four minutes later, we arrived at Alex's house in the Hamptons. He referred to his stretch of road or rather the neighborhood he lived in as The Harbour. I had seen the Hamptons on the television, and in cinema, but never in person. Without question, I was fascinated by the playground of the rich and famous. We drove through a small part of The Harbour, before turning down the road to his home. Alex called it "the main drag." It was a long stretch of posh restaurants, coffee shops, luxury retailers and charming, one-of-a-kind boutiques all situated side by side on a lovely tree-lined street. It was hard not to fall in love with this place.

The sound of gravel crunched under the tires of his Range Rover as he navigated up the long driveway, and I found myself staring at an impossibly gorgeous shingle-clad residence.

The grand two-story house was gracefully tucked away from the main road on a grassy, wooded site.

He parked the SUV and I climbed out. Sliding my sunglasses off my face, I stood there captivated, feeling impressed by the large windows and stunning wraparound porch.

"This way," Alex said, pointing his chin toward the side where we then climbed wooden steps to the back door.

Once inside, the sound of hammering echoed throughout the large empty space. The smell of sawdust lingered in the air.

"Mr. Robertsen," a deep voice boomed from behind us.

A man with a stalky build, wearing an orange polo shirt and dark brown trousers, greeted us. Obviously he'd been working hard, his sandy blond hair was sweat soaked around his temples.

"Gary, how are you doing, man?" Alex asked shaking his hand. "This is my . . . this is Ella. She's a friend."

On the inside I giggled and my stomach fluttered. I know it's something silly that girls say happens, but I know what I felt. Once I saw the blueprints unfolding across the makeshift table, made up of a piece of plywood sitting atop two sawhorses, I excused myself, allowing them a moment for business. My wandering of the open floor plan took me through three large rooms, including the mudroom, which had gorgeous slate floors. The foyer took my breath away with its impeccable millwork and the Dutch doors added a unique touch.

I climbed the back staircase to the second floor. The gorgeous dark wood flooring throughout the entire house offset the white walls and ceiling. It was a simple and clean design. My further snooping landed me in what I could only assume was to be the master suite. It had a large fireplace and lovely window bench. Smiling, I ran my fingers along the top of the wood, picturing myself curled up with a book and a warm mug of tea.

*Why would I think of that?*

Shaking the thought from my head, I turned around, and my eyes landed on a large set of French doors that led to a balcony. I pushed them open to take in the marvelous sight spread before me—a lavish garden and pool and the ocean just off in the distance.

This place was marvelous. There was no other way to describe it. It was magnificent and . . . *and* in the Hamptons, with a beach view, not to mention a guesthouse and tennis courts.

Bloody hell! This was Alex's home? The place he was going to reside. How could that be?

*How much is my brother paying him to lookout for me?*

I stood gazing out at the ocean, wondering about the man hired to keep an eye on me. He mentioned a sister and a brother, but something in Alex's voice indicated there was a deeper story there. *I know, clearly I'm the next Detective Olivia Benson, minus the whole solving of heinous crimes thing.*

"Ella?" Alex's deep voice rang in my ears, and I felt something I could only describe as a shiver tugging deep inside me.

"Yes, I'm on the balcony," I called out.

"I see you found my favorite spot in the entire house."

Twisting my head, I turned to face him. He smiled and handed me a bottle of sparkling water.

"Thank you, yes, it is truly beautiful here," I remarked, before tipping the glass bottle to my lips. Taking a long drink, I contemplated my thoughts and when I'd finished I knew how I would phrase my questions.

"So how does a bodyguard afford such a lavish new home and drive a Range Rover? Are you American royalty or something?"

He smiled and it reached all the way to his eyes. "Well, actually, yeah, you could say that."

I studied his face for a moment, because I couldn't tell if he was fucking with me, or actually serious. I cocked a brow, and stood in silence waiting for him to enlighten me on the matter.

"My mother's family was a huge part of the automotive industry in both Detroit and Cleveland. When my grandparents died, we inherited a large sum of money, and each of us grandkids was given a sizeable trust fund."

"Holy shit," I said, feeling my cheeks flush crimson. "So you're a Trust Fund Baby?"

Alex laughed. "Kind of, but there's more."

"More? What can possibly be *more* than having the good luck to inherit a family fortune?"

My words tumbled from my lips and I'm afraid I sounded like a total arse . . . correction asshat. Again, he flashed me that charming smile. The one that made my knickers wet and had me feeling a deep ache in my . . . *pussy*. Was that what an American woman would say? I am not referring to my nether region as a "flower." God, Alex has me all twisted up and thinking about what to call my vagina.

*Get a grip, Ella.*

"My father's family owns one of the largest shipping companies in the Great Lakes region, transporting everything from iron, ore and grains," he said, before taking a long drink. "The prominent Robertsen Family of Grosse Point. We have that printed on the letterhead." He gave a small laugh, and then turned to face the ocean.

I felt my eyes widen, and I swallowed a lump in my throat. Alex had been born into one of the wealthiest families in America. He must have grown up attending society parties, gone to the most prestigious university and travelled to the most exotic locations on holiday. And I bet he never had to worry about the paparazzi trying to take photographs of him and splashing them across the tabloids.

"Did you leave the company to come here and work?"

"No, I worked at the company on and off when I was a teenager," he confessed. "At the time, the family business wasn't something I was interested in. Instead, I enlisted in the military after high school."

Alex was in the military? That makes quite a lot of sense actually—threat and risk assessment. He'd mentioned that was his job last night, but I could have never put two and two together until this talk. "Actuary Science" comes to mind. I remember that from that movie with Katie Holmes called *First Daughter*. My friend, Nabila, and I used to watch that movie repeatedly.

"Are you close with your parents?"

"I suppose you could say that, we see each other frequently and manage not to annoy the fuck out of each other. Sunday dinners are a kind of tradition," he said, tapping his foot against the wood railing. "Mom has a strict rule, cocktails at six and dinner at seven. I haven't seen my parents since New Year's Eve." Tension rolled off his body as Alex drew in a long ragged breath, and then exhaled slowly. It was almost as if he was doing a breathing exercise.

My phone pinged, alerting me to a text message. It was from my brother.

"Speaking of family, mine has requested my presence for a dinner party in my honor on Saturday evening. I guess you'll have the night off."

Alex shook his head.

"What? Are you seriously going to babysit me at a family

function?"

"Yep," he answered, giving me a cocky grin. "I was sent an email about the event while we were having lunch. Dean wants me to help with security." He pulled out his phone and showed me the message.

My stomach churned, an uneasy feeling rippled through me. Security, at a dinner party? Just how many people were going to be in attendance? Is this what Ronan's life as a celebrity had become or was there a real threat of danger? Had something happened? My mind went to the darkest places, and then it hit me—his crazy ass stalker must be back in the picture.

Fame came with a price, the price being the lack of privacy. Right after Ronan and Heather Young started dating, my brother received letters and daily phone calls from a woman, Devlynn Asher. Ronan's number was changed, but the letters still came, even to our parents' home in London. One letter contained a message that threatened to kill Heather and feed her to the pigs. Heather was a mess, and Ronan was spooked by the incident and rightly so. A few weeks later, Asher was caught, after she showed up on Ronan's front doorstep.

A shiver ran down my spine at the memory. Pulling my phone from my purse, I quickly typed in her name. No new updates. She was sentenced to three years, and by my calculations, she was still in prison.

"You okay?" Alex's question knocked me out of my thoughts. I wondered if he knew about the incident. Squaring my shoulders back, I refocused attempting to push the ugliness from my mind.

"Yeah, I'm grand," I lied. "I needed to check something."

"Come on, let's get back to the city." He nodded towards the door, and then guided me through the master suite. We descended the stairs, and he called over his shoulder, "I'm staying with you and I need to grab an overnight bag."

"No, we're not living together," I shot back, over the sound of our footsteps echoing against the bare walls.

When we reached the first floor, Alex frowned at me, and said, "Ella, this is not up for debate. I *will* be staying with you. End of discussion." His tone was warning, and made me believe I'd pushed him too far.

I touched his arm. "Listen, I'll make you a deal. If something happens that makes me feel unsafe, then we'll make arrangements. Deal?"

His eyes narrowed, thoughtfully pondering my offer. After a few moments, and one sweet smile from me, he spoke.

"Fine," he huffed, expelling a deep breath. "I don't love the idea of you being alone in the city, but I'll agree to your terms."

"Wonderful," I replied clasping my hands together. "And Alex?"

"Yeah?"

"Thank you for trusting my judgement."

He gave me a small smile. "Admittedly, I'm uncertain about this, but, yeah, I trust you even if it is against *my* better judgement." He stepped closer to me, and said, "It seems, I keep breaking all my rules for you, Ella." He brought his hand to my cheek, brushing his fingertips over my skin.

I had no idea that simple touch could be erotic. That said something, because I'd already slept with him. But it made me want him again. He was breaking his rules, and I needed to keep mine or else I'd be in deep, deep trouble.

# Chapter Eight

## Alex

I stepped out of the shower and wrapped a towel around my waist. It was eight-thirty in the evening and I was exhausted from the long day. While I waited for the steam to exit the bathroom, I walked to the butler's pantry to grab a bottle of water. "Shake It Off" by Taylor Swift blared through the speakers on the radio and I found myself humming along. Now, all I heard was Ella's sweet singing voice. I hadn't been able to get her voice out of my head for hours.

I picked up the remote and hit the power button. Instead of music, I turned on the television and flipped to CNN.

I realized we were in a precarious situation.

It was completely inappropriate of me to touch her so intimately earlier today, but goddamnit I wanted to . . . *needed* to. The way she was looking at me—fuck, she was adorable. It was a miracle that I didn't take her in my arms and kiss her.

That was *epic* restraint on my part.

Even though she and I had come to an agreement about me not staying with her, I still felt that I needed to be close as a precaution. I picked my cell up off the desktop, and dialed the number for the Hawthorne Park Plaza where Ella was staying.

A sweet bubbly voice rang through the receiver, "Good evening and thank you for calling The Hawthorne Park Plaza. How may I direct your call?"

"Reservations, please."

"Certainly, sir, one moment."

When placed on hold, I was greeted with Taylor Swift's voice singing "I Knew You Were Trouble."

I hear you, Taylor. I knew I was in trouble when Ella walked into that conference room earlier today. Ella and I were a one-night stand, and now I was responsible for her safety. Conflicted doesn't even begin to scratch the surface of this crazy fucking situation.

The song cut off and a soft feminine voice chimed in. "Hawthorne Park Plaza Reservation Desk, this is Penny, how can I help you?"

"Yes, are any of your penthouses or executive suites available for the next two weeks?"

The sound of her fingers tapping on the keyboard flew at a quick pace. I could tell she had a high word per minute efficiency. She rattled off the descriptions of two suites that were available along with the prices. I opted for the one with the private rooftop terrace. The view alone would be worth the price.

I ended the call and tossed my phone onto the bed. With that issue settled, I'd sleep easier tonight. Instead of being blocks away from Ella, only a short elevator ride would separate us.

Surely, she couldn't be upset or take issue with me living in the same hotel as her. Maybe I should have cleared it with her first.

*No.*

I was already bending the rules outside my comfort zone. She would just have to deal with it. Walking back across the room, I entered the closet. I pulled on a pair of underwear along with my pajama bottoms. After I dried my hair, I tossed the towel into the laundry bag and made my way over to the bar. It was time for a drink and then bed.

Making good on my vow to change my nightly activity, tonight I'd be asleep at a decent hour and refreshed for tomorrow. Being a military man, I knew my self-discipline wasn't too far beneath the surface. Where Ella was concerned, those primal urges needed to be buried way the fuck down.

No light.

No oxygen.

No chance to develop roots and grow.

Not this time. Not a snowball's chance in hell.

# Chapter Nine

## Ella

I rolled up my yoga mat, and then made my way toward the locker rooms. The gym was deathly quiet at five-thirty in the morning. Only a handful of ladies and one guy were in this morning's class. My mind was clear and the tension that had been residing in my shoulders no longer existed.

My body was still adjusting to the time difference. After eating dinner in my room, I'd fallen asleep in my clothes last night around six. I'd woken up at midnight to brush my teeth, wash my face and change into my pajamas. Then I was up for three hours watching television before drifting off to sleep again. My hope was that within a couple of days, I'd be fully adjusted to East Coast time.

After a few sips of my water, I opened the lock to my gym cubby, and pulled out my sweatshirt, slipping it over my head. I hefted my bag up onto my shoulder and sauntered towards the doors, when my mobile . . . *cellphone* vibrated in my pocket.

My heart rate that had slowed from the post workout cool down spiked when I saw who was calling. I swiped my finger across the phone icon, and lifted the device to my ear.

"Bila, how are you?" I said, greeting my dear friend with cheerful smile. Nabila Lawson was my closest friend. We'd met at a cocktail party amongst mutual friends while at university in London. After two bottles of crappy red wine and a sensational girl crush discussion, Alexa Chung versus Mollie King, we exchanged numbers and the rest is history.

"I'm utterly fantastic, despite the fact that I miss you. This cold, spring rain is dreadful. I'm walking into Berry and Bramble now, needed another round of tea *and* espresso this morning. How are you getting on in the city that never sleeps?"

A grin spread across my face at Nabila mentioning the coffee shop around the corner from the boutique. Her art studio was in the building next to the café. The two of us would meet up at least once a day for lunch or a much needed caffeine fix.

"I miss you and London, very much. However, I must admit, I do love it here in Manhattan. I went out to the Hamptons yesterday. How are the preparations for your spring show coming along?" I took the stairs instead of the elevator as we chatted, not wanting to lose the connection.

"Oh, E, it's going to be fabulous. And Finn Carter has agreed to DJ the after party," she squealed.

My heart pinged at her giddy excitement, but at the same time, I felt a twinge of sadness because not only did I miss her, but I was going to miss her special event.

"That's amazing news! I am so incredibly happy for you."

The sound of the bells to the café jingled through the phone, and the coffee grinder came to life. I could almost smell the beans, the cinnamon and steamed milk. For a moment, I longed to be home.

"Honestly, who do I have to shag to get a drink around here?"

I smiled as I envisioned her throwing her hands in the air making her dramatic entrance. Then I heard her name shouted almost collectively. It reminded me of when Norm would enter the bar at *Cheers*. I simply adored American sitcoms. I listened to Nabila place her order and pay, as I continued to walk the stairs back to my room.

"Did you say that you went to the Hamptons?"

"Yes," I answered brightly. "And it was just as posh and decadent as you'd imagine. It wasn't bustling with activity, but I suppose it will pick up in the summer, at least that is what Alex tells me."

"Alex? *Who* is Alex?" she asked, letting out a gasp. "Have you met someone?"

My hands misted over with light beads of sweat and my heart rate kicked up at her line of questioning. What I wanted to say was yes. And gush to her about the fact that I'd met the most handsome man. Not only was he hot as sin, but Alex was smart, and sweet and I've already had the pleasure of shagging his brains out. But, instead, I kept my secret to myself.

"Oh no, nothing like that, Alex is my bodyguard while I'm in the city. My brother has gone to great lengths where safety is concerned," I admitted.

She snorted a laugh that tickled my ears. "Oh, doll, I'm sure Ronan has his reasons."

"I suppose you're right," I said, reaching for my keycard in my bag.

"Plus, you won't be totally alone in the city, and it's almost as if you have an instant friend," Nabila added in a singsong voice.

I huffed out a laugh, and pressed my forehead to the wooden door.

*The irony in her words, if only she knew.*

Alex and I were definitely on more than friendly terms. I didn't know how to define our relationship. "He's a nice guy, and he did agree to show me around the city. So, I guess that *is* a plus. Listen, Bila, I have to shower and gather my notes for my location hunting today. Let's make a date to video chat soon. I want to see the set up before your show."

"I'll text you, okay?"

"Perfect! Kisses, love."

"Cheers, doll."

I ended the call as I stepped inside my room. I tossed my bag onto the bed, and then I fell backwards onto the semi-soft mattress. As much as I loved hotel living, I longed for the comforts of my own bed. I sighed, draping my arm across my forehead.

I still hadn't decided what I was going to do as far as the expansion plans for the boutique went. Would I stay in America and let Bianca run the London location? Or would I stay in London and hire someone to manage this location? I had a bevy of questions, but I knew I wouldn't mind traveling and splitting my time between London and New York. In addition to two boutiques, I'd have two homes. Four places that would all have utilities among other bills that would need paid.

My mind whirled trying to figure out all the details before I'd even found a space. Maybe I was in over my head?

No. I've planned for this moment.

*It's going to work. I will make it work.*

It was day three of property shopping, and nothing was working out. Alex had found fault with every single storefront, building and block of the city on my list. Admittedly, it was helpful having him along. One sleazy building manager hinted that he wanted more from me than just monthly rent. I had to drag Alex out of that meeting before he punched the slime ball. Another place was in reprehensible condition, and he pointed out several structural problems. It would cost me double the value in renovations alone. Alex said I'd never get out of it what I would have put into the property.

"What's the name of your store?"

"La Vienne Rose," I replied, looking up from my laptop. We were sitting at the café downstairs at The Hawthorne Park Plaza, the place where apparently Alex and I both resided for the time being.

*Sneaky bastard.*

No matter, I was thankful to have a break from my real estate search; it allowed me to catch up on work.

He repeated the name a few times, and then took a drink of his coffee. "What made you choose that name?"

Smiling, I folded my hands under my chin and said, "I wanted something that was timeless but also reflected a personal touch. Nothing seemed to jive with Ella, and after several branding sessions with my pencil and notepad, the name hit me."

"How is La Vienne Rose personal to you?"

I dropped my hands to the tabletop, and grabbed my ink pen fidgeting with the cap. No man had ever asked me these kinds of questions before. They were more interested in getting me out of my clothes, rather than the fact that I was a prominent clothing store owner.

"My middle name is Vivienne, and my grandmother's name was Rosalie. After trying a few name combinations, suddenly there it was in bold letters."

"I like the name—it's *pretty*."

"Thank you," I said, leaning forward in my chair. "It was dumb luck on my part the French origin in the name also gave me a niche. I started buying my favorite French brands that were hard to come by in London and it . . ." I laughed, feeling foolish. "Sorry you must be terribly bored."

His eyes landed on mine. "Nothing about you bores me."

His words were warm, and the way he was looking at me sent heat racing down my belly, settling between my thighs. I shifted, feeling uncomfortable at the tingles that decided to have a dance party in my vagina.

*I sound ridiculous.*

"How many places are left on your list?"

"Two," I said, expelling a deep sigh. "I hope one is the future home for La Vienne Rose."

The worry and stress had built tension in my neck and shoulders. My muscles felt as tight as a taut rubber band. I closed my eyes, and attempted to ease pain in the back of my neck, kneading the knots with the tips of my fingers.

"You okay?"

"It's no big deal, but I have a headache," I said, pushing to my feet. "I think I'm just going to go up to my room and take a nap." I gathered my things and shoved them into my bag.

Alex lifted my handbag and laptop bag from the table.

"I can carry my own bag, Alex."

"You're completely capable. I get it," he replied, a smile tugging the corners of his mouth. "But I'm here so let me help you."

"If you must." I smiled, bumping his arm with mine. "Thanks."

I found it beyond impossible to say no to Alex, especially since he had been incredibly helpful where my real estate endeavors were concerned. I wondered if this was indeed part of his job description. We'd spent nearly eight to ten hours together. Lunch, afternoon coffee, and we'd had dinner together the last two evenings. Now he was carrying my laptop bag. It all felt very *intimate.*

As we walked to the bank of elevators, I heard someone yell my name. I spun around to find Gavin Lacourt striding towards me. Tall, dark and devilishly handsome. Along with being one of the top fashion photographers in the world, he was one of my closest friends.

In the past five years, Gavin had been my rock. He's been there through the good, the bad, and truly horrible. When I needed a shoulder to cry on, or someone to commiserate with, Gavin was there. When I needed help paying my rent, he'd given me work, assisting him with photoshoots. In the friend department, besides Nabila, there was no one I trusted more than him.

"How's my girl?" Gavin's strong hands rested on my shoulders, as he kissed both my cheeks.

"I'm good . . . but, I'm surprised to see you here," I said, stumbling back from Gavin's embrace feeling Alex's hands latching onto my waist.

Gavin's lips twisted into a wry smile. "I flew in this morning to meet with the Features Editor of *Belle Magazine*. They want me to shoot an upcoming editorial."

Not so subtly, Alex drew his arm up from my waist and draped it around my shoulders, pulling me away from Gavin and right against his body—his very taut and muscled body.

I craned my neck to look up at Alex. His eyes were narrowed and glaring at Gavin. Confusion washed through me. I needed to diffuse the situation before it became any more awkward.

"Introduce me, babe," Alex said, his warm breath fanned against my ear.

*Babe? What the bloody hell?*

Admittedly, the possessiveness in his tone made my knees weak. Alex was under my skin, it was both unnerving and completely intoxicating. *Shit!* I was slipping into deep trouble. That kind of trouble that you know will lead to no good, but you so want to see how far you can take it.

*Danger! Danger, Ella!* The words screamed in my brain, tormenting and teasing me all at once.

"Alex Robertsen, meet my friend, Gavin Lacourt."

Alex outstretched his hand to Gavin. "Friends, huh? How are you two acquainted?" Alex drawled.

Gavin gave a hint of a smile, as he shook Alex's hand. "Yes, Ella and I have been dear friends for many years, Mr. Robertsen," he answered, in his elegant voice.

"We met years ago at a Fashion Art Exhibit in London, and we've been friends ever since," I interjected.

The elevator dinged, and a mass of people rushed out. A man in a khaki trench coat bumped into my shoulder, shoving me into Alex. His grip tightened, holding me firm. Gavin's wide eyes landed on mine. There was no mistaking his look, he must have a thousand questions running through his mind.

"Are you two going up?" Gavin asked, nodding towards the empty elevator.

"*We* are," Alex answered. "Ella isn't feeling well. She needs some rest."

Again, Alex had laced a possessive vibe to his words. He

wasn't being rude to Gavin, by any manner, but he might as well have pulled out his dick and pissed, marking me as *his*. Alex released the hold he'd had on me as we stepped inside.

After pressing the button for the mezzanine level, Gavin turned back to face me and said, "Well then, you should rest, and then call me when you're feeling better."

"I will, I promise."

Waves of nausea crept up from my stomach. The bright light from the elevator stung my eyes and my head throbbed with an aching pain. I needed to get to my room and take a pill or get into a hot bath.

I caught Alex's reflection in the door. His eyes were focused and forward, much like they were the day he was introduced to me as my bodyguard. The elevator came to a stop, and the doors opened.

"It was nice to have met you, Alex."

"Likewise, Gavin."

"Au revoir, *my* pet."

My heart stuttered. That twat, he'd said that on purpose. The doors shut on him, leaving me standing alone with Alex.

"What the hell was all that territorial behavior nonsense?" I spat, spinning around to face him, headache nearly forgotten. "Calling me *babe*. Honestly, Alex, what the fuck was that about?"

"Lower your voice," he said firmly.

We arrived on my floor, and I turned and pulled my laptop bag from his strong hands. His scent wrapped around me, and I inhaled deeply. He smelled divine. So divine that I closed my eyes for a moment to take in his masculine scent, a tantalizing mix of aftershave and bergamot. As pissed off as I was, my body didn't seem to share my emotions.

"I'm not your property, Alex," I said, as I stepped into the corridor.

My breathing was heavy with every step I took. Alex followed closely behind me. I pulled my keycard from my bag, and inserted it into the slot. The green light flashed, and I pushed forward, but came to a sudden halt when my shoulder crashed into the door.

I looked up to find Alex's hand wedged between the door and its frame, holding it firmly in place. His body loomed over me, every muscle in my body froze. I tried to speak but nothing happened. No words. No sounds. Nothing.

He took a step towards me, pinning me against the door. "I don't know what came over me downstairs. For whatever reason, seeing another man with his hands on you drove me out of my fucking mind," he said, his voice was firm, but not angry. "And I didn't much care for the way Gavin was looking at you."

I held his hazel eyes, the glowing flecks of amber drawing me in, like moth to a flame. His other hand came up to the side of my face, his thumb smoothed over my lips. And I fucking melted on the inside. *Sweet Christ.*

"Why . . . why are you acting this way towards me?" The question left my lips in a shaky whisper.

He shrugged. "I can't help myself. I don't know *how* to act around you, Ella. There is a clear attraction between us." His hand drifted to my hair, where he tucked a strand behind my ear. "And I know you're having a difficult time being around me as well."

"Oh and exactly how do you know that?"

"Part of my skill set is to gather information and evaluate the facts of a given situation. In this particular case, I can see it in your eyes and the way you respond when I touch you." Leaning down, he teased my lips with his by brushing them over mine ever so slightly. Those lips . . . *his* lips, oh how I missed them and I loved how they felt against mine.

*Kiss me. Please don't tease me, Alex.*

In the next breath, as if he'd heard my inner thoughts, he granted my wish crushing his lips to mine.

I registered the echo of my laptop bag and purse hitting the floor as Alex's hand glided over my ass. My arms snaked around his neck, and he slid his tongue into my mouth. I moaned when he settled his knee between my thighs. As he pressed his big frame harder against me, I felt the solid length of his cock pressed against my stomach. I shoved a hand into his dark hair, holding him tight as I sucked on his tongue. He groaned. The sound was deep and pleasurable making the pressure between my legs tighten. I ground my pussy against his thigh as his fingers dug into the curve of my hip.

My eyes flew open, at the sound of the door opening, and I pulled back from our embrace.

"I . . . I can't do this with you," I managed to choke out, breathless from our kiss.

A frown marred the space between his brows. His eyes darkened, as he pinned them on me with confusion.

Smiling, I smoothed my palms down his chest. "What I meant to say was that I can't do this with you in public. Paparazzi or whatever, who knows who is watching us." I tossed my head towards the gentleman who was standing in the hallway a few doors down.

"I see," he said. "I guess we'll have to be more careful."

"Alex, I . . ."

He pressed his finger to my lips and shook his head. "Don't say anything. Get some rest and we'll talk later." With his foot wedged between the door and its frame, he scooped my bags off the floor and handed them to me. I could only stare as he walked away, leaving me stunned. I had a serious desire to run after him and drag him back to my bed and finish what we'd . . . *he'd* started.

My lips still tingled from our kiss. My knees wobbled and shook as I faltered across the threshold and into the hallway of my suite. The pain in my head, along with the deep ache between my thighs, was beginning to unravel me.

Once I closed the door, I sagged against the cool metal. Unsure of how long I stood there, somehow I managed to revive my jellied limbs and move towards the seating area. I placed my bags on the desk, and checked my phone for messages. Staring at the screen, my fingers hovered over Alex's name. *No, don't call him.*

As I walked into the bathroom, I couldn't stop thinking about that kiss. After turning on the water, I added some lavender bubble bath to the deep soaker tub. I stripped out of my clothes, and then turned on the sound system to a light classical station.

Sitting at the vanity, I pulled my hair into a messy bun, and my mind replayed everything that led to that moment in the hallway with Alex. This thing between us, I didn't know what it was exactly. I suppose it could be described as a sharp itch in need of scratching or a sweet craving that needed satisfied.

Alex had called it an attraction.

The last time I acted on my feelings of an attraction for a man, I ended up making the front page of the gossip tabloids. The cherry on top was having my heart broken. He said he wanted to be with me forever, but in the blink of an eye, our forever turned into over.

A wall surrounded my heart, there was nothing but darkness. It sounded all very lame and cliché. Understandably, I know I am not the first woman who has suffered a broken heart. But, I just hadn't let anyone in, in a long time. Not one man since *him* had been able to break the wall down.

A knock at the door interrupted my thoughts. I pushed to my feet and leaned over the tub to turn off the water.

"One moment please." I called out, slipping my silk robe on over my shoulders. My bare feet hit the marble in the entryway sending a chill up my spine. I pulled open the door to find room service breezing past me with a large basket.

My eyes narrowed, as the tall dark haired man arranged the basket on the table. "But, I didn't order anything," I announced, folding my arms over my chest.

"No, miss, this is a gift from Mr. Robertsen," he answered handing me an envelope.

I peeled open the card and read the message from Alex: *Here are a few things to help you get well soon. P.S. You have an in suite massage scheduled in about an hour.*

My fingers danced over my lips, and my heart leapt in my throat after reading his sweet note.

"Is there anything else I can get for you right now, Miss Connolly?"

"No, thank you," I answered, tucking the note back inside the envelope. He let himself out, and I half-skipped, half-walked over to the basket of goodies. There was a silver eye mask, a pair of fuzzy socks, an icepack, some chamomile tea, B2 vitamins, a box of Italian chocolates and an aromatherapy candle. The scent was bergamot.

I stood there feeling my cheeks heat, as I clutched the envelope to my chest. How in the world did Alex have time to put all this together? The thoughtfulness of the gift was certainly heartfelt and flattering. And he'd scheduled a massage for me.

I picked up the candle and inhaled deeply. The richness of

the fragrance slid through my blood and wound tight around my bones. My body recognized the familiar scent, and all my senses were overloaded with Alex. I craved the way I felt when he touched me. Even more, I loved the way he responded to me when I touched him.

With my hands wrapped around the candle, I sauntered into the bathroom and placed it on the stand in the corner. After lighting the wick, I turned on the hot water to finish filling up the tub. As I stepped into the water, it stung with a sharp bite—it was hotter than I preferred, almost scalding. The fiery temperature, much like being around Alex, set my body ablaze with a fevered burn—right down to my core.

*Maybe, I should take a cold shower instead of hot bath.*

# Chapter Ten

## Alex

So much for burying my feelings for Ella. I just went and sprinkled Miracle Grow all over that fucking plan. I scrubbed my hands down my face as I paced the hallway of my suite. Ella was vibrant and full of life. I liked hearing her talk so passionately about her business. What I hated was seeing that French douchebag with his hands on her.

*French douchebag?* They're friends.

There was no point in denying it, I couldn't seem to resist my feelings for her, and I'm a fucked up mess over it. All this anxiety, I needed to blow off some steam.

Blow. *Blow job.* My mind raced and all I wanted was Ella's perfect lips wrapped around my cock, staining it with that siren red color. I wanted to fuck her perfect mouth and then fuck her.

*Jesus Christ.*

I needed to relieve this tension. Since fucking Ella was not an option at this moment, I decided to hit the gym. I barreled my way through ten sets of pull-ups, doubled my push-ups and my wall squats before hitting the treadmill. I finished strong with some sit-ups, two hundred to be exact. My workout had been decent, but a lingering tension remained.

After stripping out of my sweat soaked clothes, I turned on the shower and the steam fogged over the glass. Leaning up against the tiles, my head fell back and I gripped my cock. I closed my eyes and pictured Ella on her knees in front of me, sucking her bottom lip into her mouth in anticipation. At the thought of Ella's blue eyes, heavy lidded and gazing up at me, my hand grazed up and down my cock with long, slow strokes.

In my fantasy, Ella sucked me deep, running her tongue along my tip and licking the head of my dick, lapping up pre-cum. I pumped my dick roughly, as I imagined tugging at her hair, to watch her watching me as I fucked her beautiful mouth.

She hummed and moaned, the vibrations rippled around my cock, and I went rougher picturing her cheeks hollowing, taking me deeper. My mind went into overdrive, and so did my hand, at the thought of hearing Ella begging me to fuck her. In a race to get myself off, my hand worked my cock with a brutal speed.

Our night together was burned into my memory. The vision of Ella spread wide beneath me appeared, her tight body bowing towards me as I took her mouth. My body jerked, and I came hard, growling out her name at the vision of her looking into my eyes as I slid deep into her bare pussy.

*Fuck. Ella. I need to have her again.*

I *would* have her again. When and where was up for grabs.

# Chapter Eleven

## Ella

I'd managed successfully to hideout out in my hotel suite, avoiding Alex since our kiss. Tonight was a different story. There was nowhere to escape and it didn't help matters that I couldn't take my eyes off him standing across the room, wearing an ink black suit, looking hot as sin. The ache had returned, yes, the one between my thighs. I had to tell myself to pull my shit together. I couldn't risk allowing someone to see me drooling over Alex, especially *not* my brother.

Holliday, Ronan's new "flavor of the month"—the tabloids words, *not* mine—approached me, radiating true sexiness in a black strapless gown, her ears dripping with diamond and emeralds. She was stunning, with her long dark hair and svelte figure. To my surprise, she was down to earth, and spoke with a genuine sincerity, which was quite the opposite of his twat of an ex-wife, Emma and, that cow, Heather Young.

"Ella," she said, giving me a warm hug. "I am loving this Chanel dress. You look positively stunning."

Smiling, I ran the palms of my hands over the bodice of my white fit-and-flare frock. It was one of my favorite dresses. Not only was it beautiful with its lilac embellishments, the short length, along with the jagged hemline, added some edge and allowed me to show off my long legs.

"You're too kind. I'm flattered, high praise coming from someone who looks like they stepped off a runway."

"Well, thank you, I'll take the compliment," she said, toying with her emerald pendant. "This is one of my sister's latest creations."

I knew the dress was a Ricchetti Design. I made it my business to keep up with Charlotte's collections. One day I hoped to feature her designs in my boutique.

"So, tell me, how on earth did you get my brother, the hermit, to host a dinner party?" I asked, peering over her shoulder, spying on Alex once more. From the looks of it, I wasn't the only one staring at him. My last count was ten—ten *other* women gazing in his direction.

She laughed. "We're trying this new thing where we have a relationship and include our friends and family. I'm afraid we're both guilty of hiding out."

I completely understood what she was talking about. After some embarrassing mishaps with the paparazzi, I learned very quickly to stay inside my flat, especially when Ronan had a big event. That was when they hounded me relentlessly, hoping I'd do something scandalous to sell their papers. *Assholes.*

"Before I forget, I wanted to say how much I appreciate this party," I replied gesturing around the living room of their gorgeous penthouse.

"Oh, please, it's our pleasure," she said, looping her arm

through mine. "Let's grab a drink shall we?"

As we sauntered across the room, I had to bite back a laugh. Holliday seemed quite comfortable with her place as Ronan Connolly's live-in girlfriend. I loved that she had that confidence about her.

"Are you having any luck finding a space for your boutique?"

"No," I replied with a sigh. "And I'm afraid with only two locations left to inspect, I might have hit a dead end."

"I'm sure you'll find the perfect location soon enough," she replied, offering me a reassuring smile along with a glass of champagne.

I exhaled, and took a long drink. "Thanks, I'm in need of some optimism."

We carried on like two old friends. She was sweet and very easy to talk to and I could see why Ronan was so taken with Holliday, she was beautiful inside and out.

We chatted for a while she provided an adorably hilarious story about how she and my brother once had a fight during a lightening round confessional that included shots of whiskey. God, I loved her, and I was quite positive that Ronan would marry her.

One of the catering staff approached and explained to Holliday that she was needed in the kitchen. She politely excused herself and said she'd meet up with me later. It gave me an opportunity to explore Ronan's new place.

As I moved from room to room, I chatted with a few people I knew. Everyone was having fun, talking and laughing. It was a relaxed and casual gathering, despite everyone here was dressed for the red carpet. The sound of Michael Buble's velvety smooth crooning of "Who's Lovin' You" brought the ladies to their feet. *The man's voice is pure sex, orgasmic.*

Although, there was no designated dance floor, that didn't stop Holliday and her friend Tinley Atkinson from getting the party started. At the sight of the gorgeous, tall and tattooed movie star, Matthew Barber taking Tinley into his arms and sweeping her across the floor, I pictured Alex and me holding each other and gliding across the room.

Leaning against the wall, I knocked back the rest of my drink and grabbed another from a petite and beautiful Asian woman who moved through the crowd with the grace of a dancer. Her sleek black ponytail swung, as she zig zagged around the well-dressed party-goers with ease. I lifted the glass to my lips and felt a hand squeeze my shoulder. It sent my heart racing, at the thought it might be Alex.

"Hey, Lolly," my brother said, bumping my elbow with his arm. "Enjoying the party?"

"Oh, yes, I'm having *loads* of fun," I replied, and immediately my body tensed at the sound of my words. It was evident I couldn't hide my disappointment, that I was secretly hoping to hear Alex's voice.

"Are you okay?" he asked, swirling the whiskey in his glass. Jameson Vintage or Midleton Very Rare, I suspected, his preferred choices.

"Yeah, I'm all good." I pivoted on my heel to face him. My brother's eyes were dazzling. A sparkle that I'd never noticed before. It was as if he was transfixed under some kind of hypnotic spell. My gaze followed his and landed right on Holliday. I looked back at him to find him grinning like a fool. *A lovesick fool.* Yep, he was in love, which meant he was in a fantastic mood. I took advantage of the opportunity to question him about his ex-stalker.

"I'd ask how you were, but it's written all over your face. Instead, I want to know what's the deal with all the security? Is your stalker back in the picture?"

"What?" His brows scrunched together. "No, that nut job is safely locked away in a cold jail cell."

"Then what gives?" I asked, pulling my shoulders back. "And don't you feed me some cock and bull line."

Blowing out a deep breath, he nodded towards the hallway and I followed him to his home office. He shut the door and motioned for me to take a seat. If the thought of the psycho had me spooked, this private meeting had me fearing the worst.

"The reason for the security is strictly a precaution," he replied, taking a seat across from me. "I just want to make sure that you are safe while you're here in the city."

I rolled my eyes. "Yes, so you've mentioned."

"Roll your eyes all you want, but you know that my instincts are never wrong. Alex informed Dean that a man named Charlie approached you the other day during lunch. And by his description, I'm willing to bet all the whiskey in Ireland that it was Charlie McNeil."

*Balls!* Alex had been reporting back to Dean about my daily activities. I should have known or at the very least, Alex could have told me that he would be doing that. I stared down at my champagne glass, watching the bubbles float to the top and disappear. My hands started to shake, and I didn't know whether to cry or scream.

"Ella, did he follow you here?"

"No, I asked him that very question. He told me that had to move here because he's unable to sell his pictures in the UK, which we knew about the pictures because of the trial. I guess he takes sporting event pictures now. But Charlie wasn't the entire problem," I said, tapping my finger to the glass. "Alex doesn't know about David, Charlie, and the whole trial does he? Ronan, please tell me you didn't tell him."

"No, that's your private business to tell whom you choose."

"Sometimes I feel guilty over the legal battle where Charlie was involved."

"Ella, you should not feel badly, *you* were the victim. They made their own choices and now they are living with the consequences. Do you want to get a restraining order against Charlie while you're here?"

"No," I replied, pushing to my feet. "As I told Alex, Charlie is a lot of things, but he was just an opportunist who made a bad deal with my ex."

A knock at the door interrupted our conversation. Holliday entered, letting us know dinner was going to be served shortly. Suddenly, I wasn't feeling too cheery, chatty or hungry.

"Can I escort you two lovely ladies to dinner?"

"I will catch up in a bit. I need to use the lavatory . . . *powder room*."

"Use the guest bathroom upstairs," Holliday instructed, rounding the back of the leather sofa. "Once you pass through the gallery, it's the fourth door on the right."

After they left, I took a minute to collect myself. Thinking back to that ugly and embarrassing time in my life left me feeling a little scattered. It had taken a lot of time to heal from my painful break-up with David, and the fact that it was a highly publicized scandal, splashed all over the gossip rags, didn't help matters. The only man I'd ever loved. The bastard took my heart, threw it in a blender and then pressed crush.

Behind me, I heard the shuffling of chairs smoothing across the hardwood floor as I nipped up the staircase to find the lav . . . *damn it, the powder room*. I needed to hurry, and get back before they finished serving dinner. As I strode through the gallery and down the corridor, the city lights splashed across the carpet and up the walls. The view was incredible, and I wished that the evening's weather had been warm enough to sit outside on the magnificent wraparound balcony.

I heard footsteps behind me, and pivoted to find Alex coming up the staircase. He craned his neck and my eyes met his.

"Hey, there you are."

He said something more as he rounded the railing, but I tuned him out and walked away.

"Ella, where are you going?" he asked, his footsteps growing closer down the dimly lit hallway.

"Go away, Alex. I'd rather not be around you at the moment."

"Okay, I'm gathering that you're mad, and obviously at me."

We came to a stop in front of a door, and I turned to face him. "As a matter of fact I am. Why did you have to tell Dean about Charlie? I had the situation handled. You knew he'd tell my brother, and *that* was one thing I didn't need."

"Calm down, Ella."

"Did you seriously just say that to me? I *am* calm."

"Wait, I didn't mean it that way," he said, and gently tugged my arm bringing me around to face him. "I meant keep your voice down."

"You are *my* employee, and you don't get to talk to me that way. You work for me, remember?" My voice seethed with anger as I shoved a finger at his chest. "You don't get to tell me how to behave." I wiggled from the hold he had on me, and turned away grasping for the handle of the door. Before I could open it, he slapped his palms against the wood.

He enveloped me, pinning me between him and the door.

"I am well aware of the fact that your brother hired me to lookout for you," he rasped in my ear.

"Well, you don't have to worry about that anymore because you're fired."

"Good luck with that, Ella," he scoffed, and in a fluid motion spun me around to face him once more. His bright hazel eyes narrowed, focused on me. "No one else applied for this job. *Only* me."

"I seriously doubt that."

"Trust me, sweetheart, I have the advantage here, not you. You see, I was recommended to babysit your trouble-making ass."

"Fuck you, you're an asshole," I hissed, trying to move away, but he'd pinned my arms above my head.

"Is that really what you want?" he asked his hand curling around my waist. "For me to fuck you?"

It was unbearable—how close he was to me. Anger and lust were in an epic battle of disagreement inside me. All the memories of our night together came flooding back. I could lose myself in this moment, guide him into the bathroom and . . . swallowing hard, I needed to regain my composure. But, for a little while longer, his question would wait as I relished the feel of him against me.

Panting softly, I licked my dry lips. "I don't want anything from you."

"Really?" He cocked an eyebrow, and his free hand slipped underneath my dress sliding across the edge of my panties. I jerked at the contact, and he pressed his chest against my breasts.

"Yes, really."

"Liar, you forget who you're dealing with," he replied, moving his fingers over my soaked panties. His teeth scraped across my earlobe. I wanted Alex. Everything inside me pulled in different directions.

"I'm *not* lying." My soaked panties didn't exactly help my case.

"You lied and here's how I know: we never lost eye contact, and your voice lowered an octave," he informed, stroking me back and forth. My eyes closed, as I sagged against the door. "Contrary to popular belief, most people will look you in the eye when they're lying, assuming they're less likely to be caught by doing the opposite of what was expected."

His lips connected with mine. Sliding my tongue into his mouth, I deepened our kiss. His hand fell from the hold he'd had on my wrists, landing on my waist. My arms roped around his neck.

I kissed Alex hard. Our movements were hurried and unapologetic. Everything that had built up between us over the last week came barreling through at hyper-speed, like a train whose brakes had gone out. It sent a warning light to my brain, telling me I should stop before we went off the rails, but it seems my self-control had abandoned me. And I was sure his had jumped the track as well.

I didn't want a quick fuck in my brother's bathroom in the middle of a party. One of us had to have some self-control.

Breathless, I shoved at his shoulder. "This *is* . . . I'm still mad at you and I don't feel either of us is thinking clearly."

Alex pulled back, holding my gaze. His hands smoothed my dress down. Saying nothing he turned and walked away, leaving me alone, my body clinging against another doorframe, panting and aching with need for him once again.

# Chapter Twelve

## Ella

When I returned to the party, I took my brother aside and told him I wasn't feeling well. As I expected, Ronan insisted Alex take me back to the hotel. With Holliday's help, I managed to convince him that I would be perfectly fine taking a cab.

Once I stepped off the elevator, I hurried through the empty lobby. I pulled my coat tighter around me as I stood waiting for a cab outside Ronan's building. The air was chilly, but it did nothing to relieve the four-alarm fire raging in my body. Despite the calm demeanor I displayed when I left the party, I was anything but.

As I climbed into the back of the yellow taxi I thought about what just happened between Alex and me. I'd like to say it was unexpected, but who was I kidding. It was only a matter of time before we'd have our hands all over each other again, purring and panting like a pair of wild animals.

"Where to, miss?"

At half-past eight on a Saturday evening in the city that never slept, I didn't know where to go. Well, that wasn't entirely true, I wanted to go back to Alex's suite, or mine, and shag him. And *that* was the problem. So I did what I needed to do, which was leave and get my wits about me.

"Could you drive around a while? I'll have a destination soon."

"Fine by me, it's your money."

Leaning back against the seat, I dug my smartphone out of my purse. I had a missed call from Alex and a text: *You left? Where are you?*

Before replying to his message, I fired off a few texts to Gavin. Hoping he was still in the city. My phone pinged seconds later. As luck would have it, he was staying at the Onyx SkyLofts and invited me to come over. My shoulders sagged with relief and I redirected the driver to midtown. I inhaled deeply and seriously began to think about what just happened. My eyes peered out the window and I watched as the colorful electricity of the city whirled past me in.

Alex had sent another text message: *Please talk to me. I need to know that you're safe.*

*Me: I'm fine, except for having a headache. Need some rest. Chat soon.*

After I hit send, I powered down my phone. I wasn't ready to talk to Alex yet. At some point, I would see him and we'd have to talk. I wasn't sure what I'd say. What would *he* say?

As I stepped off the elevator into the private foyer, a raven-haired exotic beauty, whom I guessed was about my age, passed by giving me a tight-lipped smile. Gavin was leaning against the doorjamb with his shirt unbuttoned and his dark hair was damp. To say he was a ladies' man, would be an understatement. I'm fairly certain that he wouldn't be giving up his bachelor status anytime soon.

"A friend of yours?" I teased, tugging on the collar of his dress shirt.

Gavin pulled me into a hug, as soon as I entered his suite. "Come in, Mademoiselle," he drawled, pulling me deeper into the room.

"Wow, this place is spectacular." I shrugged out of my coat and draped it over the back of a wingback chair. Captivated, I stood breathless, taking in the lavish surroundings accented with marigold yellow and rich reds. The space was filled with antiques and impressive artwork. "I think I could live here."

"Not me, although I do love New York, London will always be home."

"I don't know, Gavin," I replied, motioning towards the floor to ceiling windows that occupied an entire wall. "This view is impressive."

"Where's your man?" he asked, nudging me with this elbow. "You know, the one that calls you *babe*?"

Of course, Gavin was only joking about Alex, but it didn't make me feel any less awkward.

"He's working."

"Isn't his *work* guarding you?"

My eyes narrowed. How did he know that? And then it hit me, Nabila must have told him. Quickly, I switched topics unsure if I was ready to talk about Alex.

"Why didn't you mention that you were on a date?" I asked taking a seat on the couch. "I would have understood."

He laughed, and ignored my question. "Care for a drink?"

"Might as well."

With the bottle and two filled glasses in hand, Gavin joined me on the couch. He handed me one and I took a big gulp of the burgundy colored liquid.

"Something is weighing on you. You look stressed. Is it Mr. Robertsen?"

"It's a combination of things, but no, Alex isn't the reason for my stress, confusion maybe," I replied, before polishing off my glass. "But that can wait. I want to know how your shoot went."

"The shoot is Monday."

"And the lady who just left, is she the star of the photoshoot?"

"No, Isabelle didn't make the cut." He ran a hand through his wavy hair. "She was feeling upset, and so I . . ."

"You offered her solace." I finished his sentence and refilled my glass.

"Solace, yes, seems that I'm on double duty tonight."

"I don't need solace."

"Oh no?" He tilted his head, and lifted a brow. "You left your own party early, and I can tell that something is on your mind. I'm certain it has something to do with the American muscle."

"Ugh, could you please stop referring to Alex in that silly manner. It's dreadful." I laughed, leaning my head back into the sofa cushions.

"Start talking and I'll consider dropping the nickname."

Of course, I told Gavin everything. Starting with how I'd met Alex, and then what happened when saw each other the next day. From there, I couldn't stop yammering on about the trip to his Hampton's home, our sweet chats, and how thoughtful he'd been setting up a private massage when I wasn't feeling well. It had been less than a week and here I was gushing about a man that when I'd met him, I didn't want to know a thing about him.

When I finished, I tilted my head towards Gavin. He swirled the remainder of his drink, and then tossed it back.

"What are you thinking?"

"I'm thinking that's some series of events." He pushed to his feet and walked over to the bar trading his wine glass for a bottle of water. "But there's one thing you left out."

I cocked an eyebrow. "Oh and what's that?"

"Where's the problem?" he asked, extending his arms out. "You've mentioned all these wonderful things along with some crazy hot sex, but you haven't stated an issue."

I leaned forward, placing my elbows on my knees. "Isn't it obvious? He's my bodyguard, it's wrong on many levels."

"Wrong, right, what the hell does that matter?"

"I'm supposed to be here on business, not screwing around."

"Why not have both? The guy wants you, you said so yourself. And, I know for a fact, it's not the wine that's making you blush right now." Gavin lifted the bottle from the table and poured me another drink. "Just thinking about Alex has you all hot and bothered."

Perhaps Gavin was onto something. I couldn't believe I was entertaining advice from a notorious playboy. Casual sex *was* fun, so why not? As long as Alex and I discussed what we wanted, and laid the ground rules, there wouldn't be any blurred lines.

Suddenly, I was having déjà vu. Wasn't that what we'd discussed the night we met?

*Rules.* Those didn't seem to work for Alex and me.

# Chapter Thirteen

## Ella

The next morning I found myself sitting at the coffee shop around the corner from my hotel. Sunday mornings were a regular thing for me and Nabila back in London. If we weren't hungover from the prior evening, we'd hit the gym and then pop around the corner for brunch at the cafe.

Sober and very clear-headed, but nonetheless confused over my Alex situation, I sat at a table near the front, enjoying my coffee and gluten-free croissant. I caught myself reading the same paragraph again from a book I picked up at Heathrow before my flight. I'd left London a few days before I told Ronan I was coming to the States. It wasn't my intention to purposely lie to my brother, but I wanted to have a few days to myself.

"You're making my job very difficult, Ella," a low voice

whispered in my ear. "I haven't learned all your hangouts yet."

I lifted my head from my book and turned to see Alex standing there with a coffee cup in hand, wearing a pair of denim jeans and a black V-neck t-shirt that clung to his muscles. His hazel eyes were bright, and the way he looked at me sent my heartbeat racing. It's unfair how good-looking he was.

"A girl needs her morning latte and sweet treat."

"Aren't you British?" he asked, sliding into the chair next to me. "Where are your tea and crumpets?"

I laughed and closed my book. "Well, I'm not like most Brits, although I do love afternoon tea. I'm *English*, Irish, Russian, and Swedish." I tugged on my blonde hair and pointed to my blue eyes. "A mix of cultures, as I'm sure you are."

He chuckled, and his lips pulled into an amused smile. "I'm part Irish, and Robertsen is Scottish. Somewhere along the line, they changed the 'o' in son to an 'e.' My grandfather joked that the Robertsen's that spelled their names with the 'o' were the brains of the family. He had an awkward sense of humor."

He leaned back in his chair, and stretched out his long legs under the table. His arm reached for his coffee cup and the fabric of his t-shirt inched up over his muscular biceps and defined triceps. Jesus Christ, he is so damn hot. My mind retreated to the subject of casual sex.

Sex.

Sex with hot as sin Alex.

"So, about last night," he said, leaning forward.

I waved him off. "We don't have to talk about it. Clearly, we were caught up in a moment and made a mistake."

Alex's hand covered mine. "Ella, I don't feel what happened was a mistake."

The feel of his touch, coupled with his admission, returned

me to the same place I was last night and the overwhelming emotions I felt. When I'd met David, I had these same feelings; it was instant and burned white hot. Then everything around me, around *us,* was extinguished and I'd vowed not to let another man get close enough to burn me.

"What about all the stuff you said about bad things happened when you allow your dick make the decisions?"

He laughed. "I think what I said was allowing my dick to interfere with my job. It's true, I've made many bad decisions in my life, but this doesn't feel like one. Besides, you fired me. Remember? So technically, you aren't my job anymore."

*Crap.* I'd felt embarrassed and dreadful for the way I'd spoken to Alex.

"I apologize. I shouldn't have been cruel. I didn't mean any of it. You were just doing your job and I should respect that."

"I was a bit of jackass myself," he admitted. "I'm sorry, too. You *might* be trouble, but only the best kind. I like you, a lot in fact, and I'd like to get to know you better. So, for today, I'm still fired and we're just Ella and Alex. Is that okay?"

Warmth flowed through me at his words. "Okay." My heart pounded in my chest and I was sure he could see my pulse racing. Alex was observant, trained to read people. At his request, I'd agreed to just be me. This was going to be interesting.

"Come on, let's get out of here."

"What?"

"I want to show you something," he said, nodding towards the door.

"Alex, I have work to do this afternoon and I need to be ready for my appointments this week."

I was certain that when he said he wanted to get to know

me better, he'd meant that we'd just hangout and have a coffee and a chat.

"It's Sunday. You're allowed some relaxation." He wiggled his eyebrows and flashed that cocky smirk of his. "You know you want to."

Alex was adorable. Try as I might, I couldn't resist his offer. "Fine, I'll go with you."

"Good." His fingers brushed my hair away from my face.

I pushed to my feet as Alex pulled out my chair and I gathered my things. His hand fell to the small of my back and he guided me towards the doors of the coffee shop. The sun was hotter than I was used to, but I loved the way the heat felt upon my skin. We walked back to the parking garage and Alex took my hand in his. I liked this feeling because *he* was the reason I was having these feelings again.

The valet pulled his Range Rover around, and I slipped into the passenger seat and buckled up.

"Are you going to tell me where you are taking me?"

"Nope," he answered with a wry smile. "But I'm sure you will figure it out in no time."

Alex put the vehicle into gear and we drove out of the parking garage. Once we hit the Long Island Expressway my guess was that we were on our way to the Hamptons. I recognized the route from our first trip out here.

"Is the temperature in here okay?"

"Yes," I answered, settling back further into the seat. Alex took my hand in his, tracing circles against my skin with his thumb, it felt wonderful. My eyes took in the sky, painted the most incredible shade of blue with streaks of white clouds. I didn't want to close my eyes, but exhaustion took hold, or maybe it was pure contentment. Finally, I let myself relax, and I worried less about the rules.

"Ella," Alex's voice rasped warmly in my ear. "Wake up."

I shifted in my seat and managed to smack my knee against the dashboard.

"Ouch," I bellowed, rubbing at the biting pain in my knee. *Damn long legs.*

"Are you okay?"

Nodding, I cracked my eyes open, and looked out the window. I smiled at the sight of Alex's beautiful beach house. This was a lovely surprise. Alex hopped out of the vehicle and opened my door. He helped me out and I hobbled over the stones as we made our way to the porch.

"You said you had something to show me, and I've already seen your house. Did you just bring me here to show off?" I teased, nudging his arm.

Alex drew his hand to his chest, pretending to wince that I'd offended him. "I would never do such a thing." He unlocked the door, and pulled me inside. I stood in awe, feeling my jaw drop at the sight before me, the place looked quite a lot different from the last time. There were no workers milling about, and the scent of fresh paint replaced the smell of sawdust. The house was stunning unfinished, but seeing it now had rendered me speechless. My gaze was fixed to the vintage wheel mounted over a French zinc console table, simply gorgeous, and this was only the foyer. Alex tugged my arm, pulling me from my trance and I followed him down the hallway towards the living room.

Nearly everything was white, with splashes of deep blues, greys, and rich tan accents. Soft, airy drapes hung from wooden rods, and sisal rugs covered the hardwood floors. We walked from room to room, each more stunning than the previous. I wouldn't have imagined a man like Alex would have such impeccable taste in home décor. But then I remembered how he looked in that suit, and today, even as casual as he was dressed, Alex was handsome. If his personal style of dress was any indication, maybe I shouldn't be so surprised.

"What do you think?"

"It's stunning, and I think it suits you."

He shrugged. "My interior designer said the house needed to have subtle feminine touches. I wasn't sure about the curtains, and some of the candles. Do you think it's too girly?"

My heart swelled at his concern. Nothing about this place screamed gender to me one way or another—it had ideal balance. The house was amazing, and as I looked around, I could see it reflected his personality in many ways. For me, I saw a strong, safe structure that offered warmth and tranquility.

"Everything is perfect," I said reassuringly. "You don't need a neon beer sign above the mantle to say, 'I'm a man's man.'"

He laughed. "Damn it. Are you sure? I was thinking of hanging one in the dining room."

I jabbed my finger at his chest. "You better not, Alex Robertsen. I'll be furious with you."

"I've seen you get angry with me and I kind of liked it." His voice was husky with desire.

I laughed. "You only liked it because of the end result."

He stepped closer to me, cradling my face in his hands. "Ella, that's not true. I mean sure, I liked that, too, but I also enjoy just being with *you*."

I smiled. "I like being with you, too."

"Now that we understand each other, I'm going to do the thing I've been dying to do since I saw you at the coffee shop earlier."

Before I could reply, his lips pressed against mine. My arms came around his neck as he deepened our kiss. Our tongues thrashed against each other and I felt weightless, abandoning all my rules and reservations. A low moan resonated from his chest, sending a chill down my spine. My fingers tangled in his hair, tugging the strands hard as his hands smooth up and down my back. Warmth tingled everywhere we touched. His fingers skimmed under my blouse, inching their way up my ribcage.

"Ella," he whispered, breaking our kiss. "I want you to stay the night."

"You want me to be your first house guest?"

He shook his head. "I want you in *my* bed . . . all night."

"Okay," I breathed. And once again, I let go and agreed to whatever it was Alex asked of me.

"But first, we have some business to take care of, because I didn't just bring you here for a roll in the hay. Earlier, when I said I wanted to get to know you, I meant all of you. With that said, will you have lunch with me?"

"I'd love too."

Alex tilted my chin, and his lips met mine once more. He gave me a tender, lingering kiss. It was soft and sweet, full of passion, but not the need to fuck or claim me. It was meaningful on its own, it was about connecting and it spoke volumes.

I was the girl who'd sworn off men, at least the part where I allowed myself to seek comfort or find true companionship. Now it seemed the wall I'd built around my heart wasn't as sturdy as I once thought. With each kiss, the bricks just might tumble one by one. I only hoped it didn't crush me in the process.

# Chapter Fourteen

## Ella

Alex and I returned from grabbing takeaway . . . *takeout* at one of the many seafood restaurants in town. The choices were endless, but we finally settled on a place that had the largest option of gluten-free dishes. Alex stocked his place with a few groceries, mostly dry and canned goods, nothing fresh that would spoil. He'd hired a housekeeper to take care of things while he stayed in the city. When he had told me, a twinge of guilt rolled through my chest knowing I was the reason for keeping him from living in his gorgeous new home.

He pulled a bottle of white wine from the refrigerator and I watched as he reached up for a wine glass, his t-shirt lifted showing his chiseled back and I thought of his tattoo. I made a mental note to ask him about it the next opportunity.

Once he'd poured my glass and handed it to me, he

popped the top off a bottle of beer for himself. We gathered our plates of food and settled at the table outside.

"So tell me how you managed to pull all this together, your house I mean." I scooped up a bite of my grilled shrimp and vegetable dish.

"I had some time on my hands while you were locked away in your room after our kiss," he recalled with a smirk.

"Oh, by the way, thank you for the lovely basket of goodies. I'm sorry if I didn't mention before."

"You're welcome. When Gary called and said the house was ready for a final inspection, I flew out here that evening and we went over the details."

Stunned, I dropped my fork to the plate. "You *flew* out here? How is that possible?"

Alex winced. "Careful with the dishes, sweetheart, they're brand new. Flying, it's no big deal. I have connections."

"Connections, huh?"

"My brother is part owner of a small aviation company. Actually, it's not that small anymore. You could say that I'm a frequent flyer," he replied, and then took another bite of his shrimp and avocado taco.

"Your brother, the one who has offices in the city and that you used to work with? You two must be particularly close."

Breathing a deep sigh, Alex closed his eyes and shook his head. His gaze returned to me.

"We aren't that close anymore, and I'm the cause for the strain on our relationship."

I covered his hand with mine, offering comfort the best way I knew how. *Crap!* I didn't mean to make him upset.

"It's okay if you don't want to talk about it, but if you do I am here to listen."

A smile tugged the corners of his mouth, as he intertwined

our fingers. "I needed to hear that, I hope what I am about to tell you won't shatter the pedestal you hold me up on."

I laughed. Actually, I think I snorted. "Oh please, you're not *that* wonderful."

"Again, you've crushed my very fragile ego."

"Doubtful, but I can see that we might be broaching a rather delicate matter."

Alex nodded. "There is something and I'm not going to beat around the bush or sugar coat—I had an affair with my brother's girlfriend."

My eyes popped wide. "Oh." It was all I managed to say.

Moments of silence passed between us, but it seemed to go on forever. A thousand thoughts swirled inside me at his admission. Alex gripped my hand a little tighter.

"Ella, say something."

My heart raced and my throat went dry. I couldn't seem to form any words. This must be related to the "bad things happen when his dick does the thinking" matter. He was in obvious pain over the affair and my heart ached for him. I grabbed my drink and took a huge gulp, and then another, finishing the glass. I cleared my throat, and met his gaze. "If there is one thing I know to be fact, there's always more to the story. Why don't you start at the beginning?"

The beginning . . . that seemed simple enough. As I pulled my thoughts together, I took our empty cartons from lunch and threw them into the trash. I wasn't expecting to have this conversation with Ella today, but she asked, and I refused to be one of "those guys." The guy too afraid to ruin a good thing by not being straightforward, that's not who I was.

Even though Vince has since forgiven me, the affair strained our once close relationship. There were times I still hated myself for sleeping with Amanda. She was his and I wasn't supposed to have those feelings for her, but the two of us spent so much time together and Vince was rarely around. I was lonely and she was lonely, and the entire thing was stupid. Not once did I try to stop it, and when Amanda would, I'd always convinced her that I was the better man.

I grabbed the wine and another beer for myself and walked back to the deck. Ella had moved to one of the lounge chairs and I joined her.

"I want you to know that I'm not a cheater," I said, as I refilled her glass.

She cocked an eyebrow, flashing me a small smile.

"Okay, I get it," I said, before taking a giant swallow of my beer. "You have to know that Vince, my brother, isn't . . . *wasn't* always the greatest guy. He was a classic workaholic who ignored his kids and was barely a husband to his ex-wife. Their family was unraveling and Vince was too wrapped up in his business ventures to care."

"You know that his shortcomings are *his*, not yours, to amend."

"I do understand that, and it wasn't like that for Amanda and me. We *were* friends and I'd come to care about her. She was down on her luck and Vince picked her up and offered her a fairytale life. He'd given her everything but the one thing she needed—*him*."

"So you thought you'd be her prince charming instead." Ella eyed me with a mixture of annoyance and compassion. At least it wasn't disappointment.

"My brother asked me to look out for her. He trusted me and I fucked him over. She was his, for Chrissakes!" I blew out a deep breath, and rolled to my feet. "I took my job of protecting her too personally. She was in such emotional pain and asked me to take it away. I should have been a friend to her, but I saw something that wasn't there and . . . I just fucked it all up."

Ella squeezed my hand, urging me to sit beside her. "Alex, you made a mistake. Nobody is perfect, and just remember there were two people who made the decision to have an affair. You cannot hold yourself entirely responsible."

*Responsible.* The mention of that word reminded me of just how irresponsible I'd been with Amanda. She'd gotten pregnant and I could have been the father. Ella deserved to know that part of the story. After all, finding out that I wasn't going to be a dad, and that Amanda had chosen a life with Vince is what brought me here. I took a deep breath and hoped that what I was about to say next wouldn't send Ella running back to the city.

"In many ways the affair changed me, and things could be very different today." Every part of me vibrated with tension as the words came out. *Fuck.* I couldn't remember a time I'd been more nervous, not even dangerous missions had me this worked up. Ella's thumb ran smooth strokes against the back of my hand.

My gaze turned back to Ella, and I swallowed hard. "The day you and I met, Amanda had given birth to a little girl."

She gasped slightly, and her eyes closed. "And you could have been the baby's father."

"Yeah, and after I found out I wasn't my life took a tailspin. Our affair wrecked Vince and I felt this massive weight of shame. I thought I was in love with Amanda, or maybe it was the idea of us as a family. I don't know."

"I'm sorry that you had to go through all that pain. I can't even begin to imagine how you felt. You must have been in agony."

"And that's when I decided to take a vacation and it brought me out here." I tucked my fingers under Ella's chin, bringing her eyes to meet mine. "In a way, my bad decisions brought you to me or vice versa."

"And you protecting me, and this attraction we have. It all reminded you of your situation with Amanda?"

I nodded. The truth was that it was a myriad of things, but I didn't want to burden Ella with a bunch of heavy stuff today. I wanted to get to know *her*, and I only hoped this conversation hadn't placed a dark cloud over the rest of our day.

Ella drew her arms up and around my neck. Her lips settled on mine, giving me a soft lingering kiss. My arm curled around her waist, bringing her closer. She snuggled into my side, and rested her cheek against my bicep.

*Guess I have my answer.*

It was nice to have this time with Ella, she needed to step away from the everyday and just relax. We rolled up our jeans and I carried her heels as we walked along the beach.

"So tell me about your family. What's on the Connolly family letterhead?"

"Obviously you know about my brother, the Hollywood star with a hobby in real estate. He married Emma Bailey-Wilson, the fashion model, when they were quite young." She crinkled up her nose. "And thank goodness he smarted up and divorced her bitchy ass. They have two daughters, Leah and Jade. My nieces are the cutest little darlings you've ever seen."

"You don't care for your brother's ex-wife?"

"No, the minute I met her I knew she was a career climber. Emma used my brother to gain more fame. Not sure how into Hollywood news you are, but they divorced because she cheated on my brother with Dax Martin. Maybe the cheating turned out to be a good thing because that broken road led him to Holliday."

"Just like mine led me to you." I reminded her once more.

She smiled, sweeping her hair away from her face. "My sister, Molly, and her husband live in Vancouver, they have three boys. Molly was a chemist but she left the corporate world to raise her kids."

"I don't know which would be harder, raising three boys or being a chemist."

"Right? Molly worked for a cosmetics company developing new fragrances. Have you ever heard of Tallulah or Miss Victoria?"

"No, but I'll be sure to be on the lookout for them now. Wait," I paused for a moment and looked at her. "Do you happen to wear one of them?"

"Tallulah," she admitted.

"I like it a lot. I didn't let housekeeping change my sheets for two days because the scent of your perfume still lingered."

She blushed. "I'm flattered and hungry. I read an article that Praline Dreams is one of the must eat destinations in The Harbour. I need to try their homemade ice cream. I heard it's to die for."

"Ice cream, that's on the approved lists of gluten-free foods?"

"As long as there are no brownie bits or something that contains wheat, most ice cream flavors are safe. Thank fuck, because if I had a dairy allergy I think I would throw myself into the ocean."

This girl was fascinating, and I wanted to know everything about her. She was sweet, smart, ambitious, and her dirty mouth was a bonus. Ella sprinted ahead of me and scooped up some rocks and then tossed them into the ocean.

When we got to the path that led from the beach into town, we used the outdoor shower to rinse off our feet. It didn't really help matters much; sand was everywhere. So we stopped in one of the local shops and picked out some beach appropriate footwear.

"What about your parents, are you close with them?"

Ella held onto my arm as she tried on a pair of black sandals. "We're a pretty close family, I'd say, despite the fact that we don't live close to one another. My parents live in London, and travel to Cork, Ireland a few times a year. That's where I grew up. Mom is a retired school teacher. When she's not traveling with Dad she works part-time at a bakery." Ella walked around, and then stopped to study her reflection in the mirror. I couldn't take my eyes off her legs, my eyes skimmed up and down her body as she turned in different directions. If only we were in a lingerie shop. My dick was half hard just thinking about Ella in various pieces of lace and silk.

"My father started out in construction, but later moved to real estate development. While he was working construction, he started buying up real estate; foreseeing the emerging market and made a sizable amount of money. He taught each one of us how to invest our money and diversify our portfolios."

Ella and me, we were similar that way. Despite the fact that each one of us Robertsen siblings had a trust, my father was adamant about each one of us working and saving our money. "Did you always want to be a business owner?"

"Those are my favorite pair of sandals we sell." I peered over Ella's shoulder to find a woman folding t-shirts, smiling in our direction.

"Yes, they're quite lovely," Ella replied. "Can you hold them at the cash wrap for me?"

The woman nodded. "My pleasure, and please let me know if you need anything else."

"I'd like to wear those out of the store, if that is possible?"

"Not a problem at all."

She tapped her finger to her lip, and started walking. "You asked me a question. Oh yeah, I didn't know what I wanted to do, honestly." Ella and I rounded the corner, and found that the men's shoes were right in front of us. The sneakers I had been wearing were officially soaked with water and sand. I was sure that I'd be tossing them out.

"I went to London College of Fashion and studied Fashion Management. I envisioned working at Harrods or Burberry," she said, and picked up a pair of Reef flip-flops holding them in my direction.

I nodded, and began looking for my size. No such luck.

"One day I was shopping for some specific pieces and French designers that I loved. I couldn't find anything remotely close. That's when I had this idea. Ultimately, I ended up researching and then drew up a business plan for my father. He was impressed and helped me get the loan I needed to set up shop. The rest is history."

I began looking at other styles. I found a pair I liked in my size and then tried them on. "That's very cool, Ella. You should be really proud." I wasn't so much a flip-flop guy, I had a pair of Birkenstocks once, and every time I wore them my sister, Amy rolled her eyes. She made me donate them to Goodwill. Then I tried to convince her I could pull off Crocs.

That was a bad idea.

"Thanks." She pivoted and turned back to face me. "Those look good on you."

"What do you say we pay and go grab some of that ice cream you were talking about?"

"That sounds like a very good idea."

# Chapter *Fifteen*

## *Ella*

Afternoon settled into dusk and we walked back to his house where we relaxed onto the couch in his media room. During our stroll through town, I couldn't stop myself from thinking about his affair with Amanda. I understood all too well the pain he'd felt. I wanted to open up to Alex and show him the same kind of honesty he'd given me. But how do you tell someone that your ex-boyfriend was on trial for a sex scandal involving a minor? Usually, I didn't have to tell people, because they already knew thanks to the tabloids. And it was "Poor, Ella Connolly," caught in the crosshairs of the whole sick and twisted course of events. A violent shudder moved through me at the memory.

I did enjoy our conversation, though. Alex told me all about how he started his business over ice cream. I learned a little bit more about his military life, but not too much. He had answered several questions as being "classified."

"Do you want to watch *Die Hard* or *Terminator*?"

"Seriously? Is there not a more recent film we could consider watching?"

"If we watch a movie I haven't seen, then I'll have to pay attention. What if I get distracted because I'm busy kissing you?"

"Ahh, Netflix and chill?"

He laughed, and shook his head. "Not quite, sweetheart."

I grabbed the remote and started flipping through the channels. To my surprise, IFC was showing one of my brother's films.

"Oh, Ronan is in this one," I said pointing to the screen. "It's a brilliant film."

"Is this a kissing movie?" he asked, draping his arm around my shoulders and pulling me closer.

I laughed at his spin on a reference from *The Princess Bride*. "Yes, there is a bit of kissing." I nudged him with my elbow. "It's not totally girly. You'll be happy to know there's action as well." My hand fell to his chest where my fingertips had a mind of their own, tracing the hard ridges and planes of his chest.

"What's it like having a famous sibling?"

"It's interesting for sure."

"Could you imagine living your life in the spotlight, under a microscope and being chased by the paparazzi?"

Unfortunately, yes, I did know and all too well. *This* was an opportunity to share more. For a split second, I thought about spilling my guts about David and the whole mess, but for now, it seemed too much too soon. Something told me Alex would be able to handle hearing everything, but I just didn't know if I could handle telling him. Not yet anyway.

"Well, that's what I have *you* for," I leaned up so that I could see his face. "To keep me safe."

"I promise to do just that, you'll always be safe when you're with me." He lowered his lips to mine and kissed me, sealing his declaration. His arms banded around my waist and he moved so that I was lying on my back and he was on top of me. Alex's fingers grazed up the side of my ribcage and I felt my pulse race up my throat. The pull between us was intense and became stronger every time we were around one another.

Alex's tongue traced the shell of my ear and my hands pushed under his t-shirt, seeking the need to feel his skin. My fingertips caressed up his back along his spine and his tattoo flashed in my mind.

"Why the double snakes?" I asked, as he kissed my neck.

He pulled his head back to look at me, his eyes darkening. "Snakes are protectors and, for me, the two represent the duality of man."

I swallowed before speaking, "Are you saying you have two personalities?"

"No, one reminds me of the past and mistakes never to be made again. While the other represents the future and all that I aspire to."

Mistakes of the past, and here history was repeating itself. I had chosen to be with a man as opposed to working on my own aspirations. The very reason I was in the country. It seemed ironic, because I've made a lot of wrong decisions in my life. Had I not learned anything?

Do *not* dwell on the past, I told myself. Enjoy the present and this moment with Alex.

"Who knew you were so deep," I replied, allowing my fingertips to trace the ink on his muscular back.

"Deep, yes, that's me." His voice was rich and warm.

Alex hand pushed up underneath the fabric of my bra. As his clever fingers rolled my nipple, I let out a low moan. His arm came up behind his neck and he yanked his t-shirt off, tossing it to the floor. I couldn't help but admire him. Every beautiful inch of him was sculpted to male perfection.

"Buried *deep* inside you is where I want to be," he rasped, before kissing me. His tongue swept along the roof of my mouth, driving me wild with need. I ground my pussy against his cock, showing him I wanted that too. My eyes closed as his hand floated down my body, finding its way back up my shirt.

"You are so beautiful," he said, as he lifted the hem of my shirt up and over my head. "Every part of you is perfect." His lips returned to my stomach and he kissed every inch, leaving hot trails of fire in his wake. The straps of my bra came down and I lifted so that he could remove it. My hips jolted up from the couch when his mouth wrapped around my breast, sucking and licking my nipple. A low moan crawled its way up my throat and my hands found their way to his ass, his incredibly well defined ass.

"Do you have any idea what you do to me?"

"Tell me. What do I do to you, Alex?"

Oh shit, was I supposed to answer him? Or was that a rhetorical question?

*Why am I debating this?*

A hot man, a man that I'd been lusting after since I'd met him, was on top of me kissing me and told me wanted to be buried deep inside me and I was thinking about frivolous crap. My hands tangled in his hair as he feathered kisses down my neck and across my collarbone. Alex lifted me off the couch and instinctively my legs came up and around his waist.

"Where are you taking me?"

"To my bed, of course."

His tongue dipped inside my mouth, licking me slowly. He tasted like chocolate, rich and creamy chocolate decadence. With every kiss and stroke, my body hummed with desire. I was pressed so tightly against him I almost couldn't breathe. But that didn't matter. I'd give up oxygen if all I needed were Alex's kisses to keep me alive.

"I want to take it slow," he whispered against my lips. "I want to take my time with you and remember everything, your touch, your taste and savor it all."

My voice was shaky. "Yes, I want that, too."

We made it halfway up the stairs, but a knock at the door interrupted our moment. I slid down Alex's tall frame and he pulled me behind him, shielding me from whoever was outside. We were out of view, so there was no way whomever it was could see us standing there half-naked.

"What do we do?" I whispered.

"I should have hung the 'Sorry We're Fucking' sign on the door."

I let out a hushed laugh and then buried my face into the hard muscles of his back.

He turned to face me. "If we're quiet, maybe they'll go away." He brought his index finger to my lips and I ran my tongue along his skin, sucking his finger into my mouth. A smirk crossed his lips and he brought his other hand around my breast, squeezing and stroking my nipple with the pad of his thumb. Shockwaves of pleasure flitted up my spine. I took his finger deeper into my mouth, and swirled my tongue around. A moan rumbled from his chest and I felt it rush through my entire body.

"Keep doing that and I'll fuck you right here on the stairs."

This time the knock at the door was accompanied by the sound of the doorbell.

"Mr. Robertsen," a woman's high-pitched voice rang out. "I know that you're in there, I see your vehicle parked in the driveway. I need to speak to you about your landscaper."

Alex shook his head, his finger slipped from between my lips. He brushed his lips over mine, running his tongue along the seam of my lips.

"Ughh, that is Mrs. Shaw . . . I need to talk to her. She's upset about the height of my hedges."

"What do you want me to do? I kind of need my shirt, unless you want me to greet your guests topless."

"I don't think so, you're going up to my room where you will undress and wait for me in my bed." He kissed me, before turning to walk down the stairs. "I'll be quick, I promise."

I turned and ran up the staircase, when I reached the top I looked back at him over my shoulder. "You better be or else I might be forced to start without you." I shimmied out of my jeans and panties, and dropped them both onto the landing where we'd been standing.

All I heard was a groan as I sauntered down the hallway towards his bedroom.

# Chapter Sixteen

## Ella

I snapped my planner closed, and shoved it into my handbag. "Well, that was my final scheduled appointment," I told Alex, as I slid into the booth. "I don't know if I like the idea of a boutique inside a hotel."

"It's not just any hotel though, it's The York Hotel, one of the best in the world," he pointed out.

"I get that, but I think storefront would be more ideal. I believe I'd be limiting myself from foot traffic and window shoppers." I leaned forward, bringing my arms up to rest on the tabletop. Looking around the lobby, I observed people scurrying around, too busy to bother with the retail shops. No matter where the location, there was always a risk. "Besides the rent is extremely high, and, not to mention, I'd have to sign a minimum three year lease."

The waitress from the café came to our table and I ordered

a tea and a few chocolate-dipped coconut macaroons. Alex ordered a double chocolate brownie, which made me jealous, and a bottle of water.

"So, what is your next move?" he asked, settling back into his seat.

I sighed, tapping my finger against the wood. "Maybe it's just not the right time."

Saying the words left me feeling defeated. The actual thought was depressing. I'd been here a month now and nothing seemed to be coming together. My father was able to pull together half a dozen more listings after the first ten were a firm no, and Ronan was the one who found out about the space here at the hotel.

"Or *maybe* Manhattan isn't your location."

"If not the city then where do you recommend?"

"I'm glad you asked." He waved to our server for the check and changed our order to go.

"Where are we going?"

"First, back to the hotel, you're packing a bag and we are getting out of here for the weekend. It will be a nice break and, if we hurry, we will miss all the traffic on our way out to The Harbour."

The thought of spending an entire weekend with Alex at his beach house thrilled me. I needed it, too; a small break to clear my head . . . *that* sounded perfect. As I walked back to my room, I decided to text my brother. Not that I needed to check in with him, but the last time we had spoken, he seemed a bit out of sorts, on edge even, because my brother was always mild-mannered. Even during his very public divorce to Emma and the cheating scandal.

*Me: Hey, just wanted to let you know that I'm going out to The Harbour for a while.*

*Ronan: Oh, okay. Staying with friends?*

No, I'm staying with my hot as hell bodyguard, the guy you hired, and we will probably shag like bunnies all weekend. Shit. Think, Ella, think. You need something to tell him that wouldn't arouse suspicion.

*Me: Yeah, and I'm considering location scouting for the boutique. Maybe Dad was right about the Hamptons. I'll let you know when I buy a summer place.*

Not a complete fabrication. From our earlier conversation, Alex had me thinking about places other than Manhattan. Technically this answer would work for now.

*Ronan: Maybe I'll buy a place and you can stay there.*

*Me: That's a bit extreme, even for you.*

*Ronan: Have a wonderful weekend. Chat soon.*

An hour later, we were on the road driving towards the Hamptons. Nabila called me while I was packing my bags demanding I download the Snapchat app so that I could enjoy her art show in real time. I was able to create an account and not more than five minutes later, she'd sent twenty snaps. It took me a little while to figure out how to use the silly app, but it managed to keep us entertained.

"I thought we'd stop off at the market and pick up a few things before heading to the house." Alex took my hand in his, threading his long fingers with mine. "Before we left, I called my housekeeper, Mrs. Curtis, and I asked her deliver some essentials. However, I wanted to get a few special items for dinner."

"Oh, you're cooking dinner? What a treat for me."

"I'll have you know, I happen to be an excellent cook." He winked and brought our intertwined hands to his perfect mouth, kissing the back of my hand. He looked at me with that fucking sweet smile, the one that went all the way up to his eyes, and I melted. I couldn't help but stare at him—he was undeniably handsome, he was smart, charming and funny. On top of that, he could cook. This must be a dream. It was all too good to be true.

"What's that look for?"

"You're taking me to your house again. We've been with each other practically twenty-four seven over the last several weeks. This feels a lot like dating, rather than whatever relationship people are supposed to have with their bodyguards."

He laughed. "And your point is what exactly?"

"Nothing at all," I replied, squeezing his hand a little tighter. "Just making an observation."

"If you want, I'll quit tomorrow, sweetheart. I do feel a little guilty taking your brother's money."

"Why?"

"Well, for starters, I'm currently sleeping with his beautiful, smart as hell sister." He wiggled his eyebrows. "Breaking the rules and all."

I felt my cheeks heat at this compliment. "I should tell him to give you a raise, since you've taken such excellent care of me *and* my body." I slipped my hand from his grasp and slowly caressed his muscular thigh, teasing him.

"Here's an idea, what if we told him about *us*? Then I would be absolved of my guilt."

"About us? When did *we* become *us*?" I joked, feeling nervous knots form in my belly. "We've not even been on a proper date. I think it's far too soon to discuss *us*."

"Too soon, huh?" He cocked an eyebrow in my direction. "Didn't your brother move his girlfriend into his house after a few weeks of dating? I bet they'd be our biggest supporters."

Smiling, I shrugged it off, and pretended to busy myself with my phone. I knew he was saying something heartfelt, but where relationships were concerned, I tended to jump in head, heart, and feet first. Case in point—David. I've been known to also lose myself with guys and forget about everything else. Which is why I didn't see what was truly happening around me when David and I were together. On the other hand, I should just forget about him and realize no two relationships are ever the same. It should also be noted that Alex isn't David in any capacity.

My phone alerted me to another snap from Nabila. The pictures showed her putting sold tags on several of her photographs and paintings from her featured artists. And the final one was a picture of her with Finn Carter. I smiled, and sent her a quick congratulations message and told her I'd call her soon to get the full re-cap. That conversation would be rather lengthy as I had a few things to chat about myself, one such subject being Alex.

We turned to cross the bridge over to the village as storm clouds fell over the bay, shading the sky light pink and dark grey. I shoved my phone back into my bag as Alex pulled up to the market in the middle of town. We got out of the Range Rover and he took my hand in his, sending heat fizzling over my skin. Once inside, he grabbed a basket and pulled out his phone, which meant he let go of me. Immediately, a chill washed over me at the loss.

"I even made a list," he said proudly. "You're in for a treat."

I smiled as he led me down the produce aisle. He picked up fresh blueberries, oranges, lemons, broccoli and some chicken from the deli. Speaking of treats, I managed to persuade him into getting four pints of Häagen-Dazs ice cream. Before I knew it, he had a basket filled with the oddest mixture of foods.

"Grab anything you want—wine, vodka, tequila." He

nodded towards the shelves of alcohol.

"Trying to get me drunk?" I teased.

"I just want to make this weekend special for you."

"Are you sure I can't help pay for any of this?"

"Nope, it's my treat."

He set the basket on the checkout counter and pulled me into his tall frame, kissing the top of my head. While Alex paid, I flipped through a real estate magazine, curious at the value of the homes here. My eyes landed up on a listing for a commercial property on the main drag. I read the description and, on paper, it seemed perfect. The price was a little out of my budget, but that could always be negotiated, as Ronan would say.

"Ready to go?"

I nodded and dropped the magazine into my handbag. It seemed almost too good to be true. What if all this time, *this* was the place I was meant to be? There were so many factors to consider. My mind was reeling, especially since I'd just told Ronan I was actually considering space here.

*Lies imitating life. Is that a thing?*

I'd think about work, and the boutique space, later. Right now, I was more interested in exploring what the possibility of "us" might look like for me and Alex. It's all about finding balance, right?

After we unpacked the groceries, I pulled up the recipe for dinner on my tablet and began my prep work for our meal. I was cooking her dinner. This was one of my specialties and it was something I loved doing for the woman I was dating. Sometimes, if a one-night stand was lucky enough, I'd make her breakfast. That ended well for me most times, because it meant sex after pancakes, waffles, or even bacon and eggs. Now, I'm here with Ella again and it feels right. More right than anything I've felt in a long time.

Ella stood at the window, gazing at the ocean. *God, she's beautiful.* Ella's sweater fell off her shoulder, exposing her black lace bra strap and all I could think about was rolling my tongue around her pretty pink nipples. And now, I was staring at her legs, those killer stems, long, lean and attached to her perfect ass.

"You want some wine or a cocktail?"

I placed the thin slices of chicken into a bowl, adding in the onions, garlic, and soy sauce, giving it time to marinate, while I chopped the broccoli and mushrooms.

"Sure, wine sounds nice, since we're having some kind of chicken dish." Ella leaned against the island and propped herself up on her elbows.

"Yep, I found this awesome gluten-free website with tons of recipes. And for dessert, espresso drizzled ice-cream."

Her eyes popped wide. "Espresso, huh? I'll be wired all night."

"Good, I don't know that we'll be doing much sleeping."

She rounded the corner of the island and stood behind me, slipping her arms around my waist. "I thought you brought me out here to relax and now you're going to deny me rest?" Her hands found their way underneath my shirt, gently stroking my abs.

After I washed my hands, I wiped them on the dishtowel and turned to face Ella. "You'll get plenty of rest, trust me, you'll need it." My nose grazed hers, as I tangled my hands in her hair. Everything else faded into the background except the sound of her breathing, a low unsteady rhythm. I tilted her head towards mine. My thumbs brushed against her cheeks that were flushed pink; the same shade that currently painted the sky. If that sounded corny I couldn't give a shit, I'm observant and it's always served me well.

"Has anyone ever told you just how sexy you are?"

"As far as I'm concerned, you're the *only* man who's ever told me," she breathed.

*Good fucking answer.*

Ella took me by surprise when she pushed me up against the island, thrusting her tongue inside my mouth. Her hands moved to the button on my jeans, dipping her fingers inside my waistband, popping the button open. I kissed her harder, groaning into her mouth when her hand slipped down my boxers, gripping my cock.

As much as I knew I would enjoy where this was going, I turned the tables on her. Sucking her bottom lip into my mouth, I cupped her ass, lifting her off the floor. Suddenly, I wasn't hungry for food, only *her*.

She didn't seem to mind the new plan. Her fingernails dug into my biceps and a predatory smile crossed her lips.

*Fuck, those lips, they will undoubtedly be the death of me.*

I crushed my mouth to hers, and my hands gripped her hair holding her in place. Pressing her against me, wetness seeped through her leggings and onto my jeans. *Fuck yes.*

I pushed her back against the kitchen wall. My hands caressed every inch of her body. Her nipples hardened beneath the delicate fabric of her sweater. Goosebumps splashed across her flawless, creamy skin. She was like a livewire, everywhere I touched her it prompted a reaction.

I lifted her sweater over her head, tossing it over the chair.

My lips traveled over her collarbone, across her shoulder, kissing my way up her neck.

"*Alex*," she moaned. Hearing my name was like a prayer, so I got down on my knees.

Teasing her, I trailed my tongue up her stomach, grazing my fingertips up her thighs. My hands gripped the waistband of her leggings, tugging them off. I nipped her skin, alternating kisses between her thighs. Prying her legs apart, my breath fanned over her skin. Her arousal filled my senses.

"I can't wait to taste you."

Yeah, Ella and I have had sex, but I've not had the pleasure of tasting her, until now. I pulled her lace panties aside and uncovered her glistening pussy. *Christ.*

I licked her slowly, smoothing my tongue over her heated flesh. She writhed above me, her fingers dug into my hair, tugging hard at the roots. Wrapping my lips around her clit, I sucked hard, as I eased my finger inside her.

Our eyes met with a blistering heat. "You're soaking wet for me, sweetheart."

Her panties needed to go; I wanted her bare. I tugged at the fabric and removed them, then draped her left leg over my shoulder. My tongue lashed over her sensitive skin, as I massaged her clit with my thumb, driving her wild.

"Oh God, *your* mouth," she moaned, rubbing her pussy against my face. I pinned her hips against the wall and slid my tongue over her clit then dipped back inside for more of her sweetness. Nobody knows exactly what Ambrosia tastes like, but if I had to guess, this was it.

My cock throbbed, straining against my jeans. But this wasn't about me, it was *all* about Ella. Tiny moans and whimpers spilled from her lips, fueling my craving to tongue fuck her to an epic orgasm. I rimmed her harder, driving us both mad.

"Oh Alex, please . . . *I* . . ."

She arched against my mouth, my tongue circled her swollen nub, and I was rewarded with a soft wail. I wanted her at my mercy, panting and begging for more, *begging* me to let her come.

I wanted to see her lose it.

Her nails dug into my scalp pulling and tugging painfully at the root. Pleas and whispers slipped from her lips, as her hips undulated against my face. Searing pleasure wound through me, as I worked my tongue, finding a rhythm that would bring her release.

"Please, Alex," she moaned.

I felt her muscles tighten when I dipped two fingers inside, stroking and licking her in perfect unison. Once more, my tongue circled her clit and I felt her pulsing against me. I twisted my wrist and increased the rhythm. Her hips jerked and Ella screamed my name as she came all over my fingers. *Next time, it will be my tongue she comes all over.*

I lapped up every last wave of her pleasure, cooling her down with long, slow strokes of my fingers, before releasing my hold on her. I stood and adjusted my jeans. Ella clung to the wall, her skin flushed and a lazy smile crossed her face. I grabbed her panties and helped her put them back on, along with her leggings.

"Alex, my God, that *was* . . . I have no words, I guess."

"I've left you speechless and *that* works well for me."

In response, she reached for my jeans again, and I took her hands in mine. "We'll get to that later. Right now, I have our dinner to prepare."

She pressed her lips to mine, kissing me softly. I motioned for Ella to take a seat and then pulled a bottle of wine from the fridge and poured her a glass. I met her eyes and she gave me a flirtatious smile.

"Who taught you how to cook?"

"My mother." I turned on the stove and heated two tablespoons of coconut oil in a large skillet. "Despite having a full-time staff, my mom enjoys cooking. She helps in the kitchen as often as she can. I missed home cooked meals when I was in the military, especially during the holidays."

"I can certainly understand that, my whole family loves to cook and eat. If this is any good, remind me to send your mother a thank you note."

"Oh, sweetheart, there will be no *if*. I can guarantee this will be the one meal you'll refer to as the best you've ever had," I boasted, feeling quite confident in my culinary skills.

"Oh yeah and what's the best meal you've ever had?"

"*You*."

# Chapter Seventeen

## Ella

On Monday morning I'd woken up alone in Alex's bed. He'd left a note on the pillow saying he had an urgent matter to take care of and he wouldn't be long. I slid out from beneath the covers that smelled like sex and Alex and stumbled towards the walk-in closet. I glanced at my reflection in the mirror, my cheeks were rosy and I seemed to have a permanent grin attached to my lips. The weekend had been absolutely perfect and I didn't want to leave.

I rummaged through the drawers, pulling out a pair of running shorts and a t-shirt. After I threw my hair up and into a ponytail and slipped on my gym shoes, I ripped the page for the retail space out of the real estate magazine. I folded the paper and shoved it into my pocket on my way downstairs to grab a bottle of water.

"Oh, hello, dear."

Startled, I jumped and nearly fell on my ass. The floors in the kitchen were slippery and now I knew the reason—they'd just been mopped. A tall woman, wearing a floral print shirt and black pants, approached me as I rounded the island.

"Sorry, dear, I didn't mean to scare you," she said, pushing her dark brown hair off her face.

"Oh, that's okay. I'm Ella by the way," I said, outstretching my hand to hers.

"Nice to meet you, Ella. I'm Rita, Mr. Robertsen's housekeeper. Can I make you some breakfast?"

"Oh no, but thank you," I replied, opening the door to the refrigerator. "I was just going to pop out for a run. I should be back in an hour. Will you still be here?"

"Yes, I still have few more things to do. Go on and enjoy your run. I'll put some coffee on and it will be ready for you when you return."

I smiled, placing my earbuds in. After stretching my legs on the front porch, I swiped the screen on my phone until I came to my cardio playlist. It was a gorgeous spring morning and the chilly air had a bite of salt and fresh grass.

I started at a light pace as I jogged down the dirt road. Once I made it to the main road, I hit my stride when the restaurants and shops of The Harbour came into view and Selena Gomez's "Hands to Myself" blasted in my ears. Decadent memories of Alex swirled in my mind, him hovering over me, his biceps flexing, and our skin slick with sweat as we made love. *Made love?* No, we had sex.

Time to get serious. You can think about the two of you later.

The heat washed over me, as I ran across the hot pavement. Once I hit the sidewalk the canopy of trees provided some much-needed shade. Outside the North Harbour Coffee

Shop the smell of rich vanilla and caramel wrapped around me. I stopped to catch my breath, using my t-shirt to wipe away the beads of sweat that rolled down the sides of my face. After taking a few sips of water, I pulled the paper from my pocket, and then glanced at the coffee shop address. The listing said 1204 North Harbour Drive, and the coffee shop was 1600 North Harbour Drive.

Once I hit the 1500 block I started to run again and the salty ocean air whipped around me. My lungs burned, as I pushed myself the last few blocks. I slowed my stride as I came upon the home interiors store on the 1200 block corner. And then my eyes lit up at the sight of the space. It was perfect, two huge windows and the storefront was white, which I loved even more. Envisioning a plan, I paced around the front of the empty building. I could have this place up and running in four to six weeks, depending on renovations.

Panic crept in slowly and I rubbed at the pain in my chest. Dad had mentioned something to me earlier this year about looking at places in the Hamptons, but I really wanted to be in the city. If I had my space here, I'd have to live here and I was pretty positive the price range was higher than Manhattan. That was all dependent upon whether or not I decided to stay in the States. Taking a deep breath, I decided not to hit the freak out button. First, I'd need to run the numbers and then go over a pros and cons list. One definite pro was that the store in London was doing well and Bianca had everything under control.

My visa was up in five months, I honestly thought I'd have a better handle on this situation by now. Ronan said I could always file an extension if I needed more time here. More time was needed because I'd been putting more energy into my personal life than my professional one. *Perhaps, I'm overthinking it all.*

How would Alex feel about me setting up shop here in The Harbour? I pivoted on my heel and crossed the busy street to begin my jog back to his house. What were his future plans? What would happen to us if I didn't stay here? All of this might have been premature thinking on my part. Why was I even considering Alex in the decisions about my boutique?

My phone buzzed, alerting me to a text.

*Alex: Coming home in an hour. I have a surprise for you.*

Reading the message, my heart skipped a beat and a smile stretched wide across my face. Was it possible I was considering Alex in my life decisions because I wanted to? I kicked up and ran faster than I ever had in my entire life.

After my shower, Rita insisted on making me breakfast. I explained my dietary restrictions to her and she told me that it was not a problem. Turns out her youngest son was allergic to everything—dairy, wheat, nuts, and shellfish. I asked her to join me for a cup of coffee, but she declined and offered a raincheck. Once Rita finished with her work she said goodbye and hurried out the door.

After she left, I grabbed one of my favorite gossip magazines and walked out to the pool. I know I should hate the tabloids, but that's my vice. I plopped down on one of the blue and white day loungers, soaking up more sun. I'd never felt so relaxed in my life, it was almost as if I was on holiday. I was beginning to understand why Alex loved it out here. It was very calming, especially being near the ocean.

I flipped through the glossy pages, skipping over all the ongoing Kardashian drama. My eyes landed on a story about my brother and Holliday on their way to a breakup. *Rubbish.*

Skimming a few more pages, I came upon ad for Nadia's Dream featuring Gigi Ellis, my favorite actress. She inspired me to try modeling while at university, unfortunately Ronan got all the talent in that area.

"Honey, I'm home." I heard Alex call out.

I leapt to my feet, and jogged inside. Seeing him in his dark jeans and a faded New York t-shirt sent my blood pumping and fire sizzling through my veins. I jumped into his arms, pulling his mouth to mine for a wet needy kiss, I devoured him.

He nipped at my bottom lip. "I missed you, too."

I slid down his body and leaned against the counter. "So where is this surprise?" I asked, wiggling my eyebrows.

He reached into his back pocket and then placed two items into my hands: tickets to a baseball game, New York versus Boston.

"We're going to a baseball game?"

"Yes, remember the other day when you said you wanted to do something truly American?"

"I recall saying something like that."

"Well, you said it and I am here to grant that request," he said, before slapping a ball cap on my head.

"Oh, wow, but what if I wanted to cheer for Boston?" I shot him a sideways glance and tapped the tickets in the palm of my hand. Of course, I was just giving him a hard time.

His brows scrunched together, and pulled the tickets from my hand. "No way, we root for New York, *unless* they're playing Chicago, then it's always Chicago. Oh, one more thing, here is your official game day shirt." Alex tossed a navy t-shirt in my direction.

I shook my head and stared at my shirt. "Thank you so much, but I have a confession. I don't know much about the sport of baseball. I promise not to be annoying, but you might have to explain a few things to me."

He rubbed my shoulders, smoothing his hands up and down my arms. "I'll help you and I don't mind at all," he reassured, laying my uncertainty to rest.

"All right, take me out to the ball game," I said, stripping off my shirt and then pulling on the one Alex brought me.

We left the house and Alex didn't drive towards Manhattan, he began driving in the opposite direction.

"I know I haven't been here all that long, but you know the city is that way."

He laughed and flicked the turn signal and we started driving along Bay Shore Drive.

"You're very observant. We're going to the airport, because we're flying to the city."

"Are you serious?"

"I told you that I was a frequent flyer."

He pressed his finger against the screen for the music and "Kiss Me" by Olly Murs drifted through his Range Rover.

I looked around for any police cars. There were hardly any cars on this stretch of road. Bravely, I unhooked my seat belt and leaned over to kiss him on the cheek. He took my hand in his, bringing the back to his mouth and peppering my knuckles with soft kisses.

"So how was your morning?" He turned down the volume on the radio, glancing at me.

"It was good. I went for a run and well . . . I sort of stumbled upon an empty storefront shop on Harbour Drive. It's for rent and I had some thoughts about setting up my shop."

My shoulders tensed and I finished the last part of my sentence. I didn't want Alex to think I was a psycho for possibly working and living near him.

"Really?" His hand reached for the console and he pulled out a magazine. "That's ironic because I picked this up for you at the coffee shop this morning. Rita had mentioned something about one of her favorite stores in the square going out of business and it got me thinking."

I took the magazine from his hand, noting it was the same one that I had picked up at the market. I smiled as I traced the front cover with my fingertips.

"This is very thoughtful. I guess you and I are on the same wavelength."

"It appears that way. Maybe you should consider putting some roots down here instead of the city."

I felt a smile tugging at my face and my heart skipped a beat. Once we parked at the East Hampton Airport, Alex opened my door and took my hand as we walked inside. A thousand thoughts were swimming through my mind. I wondered what he was thinking. We needed to talk obviously, there were some bigger issues lingering.

As we walked outside across the tarmac to the plane, I decided it was time to lay my cards on the table, and possibly my heart. It needed to be done before we fell any deeper into whatever this was between us. I don't know why I was so nervous, talking with Alex had always been easy. It felt as natural as breathing.

The captain greeted Alex and me before we climbed the stairs. Our flight attendant, Joni, greeted us as we took our seats. The last time I was on a private jet I had been with David. It was only days after we'd come home from that trip in Tenerife that he was arrested on suspicion of sexual activity with a fifteen-year-old girl.

I leaned my head back against one of the large, white plush chairs and Alex sat to the right of me. After Joni brought our drinks, Alex told her to check on us in about twenty minutes.

"You okay?" Alex caressed my arm, capturing my attention.

"What are your plans for the future?" I blurted without hesitation.

His eyes grew wide. "That's a question out of left field."

"Well, we are going to a ball game, it seems appropriate."

Alex chuckled and it made me smile. "Let's see, I'd like to expand my business. My plan is to have an office in Manhattan, but I could also see working with clients in The Harbour."

"Yeah, and I won't need a bodyguard forever."

His jaw was tight, and he took a deep breath. Despite the serious expression, his gorgeous eyes remained soft. "You should know that I sometimes work with the military."

My heart pounded in my chest. "On missions, as in dangerous situations?"

"No, I have a team of men who volunteer for the missions. I don't usually go."

"*Usually*?" For some odd reason, my eyes filled with tears, threatening to carve a path down my cheeks, but I managed to hold them off.

The captain came over the speaker instructing us to buckle our seat belts, since we had been cleared for takeoff. The vibrations from the plane raced through me as my hands gripped the armrest. My question hung in the air, much like the clouds in the blue sky we were now soaring between.

His hand sought mine across the console, fingers intertwining before pulling them to rest on his lap. "I haven't been on a mission in years, but if I am needed, I would have to go. I hope that puts your mind at ease."

I couldn't say I liked the idea of Alex, or anyone for that matter, going into dangerous places. Nabila's dad had been a pilot in the Royal Air Force. He was killed during a training exercise in Wales. Despite her devastation from losing her father, Nabila said he died serving his country, a country he loved as much as his own family.

"I think it takes a very brave person to fight for their country—honorable. I can't imagine what that must feel like to give so much, to defend and to save so many people's lives."

He didn't say anything, he didn't need to. Over the past few weeks, I'd become quite familiar with Alex's mannerisms. From the way he expelled a deep breath and rubbed his index finger over his mouth, I knew he was thinking about something emotionally painful. He'd done that same thing when he spoke about his affair with Amanda.

I opened my mouth to speak, but Joni breezed through and asked if we like more to drink. We ordered another round of drinks just before the captain announced we would be arriving at the airport soon and we should buckle up. I was hoping I hadn't said something that would put a damper on this day.

Alex reached for my hand, squeezing tight. "Are you ready to experience your first major league baseball game?"

"Ready as I'll ever be."

# Chapter Eighteen

## Alex

Forty minutes later we pulled up to the stadium. The ride from the airport had been mostly quiet and that was my fault. Bringing up my time in the military isn't without its dark reminders. The duration of the flight my mind went back to all the people we couldn't save, including Sasha.

The guilt still chewed away at me, even after years of therapy. Where my therapist had told me I had nothing to feel guilty about. The final mission was her final day on this Earth. I tried to persuade her from going, but she insisted. And once Sasha made up her mind, there was no talking her out of it. But that doesn't mean I couldn't have ordered her to stay, I was her superior after all. I allowed her to be put in a dangerous situation and it ultimately got her killed. I'm sure she was cursing me from Heaven right now, yelling that it was her damn decision to be a part of the mission.

It had been a few weeks since I'd thought about Sasha at all. Eight years later, her death still weighed heavy on my mind. Guilt washed over me for two reasons. One, for thinking about Sasha when I was here with the woman who had consumed my every waking thought since I'd met her and two, because I wondered if one day I would forget Sasha entirely. I had loved her once and I didn't like the thought of losing the memories I had.

*Is this normal to feel this way?*

Once we exited the limo, I took Ella's hand in mine. I watched her entire face light up as she took in the view of the stadium. Warmth crept back into my chest and the iciness that momentarily gripped my heart melted away.

"Wow." She stood outside Gate Four with her hands on her hips and shook her head. "It's simply amazing."

"Come on, this way."

Immediately, my old friend, Cole Simmons, greeted us. During summer breaks he worked at my family's shipping company. He stayed with the company for many years, working his way up to the executive level. Now, Cole worked for the team, which was how I was able to get us the tickets for this afternoon's game.

"Cole," I said, gripping his hand. "Thanks for getting us these tickets today."

"It's no trouble, anything for an old friend."

After introducing Ella to Cole, he took us on a tour through the Hall of Champions and down to the field where we met a few of the coaches and players. Then Cole had arranged for Ella and me to hit a few balls with their all-star pitchers, Daniels and Griggs.

Daniels was getting a little too handsy with Ella, putting his arm around her trying to show her how to swing the bat.

She wasn't stupid. I'm sure she got it after the first demonstration. It took everything in me not to stalk towards them in complete caveman style.

Ella. Mine. Fuck you.

I didn't care if he was a professional athlete; I'd have no problem laying him the fuck out right here on the field in front of his teammates. Maybe I should take it as a compliment. After all, she looked sexy with her t-shirt knotted up, showing just a bit of her stomach, and those long legs on full display in her shorts.

On her fifth try, Ella swung the bat, driving the ball right down the middle of the field. My second swing hit high and right, lucky for me it was a fair play.

Once fans started to fill the seats, Cole escorted us to the Club Level where the luxury executive suites were located. We walked into the Champions Club Suite, where the team's two World Championship trophies were on display in a large glass case. Retired jerseys of some of the greatest players in baseball hung on the walls in large frames. The view of the field was incredible, including the Manhattan skyline in the backdrop. It seemed as if every part of the stadium was visible.

"Wow, this place is incredible," Ella remarked, as she stepped farther into the suite. "A private bathroom, a full bar and look at these beautiful chairs. This place is bigger than my flat in London."

"Listen, I have to get going, but you two enjoy the game," Cole said sidestepping around the bar to shake my hand once more.

"In here? We're watching a baseball game from in here?" Ella asked, her voice cracking with excitement.

He nodded, and then pulled the door open. "Nice to

have met you, Ella."

"You as well, Cole."

"Catering should be here in about thirty minutes, before the game starts, to set up and all your dietary requests have been met."

"Thanks, buddy, take care," I said, slapping my hand to his shoulder.

Once the door closed, I pulled Ella into my arms. "If you were a baseball and I was a bat, would you let me hit that?" My hands grabbed her ass and squeezed.

"Oh no, you did not just say that." She pushed away from me and shook her head.

"That pickup line wouldn't work on you?"

She just laughed, and walked around to the bar. "Do those not so subtle sexually charged lines ever really work?"

I shrugged and joined her behind the bar as she made a vodka soda. When she finished, she poured a scotch for me. We took a seat at the bar table in the middle of the room and I flipped on the flat screen to listen to the pre-game coverage.

"What's the worst pickup line you've heard?" she asked, before taking a drink.

I laughed. "Nice package, let me unwrap it for you."

"No way, some girl actually said that to you?"

"Yeah, but in her defense, she was really hammered. What about you?"

"This one is so gross. A guy walked up to me in a pub, he grabbed my hand, and placed it on his cock and then said, 'I made a protein shake and the straw is in my pants.'"

"I hope you punched him."

"I did better than that." She cocked an eyebrow. "My hand was still on his dick so I squeezed it and his balls—*hard*. I told him to never fucking say that to any woman ever again."

Cringing, I felt pain shoot through my own dick and balls. "Ouch, on behalf of men's balls everywhere, I want to say he didn't deserve that, but he definitely did."

"Absolutely, a total wanker, and I was sure that Nabila was going to scratch his eyes out," she said through a laugh. "What's the *lamest* line you've heard?"

That was a no brainer. "Hey, you work out?"

"That's it?" she asked, shaking her head.

"Yep," I replied, tossing back the rest of my scotch. "She said that right before puking on my shoes."

"Poor girl, she was so nervous you made her vomit."

"I don't think it was me that made her vomit." I rolled up to my feet and walked to the bar, filling up my glass with more scotch. "Okay, your turn, lamest pick up line."

"Great legs, what time do they open?"

I shook my head. Hearing this, I couldn't help but feel that the male species was a complete disappointment. Ella came around the bar and poured herself another drink. There was a knock on the door. I pulled it open to find the catering staff with four carts of food. *Damn, Cole hooked us up.*

After they left, Ella and I helped ourselves to the food. All items that were gluten-free were appropriately labeled. Everything looked and smelled delicious, from the chicken tenders, to the truffle fries and the mini bacon cheeseburgers.

"Did anyone ever use a pickup line on you that worked?" Ella asked, pouring some ketchup onto her plate.

"Now that you mention it, yeah, I can recall one. This beautiful blonde came rushing up to me on the sidewalk outside a bar in Manhattan and said, 'There *you* are! I've been looking for you all night.'"

She smiled and took a bit of her burger. A dab of ketchup landed on the corner of her mouth. I leaned over the table, brushing my thumb over her skin. She swallowed, as I swiped the sauce away. Her tongue darted over her lips, licking the ketchup off my thumb.

I moved closer and pressed my lips to hers. Her tongue swiped the roof of my mouth and she bit down on my lower lip.

"If you're lucky, you just might get to round all the bases tonight."

I smirked. "No luck needed. I'm feeling confident that I'll hit a homerun."

"Oh, are we back to the topic of you hitting this with your big wooden bat," she joked, giving her amazing ass a quick smack.

Wrapping my arms around her waist, I pulled her onto my lap and brushed my thumbs along her smooth skin. She wiggled her ass against my cock, purposely driving me crazy. For fuck's sake, I was half-hard already.

I crushed my lips to Ella's, her tongue gliding against mine. My hands wound under her long blonde hair as I deepened the kiss, needing to taste her, devour her completely. My hands fell to her perfect ass—kneading and gripping as I continued to tongue fuck her mouth. Lust filled the air as she ground her pelvis against me, silently begging me to take her. I considered bending Ella over the bar and fucking her until she was screaming my name, but as hot as that would be I needed to slow things down, there'd be plenty of time for *that* later.

Ella licked my mouth, her moans drowned out my own thoughts bringing me out of my fantasy.

"You're giving me some wildly inappropriate thoughts

right now," I murmured against her throat, feeling her pulse beating against my lips.

"Me too," she whispered.

# Chapter *Nineteen*

## *Ella*

After the game ended, Cole invited us up to the Owner's VIP suite for drinks. As if I needed more booze and food in my system. I was going to have to work out extra hard tomorrow, probably run five miles instead of my usual three.

I had one glass of red wine, as to not be impolite, plus I knew I'd drink it slower than white wine. I listened as the two of them chatted like old school mates about the game and reminisced about their summers on the lake.

We were introduced to the owner and his wife along with a few other important people. Admittedly, I was a bit nervous that someone might recognize me as David Warner's ex-girlfriend. Before being convicted, he was known as an international superstar, even having played on England's Olympic football team. I didn't know how much people in the sports industry gossiped. Although, after an hour of talking, I felt pretty confident that the prominent people among American baseball and English football did not travel in the same circles.

"Hey," I said, when Cole stepped away to take a call. "I'm going to pop over to the shops and pick up some gifts for my nieces and nephews."

Alex set his beer down on the tabletop. "Okay, I'll come with you."

"No, it's fine. I have my phone. You stay here and enjoy the chat with Cole."

His strong hands rubbed up and down my arms. I could see the worry written all over his face.

"Alex," I whispered, curling my hand over his thick shoulder. "I'll be fine, there are people everywhere. Just Alex and Ella, remember?"

"I like being just Alex and Ella." His hands wrapped around my waist, pulling me into him. He brushed his lips against mine, sweeping his tongue into my mouth with languid strokes. After saying goodbye to Cole and a few others, Alex escorted me to the door.

"I'll meet up with you in about twenty minutes," he said, before kissing me again.

"See you soon."

I made my way down to the shop and immediately spied a cute pink and white jersey that would look adorable on both Leah and Jade. I managed to only find Leah's size in the stack.

"Excuse me," I said, to the sales associate. "Do you happen to have this jersey in a girl's size five?"

"I know we have more of these in the back. I'll go check that for you."

"Thank you. I'll be over in the boy's section," I replied, pointing to the far corner of the store.

Pushing my way through the crowd of shoppers, I sorted through the logo t-shirts. My sister's boys would all need different designs or at least different colors.

"Hello, Lovie."

And before the last syllable left his mouth, my ears registered who the roguish voice belonged too. I felt my chest caving as he approached me, slowly rounding the display of t-shirts to stand next to me. My stomach lurched as the smell of beer and sweat curled around me. His hair was mussed and his pale skin was tinged rosy red.

"Charlie, I'm positive that you have somewhere else you need to be," I asserted, eyeing the press pass hanging around his neck. "Run along and annoy someone else."

"Come now, Ella, is that anyway to treat an old friend?"

My eyes narrowed. "*We* are not friends."

The sales associate I'd been talking to before Charlie graced me with his presence showed up at just the right moment.

Handing me the jersey she asked, "Is there anything else I can get for you?"

I shook my head, before going back to the task of rummaging through the stacks of t-shirts. Charlie still lingered, eyeing me like I was a choice cut of beef.

"So, Lovie, what brings you out to the game today?"

"My boyfriend. I suggest you bugger off before he gets here. He knows all about what you and David did to me. I'm sure he'd love to beat the bloody hell out of you." A white lie, but if it made Charlie leave I didn't care.

"If your boyfriend would like to buy a few pictures, I'm sure I can scour up the zip file and send him some sensational portraits. Fuck, I'll even have the photos framed at no extra charge. It would be my pleasure."

My stomach roiled with wine and grilled chicken. The thought that Charlie still had naked photos of me made me sick with disgust. I had won the case and he had been ordered to turn over everything he had to the courts. Something in his menacing tone registered fear inside me. Instead of cowering, I held my ground and stood tall so that I was face to face with him.

"I don't believe you. If you have any photos of me from that time, all I have to do is call my lawyer and you'll be hauled off in handcuffs."

"Oh handcuffs, kinky." He smirked, and his fingers curled over my wrist. "Yeah, I still have the photos of you and I give my cock a good tug session just looking at your perky tits and round arse every night. I dream about how I'd love to sink balls deep in that tight cunt of yours. David told me you were the best shag he'd ever had. Why don't you give me one night and then I'll hand over the remaining files."

"Fuck you," I spat.

"Is that an offer?"

I jerked my hand from the grasp of his rough fingers. "It doesn't matter even if you did have the pictures, like I said, one call to my attorney and I'm sure this time you'll go to jail."

He was lying. All of his equipment had been seized by the police and anything related to my case was wiped from his camera and scrubbed from his computers. If Charlie had anything, he'd be in serious violation of his agreement with the courts.

"As long as I don't sell or upload the pictures . . ." He licked his lips, then placed his hand over his cock and began stroking himself in front of me. "I'm not doing anything wrong."

Anger raged inside me. The last thing I needed was the thought of him wanking off to naked photos of me emblazed in my head. Taking a deep breath, my fingers gripped the bundle of clothing tighter.

"You disgust me. Why don't you find someone else to fixate your dirty desires on? I'm old news, get a new headline." I didn't give Charlie a chance to respond. I moved past him, dumping the pile of shirts onto the empty folding cart. Shopping online seemed like a better option at this point.

Charlie called out to me and several shoppers stared in my direction. Feeling the heat creeping across my cheeks, I skirted towards the front of the store, heading for the exit. My heart rate kicked up as I dodged through the crowded concourse. I turned a corner and ducked inside the women's restroom. There were a few ladies mingling about, checking their hair and re-applying lipstick.

I looked around before striding into one of the vacant stalls, taking a seat on the toilet. All I needed was a few moments to calm my mind. Reminders of the past would always be there. It was an unsettling feeling in the pit of my stomach.

Once the bathroom was quiet and I was sure all the people had left, I pulled open the door and walked to the sink to wash my hands. For the first time in a long while I felt helpless. After turning on the water, I dipped my hands under the running stream. My chin rested against my chest and I looked up again, only this time another face appeared in the mirror—Charlie.

My wet hands gripped the sides of the sink. I watched him as he strode towards me, his eyes falling dark as he came closer.

He stood behind me, his tall frame pinning me against the cool porcelain. "One day, sweet Ella," he whispered, grasping my shoulders with his hands. "I *will* have you." His thick fingers drifted over my shoulders and up my throat.

I counted to five. Seconds felt like minutes. I swallowed hard before stomping my foot on top of his and shoving my elbow into his stomach, forcing him back. Running for the door, I heard Charlie groan or maybe it was a laugh. I sprinted back the way I came. Not paying attention, I missed the wet floor sign. I stumbled at least a meter before strong hands caught me. *Alex.*

"Hey, are you okay?" Gripping me tightly, he pulled me into his chest.

Closing my eyes, I breathed in his familiar scent. "Yes, I . . . I'm fine."

"Liar," he said, with a wink. "What's going on?"

"Nothing, I wasn't paying attention that's all."

His hands smoothed up and down my back. I welcomed the feeling of safety that Alex was giving me. Suddenly hands stopped and all of his muscles went rigid. I pulled back and followed Alex's gaze that was pinned right on Charlie as he approached the concession area.

"Ella," he said tightly. "Tell me why I'm looking at Charlie McNeil right now and I'd think twice about brushing this off as random."

What could I say? I'd already dismissed the subject of Charlie once. To do it again would be disrespectful, especially considering my feelings for Alex. It was time to disclose the truth.

"Charlie approached me in the gift shop *and* again the bathroom."

He blew out a harsh breath and ran a hand through his dark hair. "Did he lay his hands on you? If he harmed you in any way, so help me." His body vibrated with anger as he turned back to face the beer stand. Luckily Charlie was now gone.

It was time to stop being so blasé about the ordeal and realize that Charlie posed an actual threat. "He didn't hurt me, but, if I'm being honest, this latest encounter does have me on edge."

The words that I wanted to say, they were right there on the surface, but I knew this wasn't the right place to tell him about my past. It pained me to see that keeping my connection to Charlie a secret was hurting Alex. I never wanted anyone to hurt him, ever.

"Jesus." His voice raised an octave. "What is this fucking thing between the two of you?"

"Please, let's not make a scene. I promise I'll tell you the story, the whole sordid thing." I cupped his face in my hands hoping to bring his focus back to us.

*Just Alex and Ella.*

He held my gaze and expelled a deep breath. "I'm sorry I snapped at you, Ella." His hands encircled my wrists, as he leaned forward and kissed my forehead.

Relief washed through me as the expression on his face mollified. I meant what I'd said; I would tell Alex.

"You don't need to apologize to me, and you're right, there *was* something between Charlie and me, but I can guarantee it's not what you're thinking."

He cocked an eyebrow. "Listen, I don't give a shit if he's an ex-lover of yours . . ."

"Charlie and the word *lover* should never be in the same sentence. But this does involve an ex of mine. There are things that you should know. Hopefully, you won't think less of me."

He brushed his thumb across my bottom lip and then pressed his forehead to mine. "Nothing on Earth could ever make me think less of you."

Given what I'd come to know about Alex, I am not

surprised he doesn't care about my past. Based on his inflamed reaction towards Charlie, I suspect his feelings for me have intensified the way mine have for him.

"I'd like to go to the hotel and pack my things," I blurted.

His eyebrows scrunched to together. "Do you want to leave? Go home to London?"

"No, I'm not leaving. Remember when I said that if I didn't feel totally safe I'd let you know?"

He nodded, and then pulled me closer hugging me tight. "What do you want to do?"

My mind was a mess. All the clarity I thought I had about what had happened vanished. "I don't really have a plan."

"I do. You'll stay with me at my place. It's private and Charlie won't be able to come near you."

"Okay," I replied softly. Before, I'd opposed to this arrangement, but now it gave me peace of mind. There were few things in this world I was absolutely sure of, and having Alex Robertsen to keep me safe was one of them. Not that I was some damsel in distress, but I trusted him and I really liked having that feeling again.

Alex reached for his cellphone and instructed our driver to bring the car around. The hallways of the stadium were nearly desolate, only cleaning crews remained. As we stepped onto the pavement, the warm spring air swirled around us. The limo was idling at the VIP entrance and Alex ushered me inside. I slid across the backseat and Alex settled beside me. When he took my hand in his, I felt further reassurance of his commitment to keep me safe.

We didn't speak for the duration of the ride from the stadium to the hotel. Alex just rubbed small circles on the back of my hand with his thumb. I tried to wrap my brain around how I'd begin to tell Alex about this part of my past life.

When we arrived at my suite, I went into the bedroom and began removing my clothes from the closet and the chest of drawers. All I really wanted to do was take a shower and rinse the day away. I'd overheard Alex on the phone talking to Dean. He asked if they could take a meeting tomorrow afternoon.

"Yes, she's absolutely safe. At this point, it's nothing to alarm Ronan about, but I'm taking extra precautions." He paused for a beat. "My house, yes, it's private and there's a guesthouse where Ella is welcome to make herself at home."

As I pulled my suitcase out from underneath the bed, I felt the weight of his concern for me. I loved the thoughtfulness in offering me a place of privacy to myself. Although, I suspected mention of the guesthouse was a cover story.

I walked into the bathroom and scooped up the rest of my things, there wasn't much as most of my belongings were already at his home.

"The matter is settled," Alex called from outside the bedroom. "You'll be staying with me for the foreseeable future."

He approached me from the doorway, and I stood in front of him drinking in his beautiful face, admiring every line and angle. Wrapping his arms around me, he pulled me close. I buried my face into his chest, breathing in the reassuring familiar scent of him, rich and warm like the last days of summer. It was uniquely Alex. His strong arms, they were also familiar, and day by day I felt assured that this was the place I belonged.

My fingers dug into the muscles in his back. "I don't know what I would have done if you weren't there today. I always try to be brave, but now that I've thought about it . . . I admit I was scared."

"Hey, you'll always be safe with me," he murmured into

my hair. "Talk to me, Ella. Tell me what has you feeling this way."

"You better sit down, this is a long story. Perhaps you'd like a drink as well."

He grinned and we walked into the living room. Warmth slid through my veins as he grabbed the bottle of red wine from the bar and poured two glasses. He took a seat on the sofa. I joined him, curling up and tucking my legs under me. After taking a long sip, my hands gripped the glass tightly.

"Okay, here it goes." I took a deep breath. "When I was younger, I was a party girl. If there was a hot club opening in London, I was there. Ella Connolly, tabloid darling, invited to all the posh events. There were times that I'd found myself in precarious situations with the gossip rags. Like the time I dated a rugby player and he was so smashed he fell and took my top with him on the way down."

Alex's eyes popped wide.

"Yes, there I was with my tits on display for all of Holland Park to see. Ronan Connolly's little sister's nip slip was the headline that time. 'Wild Nights with Ella' became a regular occurrence in the papers."

"I can't say I blame the paparazzi for wanting to continuously take your photo. But I'd rather have the topless ones for myself."

I looked down at my glass. "I'd like to say that was my only mishap with the papers, but the story does go a bit deeper. Just when I thought the gossips were done with me, I met David Warner, a very popular English footballer . . . *soccer* player. One thing led to another and we began dating and that relationship reignited the media's interest."

"Ah, yes, dating a celebrity. I hear that's a rough business." He tucked my hair behind my ear and dropped his fingers to my cheek. My gaze caught his and he smiled.

"A few months into our relationship, David's phone was one of many involved in the celebrity hacking scandal. What I learned later is that the Assistant Editor of *La Interviu Magazine* made a deal with David and the coach of his team. In exchange for not leaking what was on his phone and ruining his career, David agreed to provide the magazine with the kinds of photos that garner the most sales for their publication—you can guess where this is going."

He shook his head took a long drink from his glass. "Nude photos of you?"

I stood and finished the rest of my wine. "Yes, David surprised me with a getaway to the South of France and while we were there, Charlie took photos of me. Once the photos were published, I filed a lawsuit, and eventually won. A few months later, more pictures surfaced. Again, I was tied up with another lawsuit with the same magazine. They had very deep pockets."

My heart began to pound in my chest as I paced around the room. "After the soccer season ended, David's team had won the league championship and we went on holiday to relax and celebrate. A few days later, David was arrested and my life went into a tailspin."

"Why was he arrested?" He stood and walked towards me. Taking my hand in his, he gave it a light squeeze. Somehow that made it easier to say the words.

"Child grooming, and sexual activity with a fifteen-year-old girl."

Alex's mouth twisted and his eyes narrowed. "He cheated on you? He slept with a fifteen-year-old?" The look of disgust on his face mirrored the way I felt on the inside.

I nodded and felt my skin prick with heat. "Apparently,

after David's team won, the girl bragged to all her friends that she had slept with him. Without her knowledge, so she says, someone took video of her recounting the story. Once it was uploaded to social media, the young woman flipped out and said that David ruined her life."

Alex rubbed my shoulders, in an effort to ease some of my tension. "I'm sorry you had to go through all that. I can't imagine how painful it must have been for you."

"I wish that were all, but there's more." I managed to get the words out despite the fact that my throat was dry. My glass was empty, but I didn't want Alex to think I needed the alcohol to get through the memories of the past. Back then, I did need it to numb the pain, but not anymore. These days I have my head on straight. "During the trial it was revealed that both David and his coach had covered up the fact that David's phone had been hacked. Photos of the young girl, along with text messages between the two of them—it was all there. The worst part was in open court, that was how I found out that David arranged for Charlie to take the topless photos of me. He admitted that he used me."

Alex scrubbed his hands down his face, and blew out a harsh breath. "Do the topless photos of you exist anywhere? I assume David is in jail?"

"Yes and he's serving a six-year sentence. In regards to the pictures, my lawyers were very good and, along with Ronan's help, it was all buried. That's why Charlie cannot sell pictures to the tabloids any longer. He was blacklisted. Once in a while, fake nudes of me pop up on the internet, but those sites are immediately notified and the pictures are usually taken down within hours."

"Did Charlie serve any jail time?"

"No, but I think the fact that he cannot sell his celebrity

pictures to the tabloids was punishment enough. It's a big business—extremely lucrative."

"I see. What did he say to you today?

My eyes closed, and his name came out in a shaky whisper. "*Alex*, you don't want to know."

"Yes, I do or I wouldn't have asked."

A chill climbed up my legs and settled in my spine as I recalled the memory. "He said, he would have me one day and made crude references to shagging me. Not only that, but he said he still has photos of me and went into explicit detail about what he does whilst looking at them."

He touched my face, his fingertips swept down my cheek. "Everything will be okay, sweetheart, don't you worry about Charlie. This will be handled. I'll keep you safe."

"I believe that, Alex."

# Chapter Twenty

## Alex

*I'll fucking kill Charlie.*

I couldn't believe I didn't look into Ella's background after I took this job. Furthermore, why the hell didn't I investigate Charlie after that first encounter in the pub? A simple Google search could have brought me up to speed. Rookie mistake and Ella's well-being wasn't the time for me to phone in my responsibilities.

She said it was nothing and I believed her. It's not her fault I'd been breaking my own rules. I was the one who said we should be just Ella and Alex. I liked . . . *loved* being just us.

Ella slept peacefully and I powered up the laptop in the jet's office to see if there was anything I could find on my new enemy—Charlie McNeil. There wasn't much in the way of personal information. I'd found a few articles about him being involved with the David Warner scandal and that was pretty much it.

"Mr. Robertsen," Joni said, from the doorway. "The pilot says we'll be landing shortly."

"Very good. Thank you." I turned off the laptop and then returned to my seat. Ella stirred from her short nap. "Hey, sleepy head."

"Hi," she said through a yawn while stretching her legs. "Landing?"

"Yep. Are you hungry?"

"Starved."

"Restaurant or home?"

"How about some takeaway—I mean *takeout*?"

"Sounds good to me."

"I'm going to need some ice cream, too."

"You got it, sweetheart."

I zipped my Range Rover through busy streets of Midtown Manhattan. It was just after one in the afternoon and I was on my way to meet with Dean Winters. After dinner, I went to bed and I tossed and turned all night. Ella said she wasn't tired, so she stayed up to watch television. When I came back downstairs an hour later, she was on the couch fast asleep.

When I told Dean Ella could have the guesthouse I meant it with all sincerity. Ella, however, had other plans. She went straight up to my room and unpacked her bags. I couldn't help but smile at realization of having her in my bed every single night. Hopefully, there would be no surprise visits from her brother or Dean.

I hated the fact that we had to hide our relationship, although there technically shouldn't be any relations between us. I should have left Ella alone, but I couldn't. Just like I couldn't leave Amanda alone, and look how that turned out. *Fuck.* No, this was nothing like that. Being with Ella felt right, too right and it was worth the risk. *She* was worth everything.

I pulled up to the valet at The Addison and handed over my keys. The concierge rang the Connolly residence and I was escorted to the private elevator to his penthouse. Dean greeted me as I stepped out of the elevator.

"What do you have for me today, Alex?" he asked, as I followed him down the hallway to the office.

"Well, as I said on the phone, Charlie McNeil has become a threat," I began, and explained what had happened at the ballpark.

"I see." He held my gaze with steady authority. "To bring you up to speed, our original situation has been resolved, but given these new details I feel its best that you stay on as Ms. Connolly's bodyguard. I know that Mr. Connolly will agree."

The original situation was resolved, that was good news to hear. At least that threat no longer loomed over Ms. Prescott. Perhaps this thing with McNeil will be resolved just as quickly.

"Of course," I answered, rubbing at the tension knot that had formed in the back of my neck. "Normally, in this kind of situation, I'd suggest a restraining order, but I feel that would be a pre-mature move."

"For now, we'll monitor McNeil's day to day activities. In addition, my men will find out where he lives, where he works and his favorite haunts."

"Sounds good," I agreed and pushed to my feet. "You have my word, Ella will be safe."

He slapped my shoulder and smiled. "With you handling it personally, I have no doubt that she will be."

My eyes shut tight and the words took me by surprise just like *she* had that night. *Ella.* I swore I could taste her, feel her skin on mine—the scent of her. It was all crashing around me, and a split second decision meant saving my soul from being swallowed up into a pit of guilt.

"You need something else, Robertsen?"

"Yeah, *yeah,* actually I do."

# Chapter Twenty-One

## Ella

I needed some time to think about life, work and my Charlie McNeil problem. He was screwing with me and now he'd forced my hand. Telling Alex about my past was easier than I ever imagined.

Although, a cloud of worry washed over me last night at the thought of Alex going off the deep end and possibly tracking down Charlie himself. Who knows what he could have done.

*Well, I have a vague idea.*

Alex had left early this morning. He didn't wake me, but the note on the coffee table had strict instructions for me to relax. He also suggested I take a dip in the pool. I rummaged through my suitcase and began hanging my things in the closet. My swimsuit still had the tags on it. I'd purchased it a week before I left. It was a sexy, red, triangle-cut bikini with gold hardware on the ties. I bought it with the intention of impressing no one at the hotel pool, but I was certain Alex would love it.

I changed into my bikini, applied some sunblock, and grabbed a towel out of the linen closet. Once outside, I settled into a lounge chair with my favorite gossip magazines.

After ten minutes of flipping through the pages, I came across an article with a picture of Finn Carter out for a stroll in London holding hands with an unidentified female. But I knew that female—Nabila! *That little minx.* Immediately, I unlocked my phone and sent her a text.

*Me: You are so busted. Are you dating Finn Carter?*

*Nabila: Let's just say, we're having a good time. Are you dating anyone?*

I smiled at her question for two reasons. One, I knew what "we're having a good time" was code for and two, it made my heart beat a little faster thinking about Alex. My feelings for him were multiplying exponentially. I loved being with him.

My phone pinged with another text from Bila: *No worries, doll, Gavin told me all about your hot bodyguard. Your secret is safe with me.* ☺

I laughed, yeah, *safe*—safe with Bila, but apparently *not* with Gavin. Who knew he couldn't keep his mouth shut?

It was quiet here, peaceful even, only the sounds of birds and the waves of the ocean in the distance. Suddenly, it all made sense to me why Alex chose to be *here*. The water, the isolation of sorts and the near silence, it really was therapeutic.

The afternoon heat was far more intense here than back home. The sparkling water beckoned me. On a playful scream, my feet lifted off the ground and I dove into the water. I swam a few laps and then floated weightlessly on the surface as the warm rays of sunshine danced across my skin. Once more I bobbed under the water, doing a quick somersault.

When I came up to the surface and opened my eyes, I found Alex sitting on the chaise lounge smiling. "How's the water?"

"Amazing," I replied, swimming towards the edge. "You should join me."

"Maybe I will, but I'm enjoying the view from right here." He leaned back in the chair, and I heard the sound of papers scrunching.

"Alex, you're sitting on my magazines."

He pulled them from underneath his fabulous ass and then looked at them and eyed me warily. "I don't understand why you read these. I would think that you'd want nothing to do with them."

I pushed up and rested my knees on the built in ledge. "Tabloids are my sick obsession, but it's cathartic."

He looked at me as if I'd spoken the words in a foreign language.

*He's adorable.*

"What?" I shook my head. "You don't have a dirty little secret. Something odd you love that might surprise people?'

He sat up, tugging his t-shirt over his head and then tossing it onto the chair. "Here's one for you, I watch *The Bachelorette.*"

I cocked an eyebrow.

"I enjoy the epic douchery. Some of the shit that comes out of the guys' mouths is truly stupid. I can't believe women fall for it." He kicked off his shoes and next went his watch.

Laughing, I fell back into the water, watching as my own private Alex strip show continued. "I think watching reality television is more of a guilty pleasure."

"There's nothing pleasurable in watching a bunch of

over-the-top 'alpha idiots' spout off cheesy lines claiming they want to find love, but, nonetheless, it's entertaining as hell."

"Well, what do you find pleasurable?" *Yes, I know exactly what I'm doing in this moment.*

In the blink of an eye, his shorts were gone and I stood in the water admiring a gorgeous and very naked Alex. I could stare at him forever. My gaze darted around to all corners of the grounds. "Get in this pool before someone sees you."

Water pelleted my skin and rippled around my body. Opening my eyes, I used my hands as a shield from the sun, taking in his silhouette as he waded towards me. Cupping water in his hands, he poured it over his dark hair, slicking it back. His hazel eyes burned bright, and droplets of water slid down his neck and broad chest. Savoring this moment, my fingers glided along the thick cords of the muscles in his arms memorizing every rigid ripple. I know men aren't supposed to be seen as beautiful, but my God, to me, Alex was.

His arms banded around me, holding me possessively as his mouth crushed down onto mine consuming me in a deep, lush kiss.

"For the record, kissing you is extremely pleasurable."

"Well then, let me welcome you home properly," I said.

He smirked. "Yes, please, but keep the *proper* out of it."

He kissed me hard, slipping his tongue deep inside my mouth. I wrapped my legs around his waist and he ground his cock against me. Gliding his hands up my back, he tugged at the strings of my top. Lost in a haze of lust, my needy hands pulled his hair. The sharp bite of the concrete against my back added a delicious shiver to his assault upon my senses. A moan spilled from my lips as his fingers dug into my ass.

"*Alex . . .*" I whispered harshly.

The world around us seemed to disappear, all my

problems and fears washed away. I felt like I'd waited my entire life to find this man and, by some wonderful happenstance, we'd found each other accidentally on a sidewalk in New York City. I'd snuck out of his room in the early morning hours, not knowing he'd been assigned to my life in a bigger way—to protect me.

Cupping my face, he pulled me into another kiss, brushing his lips over mine. Releasing a growl, Alex pulled the strings on the sides of my bikini bottoms.

*Away they go.*

His tongue trailing across my collarbone sent shockwaves of pleasure zipping through me. In the distance, rumbles of thunder could be heard, but nothing compared to the frenzied storm brewing inside me.

I wanted this man, right here and right now.

His hands gently massaged my thighs and I shamelessly ground my hips against him. As I reached along his muscled back, clawing and pulling him closer, his mouth wrapped around my breast licking and sucking leaving me panting and wanting more.

"Please, I need *you*," I begged, as his fingers teasingly moved along my inner thighs. "God *yes*, touch me, Alex."

I heard myself moan as his lips glided up my throat and along my chin. Leaning back to look at me his beautiful eyes were filled with fire. A shiver racked through my body as I felt the magnetic pull of emotions all at once.

"I'll give you what you need," he teased, with a wickedly sexy smile.

Despite being in the invigorating water, every nerve ending in my body was burning. Unable to look away, once more, his perfect hazel eyes penetrated my soul.

"You're beautiful," he whispered. "Wars have been started

over women far less stunning than you." Sliding his hands into my hair, he grabbed the back of my neck with carnal force pulling me into a sensual kiss.

He spun around, bringing us both to the ledge where he pulled me onto his lap. His cock bobbed against my stomach. Frantic in my need for him, I gripped his cock. He groaned as I continued massaging the length of him.

Reaching up, his hands caressed my breasts, palming and then pinching my nipples in a tantalizing rhythm. His fingers created an electric trail as they worked their way down to my throbbing pussy. The feel of his touch on my clit was too much. A long moan crawled up my throat. Whimpering, I leaned back giving him better access as he slipped two fingers inside me. He pumped his fingers in and out, teasing me with every stroke. My need for him to fill me was unbearable.

"Alex," I said breathlessly. "You're torturing me."

"I suppose this has gone on long enough," he whispered in that husky tone that drove me out of my mind. His fingers left my body, leaving me with a physical ache.

"Fuck me, please, *now*."

His tongue dipped inside my mouth, licking me slowly. "Ride me, Ella." His fingers dug into my hips and I gripped his cock, holding him steady as I sank onto his erection. Working my pelvis, I gasped as I took him inch by inch. My breathing coming quick and short as I relished the feel of him stretching and filling me. Giving me exactly what I needed.

*"Alex,"* left my lips in a shaky whisper.

His hazel eyes landed on me and a wicked grin spread across his face. The sounds of water sloshing against the tiles of the pool and rumbling thunder weaved together in some kind of erotic symphony.

I only hoped I didn't look like Elizabeth Berkley's

character in *Showgirls*. However, it should be noted, that it's an awesome movie. *Why am I thinking about this whilst having amazing pool sex with Alex?*

"Ella," he moaned. "*Fuck*, you feel so good."

That amped me up and I gripped his shoulders, my nails dug into his skin. Burying his face into my neck, he lifted his pelvis matching me thrust for thrust, then surpassing my own speed.

"Yes . . . oh *Alex* . . ." I cried out his name, just as the waves of an orgasm began to take hold. He guided my hips up and down, thrusting upwards hitting my g-spot with precision, sending me soaring into oblivion. My eyes screwed shut as my pussy rippled around his cock.

"Fuck, what you do to me," he growled, rocking through the spasms of my orgasm. With the final buck of his hips, his name came out in a scream and I felt his thick cock filling me with his cum.

Alex crushed his lips to mine, thrusting his tongue inside my mouth. His hands stroked up and down my back, igniting my lust all over again. Just as I thought we might go for round two in the pool, the sky opened up unleashing a torrential downpour.

We unlocked our bodies and hopped out of the water seeking cover from the storm in the pool house. Alex grabbed two giant towels from the linen closet and wrapped me up before pulling a towel around his waist.

"Ella."

"Hmm?"

"Did I mention, I really, really like your bikini?"

"Yes," I said through a laugh, and then I rolled up on my tiptoes to kiss him on the lips. "I think you made that pretty clear."

# Chapter Twenty-Two

## Ella

Heading over to Nancy's Diner was an adventure. Instead of it being a quiet out of the way spot for me to have lunch with my brother, it turned out to be an enormous cluster fuck. It didn't help matters that The Harbour was flooded with more people than usual due to the impeding American holiday. The paparazzi spotted Ronan at the airport, so they decided to follow him here to the restaurant. In a corner booth, I sat alone while he talked to the media and sign a few autographs for fans.

*He's too polite.*

The longer I sat there, my thoughts drifted to Alex. Closing my eyes, I remembered the feel of his hands on my body that morning. He fucked me into two epic orgasms, once in bed and once more in the shower. At the memory, I felt a wonderful deep ache and I pushed my thighs together feeling the heat wash over my skin.

*Jesus.*

The chiming of bells pulled my eyes to the door. In walked Ronan and Dean, who immediately took a seat at the counter. I sucked in a breath and pushed my salacious thoughts out of my brain.

"Mr. Hollywood Big Shot," I muttered over my menu. "Don't you get tired of having to play nicey-nice with the paparazzi?"

Ronan kissed me on the cheek and then slid into the booth across from me. "Sorry to have made you wait, sis. Forgive me?"

"Are you buying lunch?"

"Of course."

"Then I forgive you."

He smirked and settled back into the booth. "What do you recommend?"

"The lobster salad is a local favorite. Alex likes the spicy shrimp tacos with the mango salsa."

"Funny, that you mention Alex."

*Oh, here we go.*

Maintaining a calm manner, I swallowed hard, before replying. My heart pounded in my chest feeling that maybe the reason Ronan invited me to lunch was because he knew I'd been screwing Alex all these weeks. Well, I guess it had been more like a couple of months.

"Funny, why is that funny?" I asked, holding my breath for an answer.

"Sorry, poor choice of words. I didn't mean anything by it."

I cocked an eyebrow. After making my lunch decision, I used my menu as a fan. It was the beginning of July and the heat was unbearable. My little white dress was definitely going to need a thorough laundering.

My stomach rumbled, just as a large platter of stuffed crabs and a bottle of sparkling water appeared before us.

"Compliments of Nancy Brooks, the owner," our server said placing the appetizer plates on the table. "Are you ready to order?"

"I believe we are," my brother answered politely. "And please thank Nancy for the stuffed crabs."

"I think I'll have the lemon-garlic shrimp and grits. And a large iced tea."

Ronan ordered some grilled salmon with avocado salsa and a beer. While we waited for our lunch, he told me about his latest movie in between bites. I didn't have any of the appetizer, but it smelled amazing, the Cajun spices combined with the onion and crab made my mouth water. Nancy was famous for mixing some of her classic southern recipes with traditional east coast seafood dishes. So Alex told me.

"Tell me, how are you doing, Lolly?"

I smiled at the nickname my brother assigned to me ever since we were kids. One summer I was obsessed with eating lollyice for breakfast, lunch and dinner. Back then, it was my favorite thing in the whole world. I'd grown out of that phase, but I don't think that Ronan plans to stop calling me Lolly any time soon.

"I'm doing well, staying busy. I'm ready to make an offer on a space here. The one I was telling you about on Harbour Drive."

I was going to have an international brand. This was the thing that I'd worked so hard for. My dream was finally happening.

At first, I thought Alex would be a distraction. Instead,

he'd helped me in more ways than I could count. By now, I expected that I would be itching to get back to London. Back to my friends and back to my flat. But, over the last few months, Alex has slipped deeper into my life and I wasn't ready to let go. Did I even have to?

Life post-finalizing this deal was filled with "what ifs." Most nights I lay in bed, staring at the ceiling in Alex's bedroom, fantasizing about him stopping by the boutique to bring me a coffee, just because. I thought about all the nights I'd make him dinner and then we'd take a walk on the beach.

We never discussed what would happen next. Alex certainly wouldn't be my bodyguard forever. He had career aspirations and dreams of his own. Did those dreams include me?

"Sis. Hey, Ella."

"Hmm?"

"Where did you go just now?"

"Oh, sorry," I said, redirecting my focus back to the conversation. "Just thinking. What did you say?"

"Do you want me to put this deal together for you?"

Shaking the cobwebs, I unfolded the white cloth napkin across my lap. "You're the only one I'd trust, well, besides Dad, of course. I have the down payment and I can have the bank wire the money or have them process a check."

Ronan nodded, tossing back a swig of beer. "Sounds good, I'll get the ball rolling today. I'll only take three percent of the commission. You keep the rest and use it towards the business."

I felt my smile grow wider. "Thank you! Have I ever told you that you're the greatest brother ever?"

He winked. "My pleasure, I guess you're an okay little sister."

Our meal arrived and, like a glutton, I shoveled in three

huge bites before coming up for air. Ronan just stared at me and then moved his plate closer to him.

"Good Lord, when was the last time you had a decent meal?"

I swallowed, and wiped my mouth. "Sorry, this is *so* unbelievably good."

"Nancy, give me some sugar!" I heard a deep gravelly voice boom out. My head whipped up, and I saw Grady James standing a few feet away. Ronan smirked and rolled his eyes.

It was no secret that Ronan and Grady were less than friendly. Last December, their club brawl was all anyone could talk about, until Ronan and Holliday went public with their relationship a few weeks later. Since then, I haven't seen much of Grady in the tabloids.

He whispered something to Nancy. Smiling, she cupped his chin in her hand and then kissed his cheek, just as a mother would. His electric blue eyes locked on mine and I quickly looked away. Dean stood as soon as he saw Grady stopped at our booth.

*Shit! Please don't fight today, guys.*

"Connolly, this doesn't look like Holliday that you're dining with today."

"You're observant, James," he drawled, and then pushed to his feet. "This is my sister, Ella."

"Ella, it's nice to meet you," Grady said, offering a gleaming smile.

"Uhmm, hi."

Grady turned back to face my brother. "Congrats on the Van Wyk movie, man. It'll be a hit for sure."

"Thanks, yeah, it's hard to believe we wrap next month."

Grady shoved his hands into the pockets of his shorts. "Will either of you be attending the Stars and Stripes Polo

Challenge this weekend?"

"No, I'm afraid not. Holliday and I will be spending the weekend at her parents' place in Malibu. They have a grand Fourth of July celebration every year."

"Oh yeah, Helen throws quite the party, you're in for a good time."

My eyebrows rose, and I studied my brother for a moment. These two are quite chummy.

"What are your plans for the weekend, Ella?" Grady asked, giving me that charming smile once more.

"I hadn't really thought too much about it," I replied honestly. "This is my first Fourth of July, seeing that I'm not an American."

That comment earned me a chuckle from Grady. With caution, I watched the back and forth exchange between them, it was very civilized. No blood spilled. No verbal assault. What was going on with these two?

"Listen, it was good to see you, Ronan, but my agent just walked in and I need to get going."

"Take care, man," he replied, giving Grady a quick handshake.

"Ella, nice to have met you, you two enjoy your lunch. Hope to see you this weekend."

"Okay, yeah, maybe."

And with that, Grady moved through the aisle of the diner and headed towards the front door. Ronan slid back into the booth, and picked up his fork. I just stared at him.

"What?" he asked, and shrugged his shoulders.

"You do realize that you were having a sweet little public bromance with Grady James, the guy you punched at a club a few months ago. The same guy who was caught kissing *your* girlfriend."

"Hardly a bromance," he scoffed, tossing back a long swig of beer. "If you must know, he's someone that's important to Holliday and it turns out he's not a bad guy."

"Yeah, apparently he is important to her." I leaned in closer, twirling my straw. "I mean *that* kiss."

"Tread lightly, Ella." His tone was warning. "Sometimes pictures can be very deceiving. They were close once and Grady helped Holliday during a rough time in her life. That's all you need to know. Satisfied?"

"Sorry, I didn't mean to insinuate or disrespect Holliday. You know I adore her."

He scooped up some salmon from his plate. "Let's talk about you. I hear that Alex took you to a baseball game and that's when you saw Charlie again. And now, you're living in his guesthouse. As it would seem, Alex is going above and beyond in his duties."

That was an odd thing for him to say, especially since it was *his* idea for me to be looked after while in the city. I suppose it was out of the norm that I was living under the same roof as my bodyguard. Usually it's the bodyguard who stays with the one they're protecting. Our family isn't exactly normal though.

"First of all, I am staying in his guesthouse." A tiny fib, technically some of my belongings are there. "Given the current situation, I think you'd find it comforting knowing that I have around the clock security. Besides, Alex is my friend. He's been really good to me."

Good to me, in *and* out of the bedroom. I felt a giggle bubble in my throat. *Grow up, Ella.*

"Friends, huh?"

"Yes, *friends*," I repeated, before taking the final sip of my drink.

"Usually one's face doesn't turn fifty shades of red, at the mention of a *friend's* name."

Alarm bells went off. *Quick Ella, think.*

"Oh stop. It's hotter than Hades in here, besides, aren't you *friends* with Dean?" I nodded towards the counter where he'd been sitting.

"I suppose Dean and I have shared a pint now and again." He pushed his plate back, and then captured the attention of our server signaling for the bill. "I wasn't trying to be a jerk, or tell you how to live your life. Truth be told, I'm very glad that you have a friend and someone that you trust while being here. I worry about you."

I reached across the table and covered his hand with mine. "You're very sweet and I love you for caring. You don't need to worry about me and, obviously, your instincts were right to hire Alex. But the good news is that I haven't heard a peep from Charlie in a month. So, as you can see, my instincts to be here in The Harbour were also correct. I love this place."

His lip quirked up. "Yeah, I can see that you do."

After I returned from lunch, I found Alex sitting in his study, scotch in one hand and something that looked like a fancy greeting card in the other. At the sound of my heels hitting the hardwood floor, his head jerked up. By his reaction, I could tell I'd startled him from deep thoughts.

"What are you thinking so hard about," I asked pouring myself a glass of vodka from the silver drink cart in the corner.

He let out a deep sigh. "I've been invited to a party."

"Ahhh, yeah, parties—total bummers."

He chuckled. "It's actually a fundraiser for a very worthy cause. A friend of mine, her family owns a gourmet candy company, Bloom Bars. Have you heard of them?"

I shook my head, and then took a sip of my drink.

"They donate a percentage of their profits to various charitable organizations that aid military men, women and their families. This year they are hosting a fundraiser for Military Women in Business. Basically, this program offers training in business, management and finance to encourage entrepreneurship for female veterans."

"Well, that sounds like a lovely event. I'm all for supporting women who want to run their own companies. Like Beyoncé says, 'who run the world—*girls*.'" After placing my drink on a coaster, I stood up while singing the chorus lyrics to the song and then went into performing my best Queen Bey dance moves.

Alex stepped up and placed his hands on my hips, stilling my movements. "You like to dance, huh?"

"I do, very much," I replied, running my hands over his chest, the fabric of his shirt soft on my fingertips.

He grinned, and swiped a remote from his desk. With a quick flip, music piped through the speakers, but, apparently, this was not the song he wanted.

*Click. Click. Click.*

The melodic sound of The Weeknd's seductive voice registered and I couldn't help but sway my hips to the beat. Alex's long fingers mapped my ass, pressing along to the sensual rhythm of "As You Are."

"You know, they say that every time one of *his* songs comes on that means someone's fucking."

Alex smirked, his hazel eyes hooded. "Is that so?" He hooked his arm around my waist, while using his other hand to bring my leg up to wrap around his waist. My body went lax in his arms, his hand slid up my back and tangled in my hair.

With a fluid movement, he pulled me back, dipping my body. I floated freely and then wound back upright meeting his eyes. It was all very *Dirty Dancing* like.

He pulled me up his body, drawing me into a deep kiss. His tongue licked mine, teasing me, driving me out of my mind.

*This seems to be a pattern.*

"I think if you listen closely, you can actually hear the sound of panties hitting the floor."

"I think that's an excellent place for your panties right now," he murmured, his lips drifting up my throat. "I couldn't wait until you came back from lunch. All I could think about was when I'd fuck you again."

His hands moved under my skirt, his fingers teasing the silk edge of my panties.

"We must be on the same page because I've been thinking about you all day." I shoved my hands into the waistband of his jeans, popping the button. "I barely made it through lunch. All I could think about was how much I'd like to suck your cock."

My greedy need for him kicked in. Consumed with want, I devoured him, catching his lower lip with my teeth. His hands tangled in my hair and he sealed his mouth over mine, licking and sucking my tongue. My hands gripped and tugged at the roots of his hair. His fingers slid over my wetness and I bucked at the contact. We were in an epic battle for control of what would happen next—who would receive pleasure first.

He groaned when I pushed him into the oversized club chair, my hands running down his stomach and over his erection.

"Ella . . . *Christ*."

After tugging the zipper down and reaching inside his

boxer briefs, I wrapped my hands around his cock. Alex was so thick and hard. I stroked him slowly, relishing the feel of him.

I licked my bottom lip. “I want you. I want to taste you, Alex.”

My hands worked his pants lower and I sank to my knees in front of him. Before I could generate a thought, my mouth was on him.

His masculine scent and the softness of his skin was a heady combination. I squirmed and moaned, his vibrating groans of pleasure driving me wild. Swirling my tongue around his cock, I continued to tease him as the thick veins throbbed against my palms.

“Fuck,” he hissed, pushing into my mouth. “Take me deep, sweetheart.”

Aroused by his request, I hollowed my cheeks and took his entire length into my mouth. His hands pushed into my hair, pulling and spurring me on.

“That talented tongue of yours is making me unravel,” he growled, gripping me by the back of the head. Our eyes met, the way he was looking at me made me slick and hot. My mind spun thinking about how much I loved giving him this pleasure. Craving for him to orgasm, I sucked him deeper, cupping his balls and massaging them gently.

“Ella, I’m going to come.” His tone was in warning and yet filled with the most superb agony. My urgency to taste him was blinding, I gripped his cock with both hands and licked him furiously.

Squeezing his eyes shut, his whole body jerked and I milked him, taking everything he had. Watching him fall apart in spectacular fashion, that was an incredibly powerful feeling.

He exhaled harshly. "Holy fuck, you're amazing."

"You're so hot," I said rising from the floor to straddle him.

"I'm going to fuck you hard, and you *will* be sore tomorrow."

"Well, I'm on top so it looks like I'll be the one doing the fucking," I challenged.

"Nope, that's not going to work for me," he growled, lifting me up and then pinning me beneath him on the faux animal skin rug.

In between kisses, he managed to kick off his jeans and then I had the pleasure of working the buttons of his shirt, feeling the light dusting of chest hair beneath my fingertips. My hands roamed along the muscles of his abdomen and around his back where I traced my nails along his spine and over his ink.

He eased up to his knees and slipped his shirt over his thick shoulders. "Ella, you have *seconds* at best to get naked or I'll do it for you. Please don't put me in a position where I'll be held responsible for the destruction of that sexy-ass dress."

I was on my feet before I knew it and striping everything off. I tossed my clothes onto the chair and turned to face Alex.

He was all over me, hands gripping and pushing back on the desk. Leaning over me, he took my face in both hands and then kissed me, thrusting his tongue deep inside my mouth. He cupped my breasts, the pads of his thumbs circling my nipples. My fingers danced along the muscles in his back. *I know I'm obsessed with his back.*

His hands fell to my ass. Gripping tight, he pulled me forward to the edge of his desk. He angled his cock and slammed into me.

"Oh, fuck yes, Alex," I moaned, my nails scratching along

the nape of his neck.

My eyes fell to his cock and I watched him pumping into me, sliding in and out with brilliant strokes. A whirlwind of thoughts zipped through me and my eyes flicked up to Alex's. Something heavy smashed right into my heart. Ripples of raw emotion flowed as I pressed my lips to his. He kissed me hard, with urgency, a compliment to the screaming of my need for him.

I needed all of him. I needed Alex. Not just in the physical sense, well, I needed that too, I wanted all of him—mind, body, and soul.

His fingers slid over my clit and I fell apart—blown to bits by a wildly shattering orgasm.

I licked my lips and met his eyes. "That was incredible."

He nodded and nipped the skin along my neck and shoulders. "You're incredible."

The pad of his thumb stroked my cheek and his lips met mine for a gentle kiss. For a long moment he stared at me, almost as if he was trying to communicate something that words just couldn't.

I felt it too . . . it was powerful. And in that moment, my whole world centered on Alex. A long time ago, I gave away my heart and today it was returned to sender. Complete and whole and full of love—love for *him*.

# Chapter Twenty-Three

## Alex

While Ella finished her shower, I took it upon myself to put together a little impromptu carpet picnic in the media room. Only one food was on the menu and that was a carton of crème brûlée ice cream from Häagen-Dazs and, of course, the bar was open. I created a romantic mood by tossing a few blankets on the carpet, stacking up half a dozen pillows and lighting some candles.

The music was still playing in the office and I trekked down the hallway to turn it off. My office smelled of sweat, of sex, and of Ella. I stared at the corner of my desk, the space where she'd spread her legs for me, moaned my name and came all over my cock. This was the woman I'd been required to protect. Now she was living in my house, sleeping in my bed, and bound to me in an entirely different manner.

As I brushed past the coffee table, the event invitation for the fundraiser fell onto the floor. After scanning the details one more time, I tucked it back inside the envelope. Then I sat down at my desk, opened my laptop and added it to my calendar. Yes, I was going to go. I owed it to Sasha and her family to be there.

I needed to tell Ella about Sasha. In fact, I wanted to.

"Alex? Where are you?"

After hitting close on my calendar, I stood up and walked back towards the media room. I couldn't help but stare at Ella. She looked beautiful wearing a pair of frayed jean shorts and a grey tank top. Her blonde hair, still wet from the shower, spilled over her shoulder.

She bopped back and forth on her bare feet. "What's all this?"

My hands came up to the sides of her face. "I thought we'd have some dessert before dinner." I waggled my eyebrows.

"Are you trying to shag me in every room in the house," she whispered, rising up to her tiptoes to kiss me.

"I'm all for having sex with you again, but I actually meant food—ice cream to be exact."

"Mmmm, my favorite."

"I know . . . crème brûlée even. Now, have a seat and I'll bring everything to you."

She laughed and then sat down, tucking her legs underneath her. After scooping the ice cream into two bowls, I sat them on a serving tray along with spoons and napkins. My mother told me presentation was everything. This surely would have exceeded her expectations.

"Here we go," I said, placing the tray between us.

She slid her hair over her shoulder, drawing my eyes to her flawless, creamy skin. I thought about marking it with my teeth just above her breast. It was an odd thing to think of, but in other weird news, I fucking loved the thought of branding her as mine.

"Oh, yummy, thank you," she replied, picking up a bowl and spoon.

"So, I was thinking. Would you like to go to the gala with me?"

Her brows rose. "You want me to go as your date?"

"I'd like to have you there with me, as my guest."

She hung her head and twisted the spoon back and forth in the bowl. My heart stopped for a moment. *Shit!* Had I fucked this up? Where this thing between us was concerned, I could be reading all the signs incorrectly. Was she feeling something *more*? It felt like something more than just sex, but I'd made that mistake before. Having my heart shredded has made me a giant pussy.

"Ella, look at me." I tucked my fingers under her chin, forcing her to look up at me. "What's wrong?"

"It's a big social affair and I don't want to embarrass you."

Her words caught me off guard. "Whoa, wait a minute." I set my bowl down, and took her hands in mine. "Sweetheart, you could never embarrass me."

"Trust me, if this is a high profile event, then I most certainly could."

"How exactly?"

"If just one person recognized me as David Warner's ex-girlfriend, it wouldn't take long before the crude jokes flowed as freely as the drinks."

"Well, the drinks wouldn't be free," I joked, hoping to ease her worry.

A small smile crossed her lips. "You know what I'm trying to say."

"This group of people wouldn't do that and even if

someone did, they'd have to deal with me. Do you worry about this all the time?"

"No, this is more of a recent development in the hot mess that is . . . *was* my life. All this stuff with Charlie has me a little unnerved. It's opened the old wounds."

My mind churned. I didn't want Ella to feel like she should go into hiding because of this Charlie situation. Life is meant to be lived fully and without fear. *Easy words to say, Alex.* I didn't have an obsessed possible stalker, making crude threats towards me.

*Calm her, reassure her.*

"I get that, I do. And hey, we'll close up those old wounds for good—together."

"Together," she repeated.

"Yeah, live fearlessly." I heard the irony of my words. I should take my own advice. "What do you say; will you come with me to Chicago?"

"Chicago? You never said it was the Windy City! Yes, I'd love to accompany you to the event."

She started rambling. "Pizza. Deep Dish. Wheat. Magnificent Mile. Shopping. Navy Pier."

Leaning close, I kissed her while grabbing at the bowl in her hands.

"Hold it right there, Mister. I'm finishing this bowl of heavenly decadence first and then I'll make out with you."

I laughed and dug into my own bowl. Settling back on the pile of pillows, I thought about a myriad of things. Ella. I loved having her in my life, and if I was being honest, I really liked having her here with me. I've been down this road before, but this time something felt different. And that scared the living shit out of me. Ella's reaction stirred up questions. I considered the possibility of *more.*

What would happen once this ordeal with Charlie ended? When he no longer posed a threat, my job would cease to exist. This job was only supposed to be temporary while I got my shit together.

Things at Robertsen Security were going very well. Patrick, my right hand man kept me updated on the day-to-day business through emails and video calls. We had a once weekly meeting, where he'd brief me on new and existing contracts. He and the rest of the team were doing a hell of a job. Of course, I'd considered having him run the office back in Grand Rapids indefinitely. For the moment, plans for East Coast expansion were put on hold as I focused on more important matters. *Ella.* Her safety was my highest priority.

Over the last few weeks, with Ella staying here, I'd studied her, watching as she sketched the layout of her floor space and coordinated color schemes for her boutique. I was in a constant state of arousal every time she painted that red color on her lips or the way she smiled at me over her mug of coffee. It was a rarity that she'd drink tea anymore and her use of English slang terms was few and far between. Gone were the days of someone being a wanker, instead douchebag was now her go to insult.

We'd fallen into an easy routine. Grabbing coffee and a box of healthy pastries at one of the cafés followed our morning workouts. There were long afternoon lunches on the pier and some lunches where food was skipped entirely for extended sex marathons. There were also nights of binge watching television, she loved sitcoms the most—*Friends* and *Will & Grace* were her top choices. I finally got her to watch *Game of Thrones*. Although she spent most episodes with her hands over her face, all the violence made her squeamish.

Tuesdays and Thursdays were becoming my favorite days

of the week. Sleep deprivation was worth it watching Ella bending and twisting her lithe body into yoga poses by the pool as the sun came up over the dunes. All the while, I tried to figure out what she was thinking.

Ella tried to give me money for rent or groceries. I explained that her money was no good here. She insisted I take some form of compensation. Offering the suggestion of trading sexual favors for room and board earned me a dirty look and a punch in the arm. One evening I found a random hundred dollar bill tucked in my underwear drawer. The gesture made me smile. More bills showed up as the weeks went by—another hundred showed up in the pocket of my dress shirt and two mysteriously appeared in the console of my Range Rover. The bills now took up space in my office safe. Maybe I'd invest in her boutique or upgrade the security system.

Ella wiped her mouth on a napkin and set her now empty bowl back onto the serving tray. "So while I was in the shower . . ."

"I like the beginning of this story already."

"My brother . . ."

My brow scrunched. "Okay, maybe I don't want to hear this."

"I knew that would get your mind out of the gutter. Ronan texted me and said his, *uh*, friend, Grady is sending over two invitations for the Stars and Stripes Polo Challenge this weekend. Do you want to go?"

"Are you asking me on a date?"

"Technically, you'd be my guest since Ronan made the donation," she said, curling beside me.

I laughed. "Touché. I'll still make a donation. Would that earn me a kiss or two?"

"Maybe, it might be worth the risk. My first Fourth of July

holiday and I get to celebrate with you."

For a moment, I pondered asking her where her mind was with the future—more specifically with us. Would it be worth the risk?

"First, we'll watch the fireworks, and then we'll come back here and make some of our own."

"Alex Robertsen," she breathed, and tilted her face to mine. "Do you think about anything other than sex?"

That was a loaded question.

"Yes," I murmured against her lips. "I think about more than just sex." My hands tangled in her hair and she dropped her cheek to my shoulder.

I've dealt with many delicate situations in my life, but this was one risk that I hadn't been fully able to assess all the details. Probability and desired outcome, those were two things I could calculate in less than ten seconds. Things were unclear and this Charlie McNeil situation needed to come to an end soon.

# Chapter Twenty-Four

## Ella

Alex maneuvered his Range Rover through the gates of The Harbour Polo Club. It was a beautiful day for a polo match. The sky was a magnificent shade of cobalt blue and the warm breeze was gently rustling the tall grasses and abundance of flowers that decorated the sprawling property. In the distance sat a huge white tent with a sea of well-dressed people mingling about underneath it. Directly across from the tent was the pristine polo field, just waiting to be torn up. White chairs under logo umbrellas lined the untouched brilliant green arena.

After Alex parked we walked towards the tent, his hand brushed against mine. Heat spread everywhere, spiraling downward, warming that deep ache I had for him. I so badly wanted to lace my fingers with his; instead, I bumped his shoulder.

We were approached by a woman in a dress with blue and white stripes holding a clipboard. The diamonds draped around her neck reflected the glint of the sun, casting dazzling flashes of light.

I presented my invitation. "Miss Ella Connolly and guest," she announced to no one in particular before pulling the paper from hand. My shoulders tensed, but I managed a bright smile. After ticking our names off the VIP list, she directed us to the red carpet, which was actually blue.

Slightly nervous, I turned to face the cameras and Alex stepped aside. I took a deep breath, and focused on something positive. I thought of all the money this event would raise for the various causes. Protecting and preserving US landmarks and the Heroes of America fund.

*"Live fearlessly,"* I mumbled to myself.

Cameras flashed and popped as I switched my up my poses. My balance faltered and I wobbled slightly. In a fluid move, Alex hooked his arm around my waist, an unspoken reassurance of security. Tingles flitted over my skin. He was my protector, hired in a professional capacity to take care of me. For a brief moment, I allowed myself to daydream that we were here as a legit couple. We were taking risks with our flirting and touching. Anyone looking close enough might believe that we were together.

"I got you, sweetheart, just breathe." His warm breath fanned across my ear, stoking the burning embers deep in my belly. Alex looked sexy wearing white trousers with a plaid dress shirt under a navy jacket. I complimented him, donning a navy pleated skirt with white and green stripes paired with a crisp white blouse.

The day before the event, I'd purchased a white pocket square with navy piping for his jacket. I told him accessories made the man. He frowned, but indulged me anyway. Standing side by side, we could have been one of those preppy couples in the Ralph Lauren ads.

Despite the event being a private, invitation only event for charity, I knew there was a chance the pictures would turn up on social media or in gossip rags, not just the society pages. Excitement and fear danced up my spine. Sweat formed on my skin, making my fingers slick against my leather clutch. Alex and I had been screwing around for months and I wondered if the soon to be published pictures would uncover our deliciously dirty little secret. Part of me wanted to take a leap and live my life the way I wanted. What I *wanted* was Alex. To be able to throw my arms around his neck and pepper him with kisses and let the whole world know. Mostly, I wanted to tell him I'd fallen for him. *Loved him. Trusted him.* Even if he rejected me, I would know that I was capable of loving someone again. That alone felt amazing.

When we stepped off the carpet we made a subtle dash for the bar. To my surprise, it was a family friendly event. The East Harbour Athletic Club had sponsored the kids' tent, complete with pony rides, arts and crafts, and organic strawberry mint and raspberry lemonade.

My eyes scanned the crowd, admiring all the fashionable couples and their well-dressed children. Little girls in gauzy dresses mirrored their elegant mothers' lace frocks. Boys dressed in colorful gingham prints paired with khaki pants. Some wore hats, others donned suspenders.

"You look beautiful." His eyes took me in with sincerity, but the raw hunger was also visible.

"Thank you, so do you."

Alex let out a low chuckle. I blushed realizing the humor in my compliment.

"I meant to say you look sexy as hell." My fingers toyed with the lapels of his jacket.

The bartender interrupted our moment. "Hello and welcome, what can I get you?"

Alex discussed potato vodkas with the bartender, which made my smile grow wider. He knew my drink order—he didn't even have to ask. Looking around the tent, I noticed several men drinking tall glasses of beer. At these events in London, guests sipped Pimm's or champagne. I wondered what Alex would order? My guess was a scotch and soda.

"Here you go . . . one vodka soda with a twist of lime." Alex handed me the glass along with a napkin, just as the bartender came back with his drink—a beer. *Damn, he fooled me.*

With his hand on the small of my back, he led me to one of the high top cocktail tables. A few of the polo players entered and I looked to see if Grady James was part of the crowd. I'd like to thank him again for the invitation.

"Alex? Alex Robertsen, my God it is you!"

A woman dressed in a pink and white silk dress nipped towards us with champagne in one hand and a pearly white box clutch in the other. She looked elegant with her wavy black hair tied up in a ponytail and tucked under a wide brimmed hat topped with delicate flowers.

"Francesca, nice to see you," Alex replied before kissing her cheek. They were appropriately affectionate, she complimented his attire and he politely thanked her.

"Francesca Baldwin, I'd like you to meet Ella Connolly."

"Hello, lovely to meet you, Francesca."

Narrow brown eyes looked me up and down as she slid her hand into mine. For a moment, I thought back to when Alex and Gavin had met. I wondered if I should wrap my arms around Alex and stake my claim just as he had done.

Was she an old girlfriend? Former lover?

"Ella, it's a pleasure meeting you." Her lips formed a sweet smile. "Alex, she's quite beautiful."

"She is," he agreed and tossed me a wink.

Glancing between the two of them, I asked, "And how are the two of you acquainted?"

"Franny here, is a friend of the family."

Approval of his answer gleamed in her smile. "Yes, we practically grew up together. In the summers, our families spent many weekends together at the lake." She turned to face me. "But I know what you're really asking; you want to know if we've slept together?"

You could have knocked me over with a feather. I wasn't prepared for those words. It's a rarity to meet a woman who's direct.

Her eyes stayed connected with mine. "The answer is no."

I smirked. "I like her, Alex."

There wasn't much time for the two of them to catch up because the bugle trumpeted alerting us the match was set to begin. Francesca scurried away, but not before giving us both a hug. The players had taken the field and the excitement bristled through the crowd. After the umpire's speech, we focused our attention to the white ball in the palm of his hand.

Alex's fingers traced along the back of my knee and my heartbeat drummed in my ears. The feel of his rough hands against my bare skin, that little bit was almost too much to take. Wetness pooled between my thighs with every gentle graze. If we were in a darkened cinema theater I would have considered removing my thong and allow him the access to finger fuck me.

After taking a drink, I whispered, "Are you having fun?"

"I am. Are you?"

Looking up at him through my lashes, I smiled.

The smack of the mallet against the ball lashed out like a boom of thunder. The players raced their horses up and down the field in an exuberant fashion. When the galloping horses rumbled past us, I spotted Grady his navy blue jersey donned with the number four. He was the primary defensive player and allowed to move anywhere on the field.

Expertly hooking his stick around the opposing player, he swung in defense. The ball flew to player number three allowing him to drive and score with ease. Whistles of appreciation and roaring cheers spilled from the crowd.

After six chukkas, there was a pause in the game for the players to change mounts. Walking briskly, we darted through the crowd. Alex gripped my hand tightly. His touch was a bonfire, melting me like toffee over an apple.

Opening the gate, he pulled me behind the stables and then pressed his tall frame against me. Before I could ask Alex what he was doing his mouth was on mine, probing and seeking entrance. A familiar hum of electricity sparked, winding its way through every inch of my body.

One kiss, one look, or just one touch from him that's all it took for him to turn me into a mass of hormones, ready to commit lewd acts in a public place.

I moaned into his kisses, smoothing my hands up his back. His fingers dug into my skin, urging my hips forward.

"What do you say we get out of here?" he rasped.

"We've been here less than two hours."

The warm breeze whipped, inching the hem of my skirt up. Goosebumps splashed across my skin. Alex smoothed the fabric of my skirt down.

"That's an observation, not an answer," Alex murmured against my lips.

"Don't you think it would be impolite to leave?"

"Answering a question with a question is not acceptable." His hands continued kneading my ass, making it impossible for me to think with any rationale. The wind was relentlessly toying with my skirt.

"Ahh, there's that arse I love so much."

I nearly gave myself whiplash when I turned in the direction of Charlie's gritty brogue. He strode past us, making a cock sucking gesture with his hand. His tongue darted over his bottom lip and then he blew me a kiss. There were two other guys with him carrying photography equipment and snickering at Charlie's crude comment. One of them looked like Tom Hardy's hipster doppelganger.

*Oh shit*. My ass was literally hanging out *again*.

"Son of a bitch," Alex hissed. He pulled my elbow, shoving me behind his tall frame. This time, my fancy footwork from years of walking in heels kept me from toppling over.

A quick mental snap along with the breeze blowing up my skirt had me smoothing my palms down over my ass. My chest pressed against Alex's back, feeling the primal energy bristling off him. Peering over his shoulder, I slid my hands around his biceps gripping tightly.

"Best tits and arse you've ever seen, mates." Charlie's words grated on my nerves.

The next thing I knew, Alex jerked his body away from me and tossed his jacket to the ground. He stalked towards Charlie, throwing the gate back. All three men turned to face Alex.

"Apologize to the lady," Alex growled.

Charlie's gaze met mine, and his lips quirked into a sneer. The tallest of the three men, squared up to Alex, as the other stood back.

"Apologize for speaking the truth? I don't think so, mate."

"Listen, *mate*," Alex retorted. "Two words to the lady and then you can be on your way."

He puffed up his chest. "And if I don't, just what are you going to do about it?"

"For your sake, I'd pray it doesn't come to that."

Charlie laughed, and shoved a hand at Alex's chest. "Piss off."

Alex's hand swung over and landed on top of Charlie's. An exchange of icy glares shot like flying arrows between the men and then Alex released the hold he'd had on Charlie.

*Crack!*

Charlie punched Alex, striking him square on the jaw.

Alex didn't even flinch as his fist connected with Charlie's nose.

"Alex!" My hands flew to my mouth, muffling the scream of his name. Everything was in slow motion after that moment. All I saw was blood spraying across the white fence before Charlie crumpled to the ground.

My throat tightened and panic rolled through me. I scooped up Alex's jacket and hurried towards him. Alex stood staring straight at Charlie and every hair on my neck stood on end.

Charlie rolled up, resting on his hands and knees, trying to stable himself. The tall man offered to help him up, but Charlie batted his arm away.

"You," Charlie snarled, pointing his finger at Alex. "You're a dead man."

Alex steeled his spine, giving him a flippant wave of his hands and stared after the men until they rounded the corner. He turned to face me after the men were out of sight.

When Alex cradled my face in his hands, I felt all the air

rush from my lungs. “Hey, are you okay?”

“Yes, I’m fine.” My gaze darted from his eyes, to his jaw. “Are *you* okay?”

“Not going to lie, I didn’t think the fucker had the stones to hit me, but he did.”

At least Alex’s humor was still intact. He pulled me into him and kissed the top of my head. Squeezing his hand, we walked behind the stables and through the sea of cars. He needed an icepack and most likely a shower and a stiff drink.

“I just need you,” he said, as he opened the passenger door for me. I stared at him in confusion.

He laughed. “You were thinking out loud just then, but that drink does sound pretty good.”

“Sorry, my head is swimming from what just happened with Charlie. Do you think he’ll make good on this threat?”

His hands tangled in my hair. “No, I don’t. That was his wounded male ego spouting off bullshit. He’ll calm down, lick his wounds and forget all about this.”

“But what if he files charges against you?”

He pressed his forehead against mine, running the pad of his thumb across my lips. “If he does, then I will deal with it. He hit me first, so I could just as easily have him arrested for assault. Try not to worry, okay?”

Giving Alex the peace of mind he needed, I nodded. “Okay.”

Today’s events certainly left me feeling puzzled. The way Charlie had approached me at the baseball game and now being so bold to state his comments out loud. Did he have a death wish? Or was he really just that stupid? I couldn’t worry about Charlie or how any of this affected him. My focus was on Alex.

# Chapter Twenty-Five

## Alex

Charlie McNeil. It was a name I had grown very tired of hearing, seeing or even thinking about.

Sweat poured down my back. I pushed myself hard the last half-mile on the long stretch of beach. The dunes that decorated my property came into focus. Beads of perspiration rained down my forehead, running into my eyes. Sweat dripped off my nose and my quads ached in pain.

I raced up the dune and collapsed on my freshly mown lawn. This wasn't the best cool down. Giving it all my strength, I pushed up and jumped to my feet. I stretched out my limbs and did a few crunches for good measure. Even though I'd just trained like I like I was about to depart for a field mission, or compete in the Olympics, tension still lingered.

My mind was a fucking mess. Maybe I should take up yoga like Ella. She seemed incredibly calm for a woman who was opening a business in less than a month. As I walked in circles around the pool, taking in deep breaths, I couldn't help but smile.

Despite how the day of the polo match had started, Ella and I managed to salvage the holiday. After leaving, she'd made me stop off at the market for some fruit and whipped cream. For dinner, we devoured steaks and the biggest loaded baked potatoes you'd ever seen. They dripped with butter and were topped with sea salt and chives. At dusk, we sat on the beach eating our triple berry dessert while watching the fireworks light up the sky over The Harbour.

For the past three nights Ella had nudged me, telling me that I had been dreaming and was stealing the covers. I'd laughed each of her adorable accusations off and then apologized by sliding deep inside her, giving us both an explosive orgasm sending us satisfied and back to dreamland.

Still, the relief was only a temporary fix.

She'd ask if everything was all right. I'd smile and kiss her soft lips, reassuring her I was all good, and that it was probably just the summer heat. I'd even suggested that I might have restless leg syndrome. *Stupid, I know.*

With her boutique scheduled to open in weeks, I didn't feel the need to add to her stress level by confessing that Charlie fucking McNeil had been taking up space in my head. Two weeks had gone by, and he hadn't even filed a complaint. I was certain that slimy bastard would have, just to make my life miserable.

Nothing but silence since the event, and it was unsettling. Maybe that was his game, to make me wonder, essentially driving me crazy. Little did he know, but I'd had training in that area. I just needed to remember how to compartmentalize that bullshit. Fuck his mind games.

In addition, I needed to keep my head clear and focused on Ella. The idea of her working long days at the boutique without me, I did not like that one fucking bit. However, I needed to respect her process while she prepped for the grand opening.

For my own peace of mind, I'd flown Marcus Blevins in from Grand Rapids to provide security. He was one of my oldest friends and top guys at the company. The fact that he'd worked the mayor of Detroit's security detail for eight years left me with little worry.

I walked up the steps of the house. Once inside, I stripped out of my workout gear and then tossed the sweat soaked garments into the laundry basket.

My phone rang just as I threw the towel around my waist.

"Marcus, what's up?"

"Man, you need to get over here ASAP." The tone of his voice had me freaking the fuck out on the inside.

"Is Ella okay?" My heart pounded in my chest. "Yes or no, Marcus."

"Physically she is fine. Visibly she is upset."

"Gotcha, I'll be right there." I swiped my finger across END CALL without another word.

Not being in control had me sick with worry. Uncertain of what had happened left me feeling a bit shaken. Although my gut told me Charlie McNeil was no longer silent.

# Ella

I closed the door to my office and then plopped down on top of one of the many boxes that occupied the small space. Once more I pulled the photos from the envelope. Coldness seeped into my body and settled in my spine as I flipped from one glossy photo to the next. That fucking douchebag had snapped pictures of Alex and Charlie's fight. I hadn't even realized the lumbersexual version of Tom Hardy was even taking photos.

The worst part was that they were manipulated in a way that the world would see Charlie as a victim. What would this do to Alex's reputation?

No pictures of Charlie punching Alex or trying to rush towards him. This is just how deceiving photos can be. Something captured in a millisecond of time means more than it does. How would the tabloids spin this?

"Ella!" I heard Alex calling out my name.

"I'm back here, in the office," I shouted, then pulled the handle opening the door.

"Hey, are you okay?"

My hands shook as I handed the envelope to Alex. Unsure if it was frustration, annoyance, or just plain anger. "Honestly, I'm not sure how I feel."

Alex's eyes captured mine and that was enough to send me rushing into his arms. Maybe exhaustion from the weight of everything had finally taken hold. Or another angle, perhaps I felt the need to comfort him before he unclasped the envelope finding the photos along with a request for five hundred thousand dollars. My guess was that Charlie and Hipster Hardy would split the money.

I managed to peel my body away from Alex. His gaze

dropped to the envelope and I nodded for him to open it. I dropped my ass back onto the box, which I'd decided would be my chair until the one I'd ordered arrived.

"That bad, huh?"

"That depends on your definition of bad." I buried my face in my hands unable to look at Alex as he rifled through the envelopes contents.

"Hmm."

I stared up at Alex, his expression was blank—no furrowed brow or clenched teeth. How could he not be angry about this?

"That's all you have to say is '*hmm*'?"

"Yep."

I shrugged. "What about the money? Doesn't that bother you?"

"No, I'm calling his bluff. I don't negotiate with blackmailing pussies."

"Ohhhh kay." I leaned back against the wall.

"Ella, the photos are of me, but he sent them here to your boutique. He doesn't know my address or even my last name. Who cares if they get published? Hell, I'll upload them to my social media page and ruin his fun." He pushed the pictures back inside the envelope and tossed them on top of my file cabinet.

I couldn't understand. Wouldn't his family be disappointed? "So you're not at all concerned?"

"If the photos were of you, hell yes, I'd be concerned." His knuckles grazed my upper arm. "I'm going to have that envelope and its contents examined. I'm upgrading your security system here. And, as a precaution, we're filing a restraining order."

Not once did I ever think I'd have to file a restraining

order, or have to go to such lengths to feel safe. Alex bent to meet my eyes, his hands framed my face. "Ella, talk to me."

"I don't think you should post the pictures to your social media accounts."

He laughed. "Yeah, I didn't think that was a very good idea." He dropped a gentle kiss on my mouth. "What else needs done around here? Put me to work."

My hands slipped up and around his neck. "Why don't you go do all the things you mentioned and I'll finish unpacking. I have some things I want to get ticked off my list before we leave for Chicago."

"As you wish, sweetheart." He kissed me again and then walked out the door.

# Chapter Twenty-Six

## Alex

The fact that Charlie had personally dropped these photos off at Ella's boutique pushed me over the edge. That motherfucker was clearly stalking her and that would end today. Although, I wasn't entirely sure how this would all work with the restraining order since Ella wasn't a US citizen.

As I climbed into my Range Rover, a million things swirled through my head. I needed more information. Normally, Marcus was my go to for research, but I couldn't have him distracted with anything but eyes on Ella.

"Patrick, I need a favor," I barked into my Bluetooth.

"Sure thing, what's up, boss?"

"Whatever project you're currently on, assign it to someone else. We have a time sensitive project. I need a top of the line, and I mean the absolute best security system installed in a building out here. The girl I've been assigned to security detail, someone is—I don't trust anyone else, and I—"

"You got it. I know this is important."

"I'll arrange a plane for you and send along all the details. I need this done like yesterday, Patrick."

"Say no more. I'm on it."

"One more thing, I'm going to Chicago for the weekend, you and Marcus update me as soon as everything is installed."

"Will do. You taking the lady with you?"

I huffed out a sigh. "I am."

"Don't worry about a thing, Alex. We'll handle it."

"Thanks, man." I ended the call just as I'd turned into my driveway. I was wound up again, more tense than I was before. At this point, would another run even help? I slammed my door shut and hoofed up the stairs.

I splashed some scotch into a tumbler and settled into the chair behind my desk. How had things become so damn messy? First, I was just a guy hired to work private security detail for a short time to de-stress and get my life back in order. Now, I had more problems than Jay Z at this point. I tossed back the drink, feeling the burn all the way down.

Charlie McNeil was playing a very dangerous game. One thing was certain; he wasn't prepared to play in my league.

Once we settled into the hotel, I'd surprised Ella with a full day of pampering. I wanted her to be completely relaxed before tonight's fundraiser. The spa director helped me put together the services, since my knowledge of this sort of thing was limited to facials, massages, pedicures, and manicures.

With Ella happily occupied, I took some time to unwind. The Bar at the Peninsula wasn't open yet, so I headed to one of my favorite Chicago hangouts, Giordano's. I sat at the bar watching the Cubs game along with several other patrons.

*Man, I love this town.*

I signaled the bartender for a refill. During the commercial break, my eyes scanned over the mass of people filtering in from the street. Most were carrying shopping bags from all the prominent stores on the Magnificent Mile.

"Just the man I was hoping to see." A strong hand slapped my back and I turned to face my old pal, Garrett "Sully" Sullivan.

"Sully, good to see you, man."

"You too, Robo."

"Have a seat." I nodded to the bartender. "Whatever this guy is drinking put it on my tab."

"Miller Lite, bottle, no glass." He leaned in, and whispered over his shoulder. "Everyone in this town wants to put my beer in a glass. Straight from the bottle or can, that's the way I like it."

I didn't have the heart to tell him that beer tasted better in a glass. Well, not so much as tasted better, more for the experience, but with Miller Lite it didn't really matter.

The bartender slid the bottle of beer in front of Sully. "Thanks, man."

"So, how long has it been?"

With his beer in hand, he bopped his head from side to side. "By my count, it's been at least five years. Rebecca's wedding."

I nodded. "Did Jessie come with you?"

"Nah," he replied, before taking a long pull from the bottle. "She's at home with the girls, and we got another one on the way in September."

"Wow, congrats. That's awesome. Do you have enough kids to start a baseball team yet?"

He chuckled. "Close. This will be our fourth, a boy. Jessie is done after this one. How about you? Married yet?"

"No, but I'm seeing someone; she's great—more than great."

I felt a twinge of guilt admitting that I had someone special. Sully had known Sasha and I were together. It was hard keeping our relationship a secret. When Sasha died, Rebecca and Horton obviously made the connection.

"That's good to hear, man. Is it serious?" he asked, before taking another drink.

Cheers erupted from the bar crowd. My eyes flicked to the TV. Cubs were up three-to-one over the Cardinals. It gave me a moment to think about my response, but, honestly, there was no need to think about the way I felt about her. I was serious about Ella, but just like my relationship with Sasha, we had to tread lightly.

"I haven't felt this way in a long while, and it feels really good," I admitted, wincing slightly at my confession. *It's not normal to feel this way.*

He cocked a brow, a signal that he had a read on me. "It's okay, man. No one expects you to not move on from Sasha. It was a long time ago, and we all know how much you loved her."

"That day still haunts me. I'm doing better now, but it was rough for a long time." I lifted my glass and took a drink. I'd never opened up to any members of Elite Eight about my feelings regarding Sasha's death and how it affected me still.

"You should have reached out to us. We would have helped."

"I appreciate that, I do. I can't help feeling a sense of responsibility over the situation."

"It's the leader in you that has you feeling that way."

"I suppose," I replied dryly.

"No one saw it coming," he said, shaking his head. "We had good intel, it was the right call. Sasha knew the risks of the mission and she made the choice that day. You couldn't have stopped her from going. She's a real hero, man."

I tossed back the rest of my bourbon, allowing his words to sink in.

Sully signaled the bartender. "Two shots of tequila, top shelf and put it on his tab."

I huffed out a laugh. "I'll have a beer, 312."

"Bottom line, no one blames you for what happened that day. And no one holds you responsible for her death. At some point you have to let it go, brother, or it will eat you alive."

"If I let it go, I let *her* go."

"Nah, I don't believe that. I think she'll always be with you—in your heart."

"When did you become such a sap?"

Three drinks appeared in front of us, along with slices of fresh lime.

He shrugged. "Probably the fact that I have three girls," he replied, handing me one of the shot glasses. "To Sasha Bloom, one hell of a woman, a great friend, and a total badass."

I raised my glass. "To Sasha." Tossing back the shot, I swallowed the liquid and along with it my guilt over her death. These few moments talking to Sully had provided more clarity than any hour long session spent with my shrink.

"Are you bringing your special someone tonight?"

"Yes, I think you'll really like her."

"I'm sure I will. Have you told her about Sasha?"

"Not yet, but I planned on it. I just don't know when the right time would be."

"Before the gala," he advised, and then took a drink.

"Having that conversation *after* could be very difficult. Just my opinion though."

It would be difficult no matter what time or place.

Sully stood up from his bar stool and threw a fifty down on the bar. "For the tip."

"Thanks, man, I'll see you tonight," I said, tipping my beer glass in his direction.

His hand clamped down onto my shoulder. "It was good talking to you, Robo. Have that conversation with your lady. You don't want something this heavy to surprise her."

After paying the tab, I glanced at my watch. It was just after two in the afternoon. Ella would be at the spa for at least another hour. I popped a breath mint as I walked down the crowded sidewalk. The air was hot and the humidity curled around me. When I arrived at the hotel, I stopped off at the concierge desk and ordered a bottle of champagne and a few appetizers with instructions for them to be delivered as close to three-thirty as possible.

Alone with my thoughts, this would be one long hour.

# Chapter Twenty-Seven

## Ella

"Alex, are you here?"

"Yeah, I'll be right out."

Alex must have been in the office, working no less. On second thought, maybe not, as I moved farther into the suite the sounds of a baseball game filtered around the grand space. Taking a bottle of water from the refrigerator, I popped off the cap and chugged half. My gaze swept to the window, taking in the tall buildings and the lake in the distance. It was a beautiful city. I only wished we had more than a short stay. Maybe we could come back again soon.

"Hey there," Alex murmured in my ear, wrapping his arms around me from behind.

"Hey yourself." I leaned back into his frame, his muscles tensed.

"How was the spa?"

"Thoroughly invigorating and very relaxing."

"Good to hear." He took my hand and led me to the sofa. "I hope you don't mind but I ordered some room service and it should be here soon."

"Oh, that sounds lovely." I dropped onto the plush sofa and kicked off my sandals.

There was a knock at the door. "Perfect timing, I'll be right back."

Along with room service, our garments for tonight arrived after being properly steamed. Once they left, Alex popped the champagne and offered me a glass. It was a good thing that I'd opted not to have the massage or I wouldn't have been able to drink tonight.

Alex took a seat on the sofa then stood. Walking across the room, he tossed back the entire glass and then poured another. Rubbing his hand over his forehead, he blew out a deep breath.

"Alex, is something going on?"

"Yes." He bowed his head, staring at the floor. "I need to talk to you about something."

"Are you okay?" My legs swung off the sofa and I stood in a rush. "Oh God, has something happened with Charlie?"

"No, it's nothing about him. I need to tell you something about my friend, Sasha."

"Oh, okay. Will I be meeting her tonight?"

He looked towards the window. "No, you won't be meeting her tonight."

"Hey." I tilted my head to meet his gaze. "Talk to me."

A few beats of silence passed. He blew out another deep breath. I sensed that he was collecting his thoughts. "Tonight's gala, it's in Sasha's honor. She died. It was a long time ago. Eight years to be exact." He raised his hand, pointing his glass towards me. "Actually, the night I met you, that date was the anniversary of her death."

I let out a slight gasp and clamped my hand over my mouth.

His hand rubbed the back of his neck. "Sasha and I, we were in a military intelligence special ops squad, Elite Eight—it's disbanded now. Counter terrorism, classified missions, I can't tell you too much, but there are things you should know. Things I *want* you to know."

*Classified missions? Counter terrorism?*

Somehow I managed to nod. Elephants were trampling across my chest. I massaged the nervous ache I felt in my heart.

"Ella, here, sit down." Alex grasped my elbow with one hand and lowered me back to the sofa. He knelt in front of me and his fingers caressed the back of my leg. "I'll just start with that day. We had been tracking a terrorist cell for a few months, that morning we'd received word a few of the leaders were hiding out in an abandoned factory in Northern Ireland. The intel checked out and command gave us the green light. Long story short, we were baited by our source—it was all a setup."

His face paled, and he rolled up to his feet. When his hands scrubbed down his face, that's when I saw that he was shaking. My heart dropped, tumbling down to the pit of my stomach.

*"Alex."* My voice was barely audible.

"Sasha didn't have to go on the mission, but she did anyway. She was days away from leaving Elite Eight. She was what we called a short timer, and traditionally . . . *technically*, when someone reaches that status they don't go into the field. Sasha was stubborn though, and she was determined to help. I think she felt it was her duty to see it through. If that was going to be the day we caught the men we'd been searching for; she wanted to help in any way she could."

He paced in a small circle around the living room, almost as if he was trapped in a cage. The sunlight passed over his face, his hazel eyes were glassy. Studying his face, I felt a sharp shudder move through me.

"Sasha and I had a relationship. It took us both by surprise and we kept things under wraps. I loved her very much." His eyes met mine. The anguish filling them pained my heart. "Instead of putting my foot down as her commanding officer, I allowed my personal feelings to interfere and that's why she was out that day. As her lover, I couldn't say no to her, but as her superior I should have."

Searing pain wound through me, watching this man fall apart in front of me. Holding back my own tears, I remained quiet allowing him to just talk it out.

He squatted down to the floor, his hands rubbing his upper thighs. "Why? Why, didn't I just command her to stay? She would still be alive!" The palm of his hand smacked against the carpet.

Before I knew it, I was on my feet and I went to him. My hands gripped his biceps, helping him to his feet. His palms covered his eyes, as he expelled a deep breath. I urged Alex to take a seat on the sofa as I scurried to the refrigerator to grab another bottle of water.

I didn't know if there was more to the story, but if he needed to sit quietly or take a break, I wanted him to know I was here for him. I settled beside him, and then handed him the cool bottle. His free hand grasped the back of my neck as he kissed the top of my head.

"That day, I'd been hit, knocked unconscious. When I awoke total chaos surrounded me. After a few moments of assessing things, I saw her lying on the ground and it was bad. I tried to stop the bleeding, but her injuries were extensive. We were trapped and I couldn't save her."

He swallowed hard, before adding, "I held her in my arms and she bled to death on the floor of a cold and dirty warehouse."

I pushed my emotions aside, realizing he lived through traumas that I couldn't even begin to wrap my head around.

He fell back against the sofa, pulling me along with him. "Months later, at the urging of my therapist, I took a vacation, a very lengthy one. I spent a few months traveling around the globe trying to cope with my guilt. I hid away on some of the most beautiful beaches in the world, trying to find some peace in any way to somehow accept that her death wasn't my fault. I can't say that I was completely healed, but I found solace being near the water."

Every single word that fell from his mouth was laced with pain. I could hear it and I ached for him. I wanted to take away his hurt and the massive guilt he felt over Sasha's death. I hugged Alex, hoping I could absorb some of the agony he felt. *It's okay, Alex.*

"The pain still lingers, but I talked to Sully . . . uhmm, Garrett, you'll meet him tonight. He was also in Elite Eight. I didn't realize until today how much I needed to talk to someone from our group . . . someone who was there." His hand brushed up and down my arm and he kissed my forehead once more.

"I'm veering off track, here. I've never been good at relationships. Actually, I'm really good at the beginning but somewhere along the way I go and screw it up. I don't want to do that with you, Ella."

My heart thumped out of sync and I struggled to catch

my breath. I leaned up to look at his face. His hands found their way to my cheeks.

I wanted to tell him that I loved him. That I wouldn't leave him, but something inside me told me this wasn't the time. Digging deep, I managed to hold back the tears that threatened. "You're a good man, Alex Robertsen."

His mouth sealed over mine, pulling me into an all-consuming kiss. Some girl's dream of a knight in shining armor is nice, but scars tell deeper stories.

Ella roped her arms around my neck as I lifted her off the ground and her legs swung around my waist. I almost had us to the master suite. A trail of clothing lay in our wake in my rush to get her naked.

For the second time in a few months, I managed to unload something heavy on Ella. There was so much that I couldn't tell her. Most of my professional life had been classified, and the reason for that was a laundry list a mile long.

Opening up to her about Sasha the way I did was unexpected. More specifically, exposing those emotions and breaking down in front of her, it just all sort of unleashed, but somehow I felt a bit lighter. She didn't say much, Ella listened, which was what I needed most. The few words she spoke meant more to me than I could have ever imagined.

"*Alex*," Ella moaned, digging her nails into the back of neck.

My tongue stroked hers, tasting the sweetness of champagne. When we entered the bedroom, she slid down my body. Taking her face in my hands, I studied every gorgeous line and angle. She was the most beautiful, perfect woman—my ultimate fantasy.

Leaning forward, I swept her long hair out of the way, kissing the soft spot between her neck and her shoulder. "Maybe we should skip the gala." My hand slid underneath the lace fabric of her bra.

She shoved at my chest. "Not a chance. I have a beautiful gown and it's not going to waste." Turning away from me, she took her hair up. "Unhook my bra."

My knuckles grazed up her arms. Goosebumps splashed across her skin when my fingers skimmed down her back just under the straps. I loved her body, but I also loved her mind and her kind heart. I loved *her*.

*I love Ella.*

I wasn't going to pretend this was a foreign feeling. We'd both fallen in love before, only to have our hearts ripped out. Everything had been a risk with Ella, but it was worth it and I wanted more. Even though she was living with me, I wanted her to move in. It sounded odd, but it made sense in my mind. Her insane shoe collection, which I was sure there were more back at her place in London, along with all her clothes, I wanted everything taking up space in the master closet.

I wanted her to have one toothbrush, not two. At this point, she had duplicates for everything. The guesthouse was merely a diversion, a setup of props cleverly arranged to disguise our truth. It was time to drag the truth out into the light. No more camouflage.

With her bra and panties now tossed onto the floor, I walked us backwards to the bed. By my calculations, we had a good thirty minutes before Ella would need to start getting ready. Drawing back the comforter, I eased her lithe body down onto the mattress.

Her blue eyes met mine and the way she was looking at me was how I supposed every man wanted to be looked at—like I meant everything to her *or* that I was a God.

She propped herself up on her elbows. "I love watching you strip."

The wicked gleam in her eyes nearly had me coming undone before I'd even had my boxers over my hips.

"I love that you're already naked." I crawled up her body, my tongue licking a line from her navel to the space between her breasts. When my teeth grazed her nipple, a gasp slipped from her lips and her body quivered beneath me.

Her nails dug into my scalp, as I sucked her nipple into my mouth. "What do you want, Ella?"

"Mmmm," she murmured. "Your cock, deep inside me."

Grinding against her, my dick was slick from her wetness. The sweet scent of oranges on her skin mixed with her arousal filled my senses. It was intoxicating as hell.

"Well, you're going to get that for sure, but that's not exactly what I'm asking."

Ella started to speak, and I pressed my thumb over her lips. She surprised me by nipping the pad of my thumb and then ever so smoothly sucked me into her mouth.

"I love you," I confessed. "I want to be the man in your life, the one who looks out for you now and always and not because of a paycheck, which by the way you should know I stopped receiving a while ago."

Her hands drifted to my cheeks, and her blue eyes welled with tears. "I love you, too, so very much, Alex."

My lips found Ella's and my fingers tangled into her hair. "I want you to move in with me."

She wrapped her hands around my wrists as I pushed

into her heat. Groaning, I sank deeper into her, the feel of her drawing me in lit up every nerve ending in my body.

"I'm already living with you." Her fingers brushed over my forearms.

"I know you are, but I want you to make my home yours, *permanently*." I sucked her bottom lip into my mouth, and churned my hips.

"You want more?" she asked, scraping her nails up and down my back.

"Yes, fuck yes, and I want it with you."

"Alex, yes," she moaned, licking her lips. "I want more."

Our bodies fit perfectly together, so in tune with another. Ella met me thrust for thrust until we were both drenched in sweat. Her eyes were hazy with lust. My teeth gritted together, as heat spiked at the base of my spine.

Ella dug her fingers into my shoulders. "Ahhh, you feel so good," she moaned, her thighs tightened around me.

I watched Ella as she went over the edge, her body going lax beneath mine. My eyes screwed shut and I let go, my orgasm charged through my veins. I dropped my forehead to her shoulder. "Holy fuck," I groaned.

Lifting my head, my gaze met hers. Ella looked deep into my eyes demanding my attention. "In case you were uncertain, my answer is yes." She pulled me closer, pressing a kiss to my lips. "I'll move in with you, Alex Robertsen."

I smiled against her lips. "Good, I'm glad we had this talk."

# Chapter Twenty-Eight

## Ella

As I pushed the back of my earring on, I thought about Alex and his confessions—the relationship he had with Sasha and basically the fact that he was some kind of American bad ass version of James Bond. At least in my mind that was how I pictured it.

Fluffing the ends of my hair, I twirled large sections with my fingers to enhance the soft waves. One last look in the mirror and I slicked my lips with a pink gloss.

Those weren't the only confessions of the evening. Alex had professed his love for me and had asked me to move in with him. There were no questions remaining, it was clear that he wanted a future with me. I wanted it all with him.

In the shower, Alex had explained that he told Dean he no longer wished to be given a paycheck. A few weeks ago, he instructed that all the money was to be split between the

Connolly Campaign and the Robertsen Foundation. I learned his family had a trust that donated money to various organizations throughout the world.

The words echoed in my head.

*"Why didn't you take a paycheck, Alex?"*

*"This job, protecting you, it was never about the money. It was about me getting my life back on track. When I started to fall for you, it didn't seem right taking payment."*

"You look fucking stunning." Alex stepped into the bathroom and adjusted his sliver cufflinks.

I splashed some perfume on my wrist. "Me? What about you? You have a body designed for fine tailored threads."

He smirked, and his hands slipped over my shoulders. "This dress . . . can we add a layer of fabric right here." His index finger slid down my clavicle and landed in the space between my breasts. I was ready to rip the dress off and climb all over him again but this event, it was important.

"Nope, you can eat your heart out all night."

"Change of plans. We make an appearance, dinner, a few drinks and I hand over the donation." His fingers danced over the curve of my hip. "Two hours, tops. Then we come back here and I make love to you all fucking night."

I laughed. "Aww, honey, it's cute that you said, 'make love.' I didn't know that term was in your vocabulary."

He offered me his arm. "Fine, I'll fuck you all night long. Better?"

I smiled, looping my arm with his. "I love you." Three simple words, I was elated to say them out loud.

He kissed my cheek. "I love you, too."

We almost made it to our table, but not before I heard a sweet feminine voice call out to him. "Hello, Alex."

Turning, I was confronted by a very beautiful woman. She was tall and curvy in all the right places with gorgeous brown hair that fell in waves over her bare shoulders.

"Laura, hi," Alex replied, before kissing her cheek.

She flashed a smile at me. "Hi, I'm Laura Bloom-Olsen."

As I shook her hand Alex smoothed his hand up my back. "Laura, I'd like you to meet Ella Connolly."

"So nice to meet you, Ella, I'm Sasha's sister." Her lip quirked up and she shook her head. "I apologize, Sasha was my sister. I never know how to address the relationship, especially at this event."

Alex gave her a sympathetic smile. "It's okay, Laura. Sasha is your sister and always will be."

"It's very nice to meet you," I interjected politely. "I'm so honored to be here with all of you on this special night."

"We hope to raise a lot of money this evening." She nodded in the direction of the bar. "Well, don't let me keep you, have a drink and enjoy yourselves."

We exchanged goodbyes and then Laura skittered off to greet a small group of people at the door.

By the time the second hour of the party rolled around, Alex nor I seemed to care about rushing out. This gala gave me the opportunity to see the other side of him, Lieutenant Alex Robertsen, the man who served his country with pride. He spoke with such passion about what it meant to him to serve, but his interest in dedicating free time to veteran's charities amazed me.

There was something in his voice that warmed my insides when he introduced me to his military family—Sully and Rebecca. There was no mistaking the three of them shared a strong bond.

As if I slipped into some alternate universe, I found myself surrounded by people who didn't see me just as being Ronan Connolly's little sister. Even though I had been asked about my brother and his movies, it didn't consume the evening's conversation. And there was no hint of anyone knowing about my past with David.

Alex carried on about all my accomplishments, informing them I was an international entrepreneur. Any nerves I had before settled and that was all because of him. I was stunned to find that people were interested in me and why I decided to start a business in the states. As a bonus, Rebecca's wife, Sara, told me she would be making a special trip out to shop at my boutique.

During dinner, the trio of friends shared heartfelt memories of Sasha. More and more, I was fascinated by the affection they all regarded for Sasha, it was incredible. It made me feel as if I'd known her. Much like Alex, she wanted to serve her country rather than the family business. She was a lover of languages, fluent in French, Spanish, German and Arabic.

After dessert, I stole a moment for myself and walked around the ballroom admiring the tabletops decorated with large cylinder vases holding calla lilies, which I learned was Sasha's favorite flower. Pretty silver frames adorned each table containing quotes from notable woman including Condoleezza Rice, Amy Poehler and even Coco Chanel.

Stepping out onto the patio, I absorbed the air of the gorgeous summer evening. The lights of Chicago were bright and the skyline held one of the prettiest views in the world.

"There you are."

I turned to face Alex, feeling heat stretching across my cheeks. "I just wanted to check out this impressive view."

"It doesn't hold a candle to the stunning view I have," he

said, resting his hands on my waist.

My fingertips smoothed over the fabric of his shirt. "How's it going in there?"

"The party is winding down. Sully, Rebecca, and a few of the guys invited us to play poker, but I told them we had other plans."

"Poker, huh?"

He cocked a brow. "Do you play?"

"I may have played a time or two."

"Well then, shall we adjourn to the after party?"

As he pressed his tall frame against my body, I stared back at those impossibly gorgeous hazel eyes searching my face. Before I could open my mouth to reply his lips were on mine, kissing me softly. My tongue slid across his, stroking it greedily.

"*Alex*," I breathed. "I need to freshen up first. Meet me by the staircase?"

"You got it, sweetheart." His hands came up and framed my face. "One more thing, I want to thank you for being here with me and celebrating Sasha's life."

Swallowing the lump in my throat, I nodded. "Of course, thank you for inviting me. I really loved meeting your friends. Sasha was lucky to be loved so much."

A wide bright smile crossed his face. "I love you."

"Say it again," I whispered.

"I. Love. You." He pressed his lips to mine.

There was a time in my life where I didn't think happiness or love was a possibility for me again, but it ended when I met Alex. Despite my original plan to move to New York to make something for myself without the complications of a relationship, I'd managed to fall in love. Not only that, but I'd fallen for someone who supported me and my dreams.

When I reached the ladies' room, I leaned against the cool tile. My body was all hot and tingly from kissing Alex. After taking a moment to collect myself, I sat at a vanity and applied some lipstick. At the sound of heels clacking onto the marble floor, my eyes drifted to the door. Laura appeared and sauntered my way, the fabric of her red gown floating elegantly with every step she took.

"Hey, Ella," she said, taking a seat next to me. "Look, I just wanted to tell you that Alex seems very happy."

My brows crinkled. "I'd hope so, but what are you getting at exactly?"

"No, please," she began, her palms crossed over her chest. "I didn't mean for that to come off in a negative way. I just wanted to let you know that my sister, she loved Alex very much. Did Alex tell you that the two of them had a relationship?"

Straightening my shoulders, I nodded. "Yes, he told me how much Sasha meant to him. I feel very lucky to have been included in tonight's event. I could tell that your sister was an amazing person."

"This night stirs up so many memories and feelings," she sighed, fanning her face with both hands. "When they were on leave, or in between missions, I honestly don't know what to call it. I met Sasha in Berlin and that is when she introduced me to Alex. They didn't say one way or another, but I gathered they were in the same line of work."

"Oh, so you know about Elite Eight?" I whispered the question, treading lightly.

I kept looking around the ladies' room, for cameras or people listening in on our conversation. All the while hoping to God that Laura and I weren't divulging military secrets. I had a feeling I was going to have some freaky dreams over the next few nights.

"Yes, half the room out there thinks my sister died in a military training exercise but there is so much more to it. Instead of worrying about one person in Elite Eight, I suddenly had two." She cleared her throat and used her index fingers to swipe away the tears.

My heart went out to her. "I can't imagine what that must have been like for you. Keeping that part of your sister's life a secret and then realizing Alex was in the same situation."

She nodded. "I'm sorry, I am such a mess right now."

"It's the powder room," I replied softly, handing her a tissue. "I am sure this place has seen its fair share of tears. No apology needed."

She laughed, dabbing her eyes. "What I'm trying to say is that my sister loved him so much and I haven't seen him happy in a long time. I know Sasha would be thrilled he's found love again."

Startled by her words, I took a deep breath. "You can see that Alex loves me?"

"Absolutely, he's totally taken with you." She clasped my hand in hers. "Alex has never brought anyone to the gala. We host this event every year and he shows up with a donation, has one drink and then leaves. He's *never* stayed."

A thousand emotions flickered inside me at her admission. My mind carried me back to the conversation I had with Alex, he had just told me he loved me and wanted me to move in with him. I had known for a little while that I loved him, but to have the outside world take notice that made my heart melt.

# Chapter Twenty-Nine

## Alex

"You held your own during poker. I still can't believe you took Sully for two hundred bucks," I called over my shoulder.

She laughed through deep breaths as we ran along one of the dirt roads outside The Harbour. "He was very sweet about losing, and a worthy opponent."

I shifted and started to run backwards. "I enjoyed watching you put him through the paces. It was very sexy."

She blew me a kiss. "Turn around, baby, I love watching your tight ass whilst we run."

Shaking my head, I turned back around giving her what she wanted. I loved her dirty mind. The morning sun poured through the overgrown trees and the breeze whipped over the tall grasses that lined the road. For whatever reason, Ella had started running with me, and while I enjoyed having her along, it was proving to be quite distracting. I began running in front of her, because watching her tits bounce and the sway of her ass along with her breathing all reminded me of sex.

*Running with a semi chub is not recommended.*

Even though we'd been back in The Harbour for a few days, the past weekend was fresh on my mind. Telling Ella I loved her and asking her to move in, it all felt right, more right than I ever anticipated. Not only that, but she loved me.

Sweat trickled down my chest and I slowed my pace. I was pretty far ahead of Ella.

"You okay back there?"

She waved me on and pointed to her ears. I picked up my pace again, feeling the burn in my lungs. Looking at my watch, I noted we had logged about five miles and we had two more to go. Speaking of two, we had just over two weeks until the grand opening of her boutique.

There was no word from Charlie and all was quiet while we had been in Chicago. But quiet wasn't what we wanted anymore, at least where our relationship was concerned. When we returned, Ella called and invited her brother over for brunch and that was when we planned to tell him about the two of us. Unfortunately, Ronan was out of town filming a movie and wouldn't be back until a few days before her boutique opened. That suited me just fine, I was totally okay with having a few more days to prepare what I'd say to him about shacking up with his little sister over the last few months.

Pushing forward, my quads vibrated with superb agony. I nearly gave myself whiplash at the roar of an engine and gravel crunching underneath rubber. A maroon colored van barreled down the dirt road heading straight for Ella. I sprinted towards her, waving my arms for her to get out the way. "Ella! Move!"

I was about a hundred feet from her, but the van was closer. "Lookout behind you!"

Shrugging, she slowed her pace and took out her earbuds. She stopped completely and then turned around upon hearing the sound of the engine and gears grinding.

"Oh shit!" Ella kicked up and started to run towards me.

My calves ached, and my chest shook as I pushed myself faster to get to her. "Hey, motherfucker! Slow down!"

The van increased its speed, chasing Ella sending dust swirling and swallowing her up. My feet slipped from beneath me, but I managed to keep my balance.

The dust cloud thinned, and I rubbed the sweat out of my eyes. "Hey, asshole, get the fuck out of here!"

Still, I couldn't see anything, but I heard the van come to a stop and start spinning its tires. The passenger window was tinted, blocking me from seeing who was inside. The insane driver revved the engine, and through the dust I searched for any sign of Ella.

*Please be all right.*

Seconds felt like minutes.

"Ella, call out to me, sweetheart!"

As I slammed my hands down over the hood, I felt the rumbling of the engine. "Do we have business, asshole?"

The engine revved again. My eyes focused on the driver, wearing a black shirt and dark sunglasses, his passenger wore red shirt with a zigzag pattern. Mentally, I took in every single detail I could before the driver sped backwards down the road. The word Ford was splashed across the grill.

*The license plate. Fuck!*

I charged towards the left side of the road calling out for Ella. As I got closer, my worst fears hit me, seeing her long legs unmoving. My heart slammed against my chest.

"Alex," she cried out softly.

"Goddamnit, careless fuckers, what have they done to you?" My throat went dry.

Ella lay in the tall grass, coughing and struggling to push up on her hands. She jerked her head towards the road and sucked in a deep breath.

"Hold on, sweetheart. I got you." I pushed her hair away from her face, and then lifted her into my arms. She snaked her arms around my neck.

"Do you think you can stand?"

She nodded and I helped set her feet to the ground. "Who were they?" She winced, clutching her side.

"I don't know, probably some townies looking for trouble." I shook my head, trying to stay calm and keep my anger at bay. But rage filled my veins. I should have been watching out for her. To keep her safe, I should have been behind her, eyes wide open.

"Gold license plate," she mumbled. "FAA, those were the first three letters."

I turned to face her, noticing the cut on her arm. "What?"

"I'm sorry FAA, the color gold and it said Empire State on the bottom; that was all I saw."

"Babe, you did good."

She looked up at me, smiling and her blue eyes were bright. "I did?"

Sighing heavily, I kissed her temple. "Come on, let's get you to the hospital and make sure that you're okay."

Back and forth, I paced across the same section of carpeting in the waiting room, feeling my nerves combusting with every single step.

One of the nurses urged me to take a seat. Leaning back in the chair, my legs bounced up and down nervously. I could feel Ella everywhere, deep in my bones, on my skin, and in my heart. Exhaling a deep breath, my eyes screwed shut tight.

Every time I closed my eyes, my mind ricocheted from Ella lying on ground to Sasha bleeding out on the warehouse floor. I swallowed the lump in my throat and scrubbed my hands down my face. Adrenaline coursed through my entire body, vibrating with tension. I wanted to slam my fists into a wall to ease the pain.

*Fuck.* Another woman I loved was suffering because of my inept ability to look out for her.

As I waited impatiently, I pulled out my phone and made more notes—the color of the van, the license plate information and the weak description of the two people inside. I swiped Patrick's name and sent him a message.

*Me: Sending you some information. I need anything you can tell me about this vehicle.*

*Patrick: Will do, boss.*

*Me: Great thanks. Any word from McNeil?*

*Patrick: Nope, nothing at all.*

It still didn't sit well with me that McNeil had been silent. On the upside, it took no time at all for Marcus and Patrick to get the security system up and running at La Vienne Rose. They'd had everything installed by the time we returned late Sunday afternoon from Chicago. That was a relief.

"Mr. Robertsen, Ella is doing great."

My head jerked up at the sound of Dr. Carpenter's voice. I stood, feeling the relief washing over me.

"We patched up her cuts and scrapes. No broken bones, however she has some discomfort in her shoulder and inflammation in her ribs. She was jostled pretty good."

"Thank you, Doctor. Can I see her now?"

He nodded. "My recommendation is that she rests the next few days and absolutely no working out."

After shaking his hand, I made my way down the hallway to Ella's room. I stood in the doorway watching the rise and fall of her chest as she lay in the bed. She was alive, no thanks to me and my carelessness on the job.

"Hey, you," she said weakly.

"Hey." I walked over to her bed and took a seat in the chair. "How are you feeling?"

Reaching for my hand, she smiled. "A little sore, but nothing I can't handle."

That was true enough. I thought about all she'd been through—her history with David, the scandal, public humiliation, the trial and how she managed to overcome it all. She did all of that on her own, because Ella was a fighter.

I let go of her hand and stood. "That's good to hear and I'm so glad you're okay." Touching her was almost too much to bear right now.

"Are *you* okay?" she asked, her voice was shaky.

"I'm fine, just worried about you."

I stared at the bandages that covered her arm and the bruising along her neck and shoulder that turned her creamy skin red and purple. My stomach rolled and I felt sick. This was bad, and things could have been a lot worse than a few bumps and bruises.

*So much worse.*

My main concern was to get her home, but there was no denying other factors weighed heavily on my mind.

Once we got home, Ella wanted to soak in the bath, so I let

her and then redressed the bandage on her arm. After that I helped her get dressed and then get into the bed. Leaving her to rest, I walked downstairs to my office.

Taking a seat at my desk, I blew out a deep breath. I grabbed my phone and tapped the screen, a message from Patrick appeared.

*Patrick: No go on the van, emailed you some information.*

I powered up my laptop and then opened my email. There wasn't much to the message, and nothing solid to even start an investigation. The screen on my phone flashed, it was another text from Patrick.

*Patrick: McNeil was spotted in Newark this morning. I checked, just in case.*

*Me: Thanks, man.*

*Patrick: Not a problem, that's why you pay me the big bucks. How's Ella doing?*

*Me: Remind me to give you a raise. She's okay despite being a bit shaken. She's resting now.*

*Patrick: Glad to hear she is okay. This was probably just some locals being dipshits and completely random. Don't sweat it, buddy, and tell Ella I said to get well soon.*

*Me: Will do. I'll check in later.*

After I sent my last message to Patrick, I walked to the bar and poured a drink. It was after noon on a Thursday. Besides, it's five o'clock somewhere.

I tossed back the contents of the glass and poured another. Concerned for Ella's safety, I was on high alert, and every sound I heard triggered a flashback. My mind fogged over with worry.

Maybe I should take a step back from this job. I slumped into the chair and mentally kicked myself.

*Ella is not a job, you love her.*

And that right there was the truth, but if I *didn't* love her I would have been doing my job and protected her effectively keeping her unscathed. Now, she was lying upstairs covered in cuts and bruises and it was my fault.

# Chapter Thirty

## Ella

As soon as Alex left me alone in his bed, the tears spilled down my cheeks. My heart thumped and I buried my face in the pillow. On top of being drained and tired, I didn't want Alex to see or hear me cry. I don't know what I would have done if I had been running alone.

A mixed bag of emotions rained over me. I wanted to wail and let out all the fear and relief. Perhaps it was only the medication leaving me feeling emotional and a bit loopy.

When I couldn't see Alex through the dust, it had scared me to death. In that moment, the worst fears washed over me, that he was injured because those assholes had run him over.

Tossing onto my side, I couldn't turn off my brain. All I thought about were the tasks I needed to finish at the store before opening day. And then my thoughts shifted to Alex, seeing the pained look on his face as I lay in the hospital bed made my heart crumble.

My phone lit up, Nabila's name flickered. I studied the screen for a moment before answering.

"Hey, girl," I chirped trying to sound upbeat.

"Ella, my love, I miss you so much."

"I miss you too, doll." I sat up in the bed leaning against the headboard.

"How are you?"

"I'm okay," I sighed, feeling the rush of tears prickling.

"Cut the crap," she scolded. "You sound dreadful. Have you taken ill?"

Pain radiated in my chest, at the memory of the van barreling towards me. "No, kind of, I guess . . . I was in an accident this morning."

She gasped. "Oh my God, Ella. What happened?"

"Alex and I were out for a run and this van almost ran us over. I dove out of the way and landed in some weeds, I cut my arm on a branch or something. Nothing major, I was in and out of hospital."

"Christ, that's awful. I'm so sorry."

"I'm okay, truly," I answered reassuringly, then glanced at the bandage that covered my arm. "Thank God Alex was there. I wasn't sure what I would have done if I had been alone."

"It sounds to me like your bodyguard boyfriend wasn't doing his job well enough, if you were injured." The sarcasm in her voice irritated me. I hoped she was only kidding.

I dropped my head to the pillow, and stared up at the ceiling. "This wasn't Alex's fault, Bila. There's not much one can do when idiots get behind the wheel and act like total wankers."

"I suppose that is true enough. Alex better take better

care of you or it will be him that ends up in hospital."

I laughed. "Alex always takes good care of me. Now, what's going on with you?"

Nabila yammered on about her latest art collection and Finn. For the most part I listened, but I found myself becoming distracted and unable to contain my yawning.

"Let me tell you, his long fingers aren't just useful spinning the tables. That man can massage a g-spot with glorious precision, like you wouldn't believe."

Shaking my head, I let out a long set giggles that morphed into tears. I ended our call with a promise to call her in a few days. It was good to hear from Nabila, and I'd been a terrible friend not keeping up with what was going on in her life. Clutching the phone to my chest, I vowed to make time to catch up at least once a week.

Darkness fell across the room. Thunder cracked and my gaze darted to the window. I swiped away the tears. The tapping of rain soothed, reminding me of London. Somewhere in between tracing designs on the comforter and playing Tetris on my phone, I fell asleep.

By day five, post-accident, I was certain I was going absolutely mad. It didn't help matters that I still couldn't run or even do yoga. If I had been at my flat in London, I would have gone on a total cleaning spree by now. To my amazement, I had a desire to mop floors and scrub the shower. Even dusting sounded appealing.

As for Alex, he spent most of the time tucked away in his office. He checked in on me, almost as if we'd slipped into some odd roommate agreement. Was he bored of me already? Bloody hell, the man had just asked me to move in with him. To make matters worse, we hadn't had sex in days. Our kisses were now chaste, the passionate ones were few and far between. Even at night, we crawled into bed separately. I wondered how things had changed so quickly.

My heart stuttered, dreading that the honeymoon phase had fizzled out already.

After lunch, I found a way to sneak out of the house without him knowing. I'd deal with the consequences later. In addition to checking in on the boutique, the need for a large salted caramel latte and one of those delicious gluten-free, orange cranberry muffins from the bakery had been elevated to a level five emergency.

I'd convinced Marcus not to tell Alex that I was at the boutique, a box of sugary treats and a black coffee was my only bargaining tool and yet it worked.

After a few hours of steaming garments and merchandising a few display walls, I sat at my desk checking in the latest shipment of clothing. Despite my several days' absence, things were running on schedule with the grand opening. On top of that, the London store was doing well and the sales were up six percent over last year at this time.

*Knock, knock.*

When I lifted my head, my eyes took in a very sexy Alex leaning against the doorframe, with his arms crossed against his broad chest and his hazel eyes narrowed.

"Marcus, there's a very tall man who looks a lot like Alex standing in my doorway," I called out, my voice cracking with laughter.

"Sorry, Ella, he *is* the boss."

"But I gave you donuts. I thought we were friends."

"Blame it on my sugar crash."

Alex nodded his head towards the front of the store.

"Come on, Ella, let me take you home."

"But I . . ."

He cut me off. "No buts, besides I need to talk to you."

The serious tone of his voice caused fear to roll through me. I finished entering the last item and made a note where I'd stopped. After shutting down the program, I grabbed my bag and then closed the door to my office.

Swallowing the lump in my throat, I looked at Alex. "What's going on?"

He led me out the door to his Range Rover. "Not here, we'll talk at home."

I had a very bad feeling. Every single nerve ending in my body was lit up like a live wire. Despite the sound of my heart pounding in my ears, the ride to the house was much too quiet.

*I recognize the weight all around me; this is what the end feels like.*

I didn't wait for Alex to open the passenger door. I hopped out and then made a beeline up the back steps, taking them two at a time. Nothing about this felt good, I could practically feel the bile rising in my throat.

"Okay, Alex, what is going on?" I demanded. "You've been acting odd ever since the day of the accident."

He scrubbed his hands down his face. "You're right, and I apologize for being so distant."

My shoulders tensed. "Distant, yes, and not to mention quite cold—things between us have been a little frosty. So what gives?"

We moved through the kitchen and as I passed by the hallway leading to the front doorway, that was when I saw his suitcases sitting in foyer by the staircase.

My heart fell into the pit of my stomach shattering into

heavy pieces. “Alex? What is going on?”

Silence filled the space between us, and then, “I need to go to back to Grand Rapids.”

“Oh.” My brow crinkled. “Has something happened with your family?”

“No, this has nothing to do with my family. I need to go back for me.”

For him? Did he mean permanently? As much as I tried to fight back the tears, I couldn’t. Alex strode towards me, and then pulled me into his frame. “Ella, please don’t cry. My heart can’t take it.”

The sobs grew stronger as I fisted his shirt in my hands. “How can I not cry? You’re leaving me.”

He pulled back from our embrace, and then dipped his eyes to meet mine. “I need some time to think and clear my head.”

“But this is your home, the place you bought to think and get away from things. Don’t do this, Alex.”

He stared at me, agony washing all over his face. “I’m worried that I’m not the man who can take care of you. I just need a little time.”

*He’s not going to leave. I just moved in.*

“Please don’t run away. Let’s get some ice cream and talk.” The words were coming out of my mouth, but I had no idea what I was saying. As I paced the kitchen, I went on, babbling about flavors of ice cream.

He caught me by the waist. “It’s a deeper issue, and it’s mine. You’ve done nothing wrong.”

“I know I’ve done nothing wrong, I’m just talking about ice cream. Come on, I’ll change and then we can go.”

I turned to walk away, but he grasped my arm. “I need to leave.” His eyes pleaded with me, and his hands came up to frame my face. "Before it's too late."

"Too late," I repeated, anger vibrating in my voice.

He said it was worth the risk. That *I* was worth the risk. I loved him and he loved me. Everything about this was too late.

He swallowed hard before speaking. "Ella, I need to get my head on straight. I've arranged for Marcus to be my replacement, it's all taken care of. I asked you to live here and I want you to stay."

The words echoed in my brain. Every fiber inside me screamed in agony. I looked down at my faded bruises where I'd been cut, and then it hit me.

"This is about Sasha, isn't it?" I eyed him with a sympathetic stare.

He stood in silence, as his eyes dropped to the floor. As much as I was hurting, this was a thousand times worse for him. As anger left my body, I realized, as much as it cut into my heart like shards of glass, I had to let him go. My hands shook as tears cascaded down my face.

The back of his knuckles grazed over my cheek and the pad of his thumb swiped away the tears. "I can't be responsible for your pain."

"It was an accident, these things happen," I choked out, my heart aching for him. "You shouldn't blame yourself. I wish you didn't."

All at once, a multitude of emotions stirred inside me. I blinked up, and then he crushed his mouth to mine. If he'd let me, I'd swallow his torment and drown all of his fears. His hands tangled in my hair and he deepened the kiss, it was impatient and generous. How could this be over? It barely started.

Gripping him tightly, my fingers dug into his shoulders.

I closed my eyes, inhaling his scent, savoring the feel of his body against mine, needing to catalog everything to memory.

After a few moments, I placed my hand over his heart, immediately his hand covered mine squeezing tight. "You are here," he whispered into my hair.

# Chapter Thirty-One

## Alex

My apartment in Grand Rapids was much too cold and much too empty. There wasn't a physical trace of Ella anywhere, but that was exactly why I'd come to this place—detox, to get her out of my system. Out of sight, out of mind, right?

The last time I had been here, my sister, Amy, was sobbing on my couch and begging me to reconsider leaving. Maybe I should have stayed here. I could have spared Ella the pain of loving me and all my fucked up glory. She was too good for me anyway.

When I'd finally rolled out of bed on the third morning . . . *afternoon*, I had no fucking idea why I was even back here. My plan to erase Ella from my mind wasn't working. Not in the least. Despite never physically being here, she was everywhere. I saw her reflection in the mirror. That flowery scent lingered on my clothes and stained my skin. Anything the color of red morphed into her luscious lips.

I stared at my ceiling and it occurred to me that I was a first class asshole. Ella deserved a better man than me.

When I arrived the place was spotless, but today it was in serious need of cleaning. Empty beer bottles lined the island, along with empty pizza and carryout boxes. All thanks to the modern conveniences of apps like Drizly and Grub Hub.

All my calls had gone to voicemail and I had no desire to listen to any of them. The only thing I wanted to do was drink and fill up the emptiness that was inside me.

*Jesus, Alex, you sound like a fucking pussy.*

The reality was that I *was,* in fact, a fucking pussy.

"Alexander William Robertsen, you have thirty seconds to open this fucking door or I am breaking it down!"

"Shit," I groaned, and stumbled up to my feet.

"Alex, get off your ass and open this goddamn door!"

I pulled open the door and dragged my sister inside by her arm. "Amy, was all that swearing really fucking necessary?"

"Relax," she scoffed, jerking her arm from my grip. "Besides you're the only resident on this floor."

While that was true enough, it didn't warrant her uncouth behavior. I scrubbed my hands down my face and dropped to the sofa. Amy's blue eyes scanned over every surface and corner while she tapped her foot against the hardwood floor.

"What are you doing here?" she asked, tucking strands of thick brown hair behind her ears.

"Better question," I shot back. "How did you know that I *was* here?"

"Our brother told me."

My brow crinkled. "How the hell did Vince know I was here?"

"Seriously?" She threw her hands up. "You flew in on one of his planes. His office gets a copy of all the flight manifests, dumbass."

My fingers rubbed at my forehead. Yep, I should have flown commercial.

"Alex," she sighed, taking a seat beside me. "What is going on?"

"It's a long story."

"Well, I've got time."

"Shouldn't you be at work? I am sure there's an intern that needs yelled at."

She glared at me. "College interns completed the program last week."

"Smartass."

"Why don't you grab a shower," she instructed and pointed down the hallway. "I'm going to tidy up, and then we'll talk."

"Maybe I don't want to talk. I came here to be alone."

"Is this really how you want to play it?"

"Fine, if it will get you out of my apartment."

She folded her arms against her chest, giving me a cold hard stare. "March to the shower, right now or I'll kick your ass all the way there. And we are *soooo* talking about why you are here and look like fucking shit."

Amy was damn stubborn and for that I was grateful. I'd like to put up a fight, but I was much too tired and maybe I should have that conversation.

My hand rubbed at the back of my neck. "Actually, could you call Ethan? For this problem, I'm going to need his advice."

Amy stood up and took my hand in hers giving it a tight squeeze. "Consider it done."

Thirty minutes later, I emerged freshly showered and found my apartment was back in order. Amy was a godsend. She smiled at me and, for a moment, I thought about confessing everything. My military career, Sasha, and how I nearly died on a mission in Istanbul. But, if I'd told her, she'd never have a restful night's sleep again.

I took a seat at the island. "You're the best."

She leaned her hip against the counter, nodding slowly. "I am, and don't you forget it."

The doorbell rang and I slid off the barstool. Amy rounded the island and I walked a step behind her down the hallway.

After grabbing her bag, she opened the door. "He's all yours, Ethan."

I caught her by the arm, and pulled her into a hug. "Thanks, sis, I owe you one."

"You'll let me know if there is anything I can do?" she asked.

"I will, I promise."

A few days ago this place had sat empty for months, and now it had been filled with one visitor after another. I welcomed my old friend inside and took the bottle of scotch from his hands.

"Is Charlemagne branching out and making scotch now?"

He laughed. "Funny, maybe brandy though."

He slapped my back as we walked into the kitchen. "Why didn't you tell me that you were coming back?"

I shrugged. "Honestly, I didn't think I would be back unless it was a holiday or a high school reunion weekend."

"Didn't you go to high school in Detroit?"

I shook my head, and pulled two glasses from the cabinet. "Dude, I went to boarding school in Bloomfield Hills."

"Sorry I asked." He held up his hands and nodded towards

the bottle. "Just pour."

"It's good to see you, E," I said handing him a tumbler. "How's the relationship?"

"Good to see you too, buddy, but today's not about me. Now, what is with all the Howard Hughes theatrics? You're not pissing in mason jars are you?"

"Fuck no. I haven't gone off the deep end, *yet*." I raised my glass in a toast, and then took a long sip. It burned all the way down, and it felt fucking good. I walked towards the window and stared down at the street below. People walked along the Riverwalk possibly arguing politics for this fucked up election or discussing their futures. Some could be breaking up, while others were making up.

Who among them was hurting? Who among them had something to look towards?

On that chilly spring night, all those months ago, I felt I'd hit my lowest low. Vince and Amanda had a baby girl and all the happiness in the world. Wracked with guilt, I still couldn't shake the affair or Sasha's death. Then Ella bounced into my world and suddenly I didn't seem fixated on my guilt or broken heart.

"So, what brings you back here? I'm assuming it's a woman and it better not be Amanda."

I laughed. "No, I'm over her. But, yeah, I'm fucked up over a woman."

"Great, I can't wait to get all sensitive and talk about *your* feelings."

"Strap in." I smirked, swirling the contents of my glass. "It's bound to be a bumpy ride."

Two hours and half a bottle of scotch later, I had sufficiently disclosed my feelings for Ella, and explained how the accident had paralleled how I felt the day that Sasha died.

Ethan leaned forward, resting his elbows on his knees. "I gotta be honest, you need to let Sasha go. You didn't get her killed, and you most certainly weren't the cause of Ella's injuries."

"If I had been doing my job, Ella wouldn't have been killed."

He stared at me wide-eyed. "You mean *Sasha* wouldn't have been killed."

"Of course, that is what I meant, I said it didn't I?"

He shook his head. "No, you said Ella."

*Well, shit.*

I let that sentence roll around in my head for a few minutes. It didn't take a therapist to tell me what that meant. Actually it did, because my own therapist had explained that loss of control was my weakness. Dying was something I couldn't control, but as my profession—a protector, I'm constantly battling for the control. I'm human and I'm supposed to control death. That was one sharp, double-edged sword.

# Chapter Thirty-Two

## Ella

"I've decided that my next place will most definitely have a pool," Nabila announced, slinging her legs over the lounge chair. She tossed her sunglasses onto the table and then jumped into the water.

I smiled and continued reading the article about Charlotte Ricchetti's new boutique opening around the corner from mine this fall. We would both have shops here in The Harbour. Still, I couldn't believe it, and she'd even attended my grand opening party a few weeks ago. Charlotte told me I had a real eye for style and loved the French aesthetic of the store. That was enough to put me on cloud nine for a few days.

My parents, my sister, Molly, Ronan and Holliday, even Gavin showed up to support me in my new adventure. Nabila had told me that she couldn't make it, but the little hussy ended up surprising me. On top of that, since it was August and with all of Europe on holiday anyway she decided to stay a little longer. Having her here made me feel a little less lonely.

I didn't hear from Alex the day La Vienne Rose opened. Not directly, anyway. He'd sent a bouquet of flowers with a note that said simply said: *Congratulations. Love, Alex.*

Nabila attempted to dump the bundle into the trash, but I managed to save them from an early grave. At least the flowers let me know he had thought about me.

I had certainly thought about him. How could I not? I was here living in his house and the reminders of Alex lingered in every corner and on every surface. At first the nights were the worst, I cried buckets. One night, I broke down and had that ugly shower cry. I missed him that much.

It didn't help matters that HBO Family was apparently running some adorable mouse themed movie marathon where I bawled my eyes out whilst watching *Cinderella* and an *American Tale.*

Nabila was doing her best in helping me to find a new place, but I found fault with every space. My default excuses included cost and distance to the store.

I would never admit this to her, but I continued to stay here in case he came back. He would come back, right? A little bit of time was what he said he needed. I couldn't be mad at Alex for leaving.

Was I frustrated? Absolutely, but this was something that he needed to work out.

"It's just not a proper Sunday unless you're sipping champagne in a bikini." My eyes lifted to see Nabila walking back from the pool bar with a drink in her hand. I hadn't even heard her get out of the water. I picked up my phone to check the time. Why hasn't Alex even texted me? I know he needed time to clear his head, and I was trying to respect his wishes, but I felt myself crumbling more each day.

*No, you're fine.*

"Ella, you need to turn that frown upside down." Nabila grabbed the towel off the back of the lounger and then wiped off her face.

I flashed her a smile. "I'm fine."

*I'm fine.* Everything was fine.

After toweling the ends of her hair, she dropped back onto the chair. "It's been over a month since he left. It's probably safe to say he is *not* coming back."

After shoving my phone underneath the towel, I placed the magazine on the table. "He has to come back. It's his house."

"Are you going to stay here or come back to London?"

I hadn't thought about returning to London permanently. The weekend Alex asked me to move in with him, I spent the flight home compiling a list of things I needed to do in order to move. I wasn't going anywhere.

"As I told you before, Alex asked me to move in with him and I intend to do just that."

"Yeah, and then he took off a week later to get his head on straight." She said the last three words with air quotes attached. "Honestly, Ella, I don't know how you are putting up with this man's behavior right now."

Actually, he "took off" closer to two weeks later, but that wasn't really the point.

"I don't believe I am putting up with anything. What I do believe is that this man is hurting deeply and needs some time away to heal. I love him, so until he gives me a reason to not trust in his words. I choose to believe he will be back and we will start our life together."

She gave me a sympathetic smile. "You don't think that

makes you weak, waiting around for a man?"

I narrowed my eyes. "I'm *not* waiting for him. My life has gone on. I could have pushed back the opening of the boutique, but I didn't. It's not as if I'm sitting around crying or drowning my feelings in ice cream."

Yes, I did that at first, but could anyone blame me? One morning, after feeling the regrets of swallowing a pint of cherry-vanilla ice cream, I decided I wasn't going to be the woman who wallows in tears and eats myself sick. And I most certainly didn't want to be the woman who says to herself, "I should have known better. I should have known that he would break me." Loving Alex was a good feeling, better than good, it was wonderful.

"It's my last night here before I fly back to London. Can't we put on some cute dresses and go dancing in the city? I've heard amazing things about Indigo Row."

I groaned. "Do you really want to be out dancing and drinking all night and then get on a plane for a seven-hour flight?"

"We can stay in the city overnight and then I can get a cab to the airport."

Picking up the magazine again, I mulled the idea over while skimming an article on a list of the hottest yoga retreats. Even reading about post yoga activities in Turks & Caicos and hot stone massages couldn't hold my attention. All I thought about was the last time that I was in the city drinking and dancing I had met Alex. I'd much rather go to one of the quiet wine bars in The Harbour. Even though I was putting on a brave face, I didn't know what trigger would take me down.

*Remember, you're fine.*

"Come on, it will be a total blast."

"Let's do something here. I could make your favorite

meal, and then we could have a bonfire on the beach and drink copious amounts of wine."

She waved her hand at me. "Ella, even if you're not being honest with yourself, I know that you are hurting. You need to leave this bloody house, and I don't just mean for work."

*Shit.* I really hated that Nabila could see right through my bullshit, but I also loved that she cared enough to call me on it.

"Okay, fine, but it's your fault if you're hungover and tired on your flight."

She smiled and then muttered something in French. I assumed that she was cursing, but the French accent made it seem like beautiful poetry, even if she might have suggested that I suck a dick.

"Hey, Marcus," I called towards the guesthouse where he'd been residing since Alex left.

He emerged from the doorway shirtless, his six-pack on full display and his black basketball shorts hanging low off his hips, totally the professional bodyguard wardrobe.

Nabila turned to me. "Fuck me, how did you get lucky to have that delicious man looking out for you? Seriously, what is in the water around here?"

I chose to ignore her comment, but she wasn't wrong in her opinion. Marcus was handsome, he had gorgeous, golden brown eyes, light mocha skin and if that wasn't enough to catch your eye, his height of six foot five would easily.

"How can I help you?" His voice was cool, as he gazed the grounds. I'd seen this look a hundred times, another reminder of Alex.

"Nabila wants to drive into Manhattan tonight for some cocktails and dancing. Do you think we can make that happen?"

His hand scratched at the back of his neck. "I don't see

why not, but I did hear there was pretty killer end of summer party happening over at Castle Hill Beach House."

I eyed him over the top of my sunglasses. "How do you know about this party?"

He smirked, stretching his hands above his head. "I know everything, Ella."

That was true enough. Marcus was a trained professional through and through. And apparently that included having his ear to the ground where cocktails and parties took place.

Nabila was practically frothing at the mouth, and crawling out of her skin at the mention of this party. "Okay, that settles it. Tonight, we party on the beach." She jumped up and then twirled around on the deck.

"Fabulous," I said, settling back in the lounger. "Marcus, can we make arrangements for Nabila to get to the airport tomorrow?"

He cleared his throat. "She's on the jet's passenger list for a flight to Manhattan. Miss Nabila will arrive in plenty of time to board her flight. Weather reports show no delays. I can escort her, if you like."

I tilted my head. "I thought the jet was in Grand Rapids?"

"It was, but Alex thought Nabila might be more comfortable flying to JFK. He also arranged for a town car if you prefer."

Nabila cast a wide-eyed glance my way. "Well, color me corrected. I like Mr. Robertsen a whole lot more now. I'll take the jet, *dahling*."

The blush crept across my cheeks and I used my fist to hide my smile.

A glimmer of hope was all I needed. I believed in the sun even when it wasn't shining, and I believed in Alex even when he was silent.

After two hours of dancing and drinking, my feet were killing me.

"I need another cocktail," Nabila called out as we made our way back to our booth.

I plopped down into the chair. "I am so tired. Are you sure you want another?"

She nodded, sipping the rest of her drink—a Blushing Kiss Martini, the signature drink for tonight's party. I asked that they substitute the gin for grain free vodka. The bartender gave me some attitude, but after Marcus gave him a helpful suggestion he was all too happy to make my request. I was going to find this recipe on Pinterest or call the bartender and make him give me the recipe. Perhaps Marcus should make that call.

Loud screams came from door as a bridal party entered and the DJ flipped the tune to "Celebration" by Kool and the Gang.

*So fucking cliché.*

As much as I wanted to hate it, I couldn't and I found myself bouncing and clapping along with the rest of the bar.

"Ella, will you please be a dear and get me another pretty drink?" She gave me a pouty look and I nodded.

I motioned to our server and ordered another round of drinks. Glancing over my shoulder, I saw Marcus standing a few feet from the bar. I nodded and held up two of my fingers. Earlier, he requested that when we ordered drinks to let him know so he could keep an eye on the bar activity. Apparently, there was a rumor some bloke had slipped Klonopin into a young woman's drink a few weekends ago and she was rushed to the hospital. Marcus didn't say as much, but I knew that was code for possible date rape.

"I'm going to use the loo," Nabila sang out, as she pushed to her feet.

"I'll go with you."

"Ella, I stopped using the powder room with my girlfriends after university. I'll be fine."

I watched as she twirled through the crowd, and I looked towards Marcus whose cool steady gaze was on her as well. Just like Alex, always aware of everything.

When our drinks arrived, I immediately pulled out the sprig of thyme and tossed it onto a napkin. I twirled the grapefruit wedge in the glass. I hated thyme, the smell was awful and it tasted like dried mold to me. Rosemary, sage and oregano were high up on that list of herbs I hated. In fact, I couldn't think of a single dried herb that I didn't hate.

Sipping my drink, I watched people spill onto the beach from the dance floor. The taste of grapefruit on my tongue reminded me of bergamot and bergamot reminded me of Alex.

*Stupid thyme.*

"Oh good, this drink is exactly what I needed," Nabila confessed, and bopped her head to the beat.

Secretly I was hoping she'd come back from the bathroom and decide she was tired. I glanced at my phone screen, it was half past nine.

"Get this," Nabila said, leaning across the table. "On my way back from the loo, some bloke asked if you and I were fashion models."

I tilted my head away from her. "What? You can't be serious."

"Right? I laughed in his face." I watched as she twirled her thyme sprig. "Even after I told him that we weren't, he still wanted to know if he could photograph the two of us."

"That's not creepy at all," I replied, before taking another drink.

She giggled, and shook her head. "No, not at all."

"Is he still here?"

She stood and gazed around the bar. "No, I don't see him. He was tall, about two meters in height . . . six feet or so with dark hair."

"So odd, but good to know in your slightly intoxicated state you can identify a potential weirdo."

"Are you a fashion model? Seriously has to be the lamest pick up line in the book."

I nodded and took a long drink. "*There you are! I've been looking for you all night.*"

Despite not venturing into New York City tonight, a previous reminder from that truly amazing evening washed over me. I guess Alex and I would always have a little piece of that Manhattan sidewalk in our hearts. At least I knew I would.

I stared out in to the night watching as the moon and stars sprinkled the waves and sand with light. And as stupid as it sounded I really hoped Alex was looking up at the same sky.

*I hear you Fievel, I know he's out there somewhere.*

I sat at my desk tapping a pen to my lip as I stared blankly at my computer screen. There were at least fifteen things that required my attention, but I couldn't focus on any of them for more than five minutes. At least the store was operating with the exquisite precision of a ship at sea. Daily operations rarely needed my attention because Mary-Ellen was the Chief Officer, Second Officer and Third Officer all rolled into one. The sales associates respected her, but I think they were also secretly afraid of her, which is why there were very few slip ups on her watch.

Sales were up three percent since opening day and we could hardly keep up with the demand for the leather moto jackets and circle skirts we carried. Dressing like a French woman was a hit in The Harbour. I was making a statement here. Professionally, everything was falling into place, better than I ever dreamed. Personally, that was an entirely different beast.

*Knock, knock.*

Tiffany appeared in my doorway smiling and holding a glossy pink envelope in her hands, along with my afternoon tea order from the bakery. At eighteen, Tiffany was my youngest employee. She was bubbly and was very good with the customers. She had mad add-on skills and knew how to accessorize a look to perfection.

And it didn't hurt that she was a member of a highly respected and well-connected family, which was good for business. The Buchanans owned half of The Harbour and it seemed as if they were a small elite army of sorts. Tiffany's immediate family tree was filled with marriages, divorces, re-marriages, and that was just her father. Not only that, she had half-siblings and step-siblings out the ying yang.

"Ella, this package arrived for you."

I took the envelope along with my tea. "Thank you, Tiffany." I noticed she had a tattoo on the inside of her right wrist, an adorable black bow, tiny and tastefully done.

"When did you get your tattoo?"

She ran her index finger over the ink, and smiled. "Last weekend, my friends and I, we all said that we would get one as soon as we all turned eighteen. It was Fiona's birthday last Saturday—oh, she's my best friend and the last one in our tribe to turn eighteen so that's when we did it."

My brows rose. "Your tribe?"

She laughed, and tilted her head to the side. "Oh, sorry, that's just another way of saying group of friends."

"I see, that's cute and your tattoo is lovely. Why did you choose a bow?"

"Thank you," she replied with a smile. "It might sound dumb, but I read somewhere that bows signify love and femininity. I just thought of it more as another accessory like a bracelet or ring. Do you have a tat?"

"Me, a tattoo? No, but I'm giving serious consideration to the idea."

"Well, if you want to get one, I'll go with you."

"Thanks, Tiffany. I'll let you know."

"Okay, gotta go. I need to get back on the floor." She pivoted and headed towards the stock room.

"Have fun." My eyes dropped to the envelope on my desk.

"Talk to you later, *bye*," she chirped, as she raced past my door with a stack of sweaters.

Smiling, I shook my head, and then took a sip of my tea. Flipping over the envelope, I noticed the return address was Manhattan. I didn't recognize it though. Using my letter opener, I sliced through the pink paper.

It was an invite for Holliday's birthday and the event was going to be held at Lorenzo's in Manhattan. Further down the invite I noticed it said that I could bring a guest.

I let out a deep sigh. *If only I had someone to bring.*

I picked up the phone and hit the intercom for the cash wrap. "Hey, Tiffany, on second thought, take your break now. We need to discuss that ink issue."

"Okay, Ella, I'll be right there."

# Chapter Thirty-Three

## Alex

My previous mental snap, breakdown or whatever you wanted to call it landed me at the western edge of Fiji on the Yasawa Islands. The islands are only accessible by boat or kayak. To say the twenty or so islands that made up the chain were sparsely populated was an understatement. No roads, no cars or banks. The resorts serve as the only source of income to each island.

After twenty-four hours of travel, I was exhausted and I decided to stay on Barefoot Island. I hiked, swam, snorkeled and spent a lot of time in the hammock outside my bure that was thirty feet from the beach. It was probably the worst idea of my life to stop there first. Turning off the noise in my head was a challenge.

After three days of being alone with thoughts that I couldn't escape, I hopped on the boat and headed north to the

Blue Lagoon resort. I needed some modern conveniences and human interaction. Another mistake—surrounding myself with couples in love. Worse yet, honeymooners.

After several drinks, I called my therapist and found very little satisfaction in telling her that this was a fucking terrible idea. Additionally, I told her that I wanted back every penny that I ever paid her and thanks to her idiotic suggestion, I was more miserable than when I'd left.

She laughed, and told me to take back the control. It was up to me to decide how to heal and get back to neutral. How the fuck was I supposed to do that?

Now, I found myself sitting on the patio of Ethan's beach house, staring out at the waves on Lake Michigan, pondering the same question. The leaves had begun to change and hints of fall started to crackle in the air, despite the fact that it was eighty-two degrees in mid-September.

As I took a swig from the beer I was drinking, I heard the door to the patio open. Craning my neck, I expected to see Ethan, but instead Amy appeared.

"Hey, sis." I stood, and then pulled her into a hug.

Amy had been coming by most evenings while I'd been staying here, always bringing food and making dinner. It was all unnecessary, but she insisted. I glanced at my watch, it was just after four and she made very good time leaving Grand Rapids for South Haven on a Friday.

"This weather is unbelievable, but I'm still making lasagna for dinner tonight."

My sister designated all meals for certain seasons of the year. Lasagna was a winter meal, but anything after Labor Day was fair game for comfort foods. Any day now she'll be making butternut squash soup and cheddar penne pie with apples.

"You really don't need to do that. I was going fire up the

grill and make burgers." I popped off the cap of a bottle of beer and handed it to her. "Wait, are you eating meat these days? Or is that not allowed?"

She waved me off and dropped into one of the chairs. "Yes, I am eating meat. If my memory serves correctly, I recall you grilling on a December evening one year with a snowstorm on the way."

I laughed. "To be fair, it was fifty-five earlier that day."

"The Midwest, the only place where you can experience all four seasons in one day."

Her phone rang and she stepped inside to take the call. Silence surrounded me once more, and I watched a large tanker in the distance as it glided through the pristine blue waters. The color reminded me of Ella's eyes. My fingers scratched at the curve of my jaw, I'd let my beard grow in. For a moment, I allowed myself to wonder how Ella would like it.

"I went to see my psychic the other day," Amy informed, before taking a long sip of her beer.

I rolled my eyes. "I don't know why you listen to that horse shit."

"Always a skeptic." She shook her head. "I listen because it brings a different perspective into my life. I like Michele's wisdom, and she has helped me to solve countless problems just by re-framing the issue."

I peeled the label from my bottle. I didn't know what to say, I stayed quiet hoping Amy would move on to another topic of discussion realizing that I wasn't interested.

"Michele invited me to sit in on one of her group discussions. The topic was love and fear."

My brows rose. "Oh here we go."

She turned to face me. "Just listen, this makes sense. The core of the conversation centered on the fear that one will lose love or never be viewed as lovable. Most of the time when we have a problem in our love life the root cause is fear."

I stared at her blankly. "Yeah, and?"

"Michele told us that love and fear should never share the same energetic space."

I shoved a hand through my hair. "Get to the point, Amy."

"Look, Alex." She pushed to her feet, and smoothed her ponytail. "I am well aware that you think I am a bit of a whack-adoo for seeking the guidance of a psychic. I am sure you roll your eyes when I read daily affirmations and recite mantras. I know I don't have all the details about what happened with you and the time you spent in the military, but I do have a pretty good idea that the reason you moved hundreds of miles away from your family and friends was to avoid Vince and Amanda because *you* fucked up. It seems to me that you need to get over yourself and your mistakes. Get back to The Harbour and tell Ella you love her—it's as simple as that." She slammed her beer down and headed towards the door.

Realizing I had pushed her too far, I stood and grasped her arm. "Hey, I'm sorry and I don't think that you're a whack-adoo . . . a bit eccentric, maybe."

"Alex, you're my big brother and I love you, but *you* need to love fearlessly. Trust in the universe. Don't you understand that you were fated to meet Ella? I believe you should spend time creating your destiny rather than running away from it."

"What?"

"Yeah, you heard me," she said, lifting a single brow. "Your first response is to run away from emotion. It's become a pattern. When you came home from your military tour, you took off for three months, although that may have been warranted. When Amanda chose Vince, you escaped to New York. And now, you've left Ella behind instead of staying to work it out.

You might fuck up and make some mistakes, but when you go away to 'clear your head' you're not solving the problem."

Did all of that make sense or had I been around Amy and her new age mumbo jumbo for too long? If I was being honest, she was right about the running away. It was possible that I wasn't giving myself the opportunity to resolve my issues on an emotional level, which was probably why I couldn't see past my guilt.

Amy grasped my shoulders. "All you have to do is ask yourself if Ella is worth the risk and if the answer is yes, then stop letting fear dominate love."

I was beginning to think Amy was a mind reader. When this whole thing started, I had told Ella that *she* was worth the risk.

"You make it all sound so simple, sis."

"I'm very wise."

It had been almost six weeks and I still hadn't arrived at any kind of clarity. No amount of time would explain why Sasha's life ended that day. Like Sully said, no one blamed me for her death. Amanda, I was over her, so there was no need to rehash. She and Vince were happy and that was all that mattered.

Instead of me going away, perhaps it was time to send away the remorse, shame, and liability—all of it and lock it away for good.

# Chapter Thirty-Four

## Ella

Gorgeous shades of orange and pink painted the evening sky. My mood was black, and it perfectly matched the ink lettering that now adorned my upper thigh. The tattoo had healed nicely, and I relished the pain when the needle pricked along my skin. The physical sensation was nothing compared to the ache in my heart.

I'd stopped counting how long Alex had been away. All I knew is that September was sliding into October and he had not returned to The Harbour, to his home or to me.

The Range Rover pulled up to the valet stand at Lorenzo's and the door opened. I slid out, and then Marcus handed me the gift I'd brought for Holliday. I twisted the silver bow and used my fingers to fluff it up. Although my gift was pretty cool, nothing could top the fact that Ronan had our sister, Molly, develop a special fragrance for her. Molly sent me a sample to test out and I absolutely loved it.

"I'm not working tonight, but I'll be around if you need me. I'll be ready to take you home whenever you like," Marcus said, as he opened the door.

"Thanks, Marcus, are you allowed to have a drink with me since you're technically not working?"

He shot me a sideways glance. "You really want me to drink and then drive you to your hotel?"

"Fuck it, we can grab a cab or one of those Uber things people keep talking about." I handed over my coat to the attendant. The place was empty, not a soul in sight.

"I'm not allowing you to get into an Uber." He crossed his arms against his chest. "Have fun, and if I'm not inside, that probably means that I stepped out for a smoke."

"You should really quit those cancer sticks," I called after him. "They're no good for you!"

He waved me off and I dropped my present off at the gift table. This was some spread. I stood alone in the doorway admiring the mini winter wonderland that lay before me. Tiny cupcakes with white frosting in silver foils lined the dessert table and there was a jar of sparklers off to the side. There was a candy bar with rock candy, pretzels dipped in white chocolate and blue and white candy cane sticks, and there was even a station to make s'mores. Everything around the room was layered in white, silver, and sensational shades of icy blues—even the candles.

"Would you care for a drink, miss?"

I turned around and came face to face with the same petite Asian gal I noticed at Ronan and Holliday's party months ago. "Hi, I assume that there's a signature cocktail?"

She smiled. "Does open bar sound like a good signature drink?"

I laughed. "Vodka soda with a twist of lime, oh, I have a gluten allergy, potato vodka please."

She nodded. "Yes, I remember. I'll return shortly."

I sagged into a chair near the back, and I watched as people filtered in with their drinks. I felt my mood slipping deeper into melancholy and I should not be sad. This was a celebration. It still freaked me out that I was only seven months older than Holliday.

"Here you go, miss," she said, placing my drink in front of me. "I'm Lila, by the way, and if you need anything just let me know."

"Thanks, I'm Ella. Cheers."

I sipped my drink, and watched as more people filtered in, including Tinley Atkinson and Matthew Barber. They had their hands all over one another. *Fuck*. It made me miss Alex. My phone vibrated. I had twenty notices from Snapchat, all Nabila. Aside from a few fashion designers, she was the only person I really followed.

Swiping my screen, I scrolled through the endless stream of pictures and videos. There were sweet images of her and Finn—laughing over coffee, making brunch, hanging out at her studio and the last picture was of the two of them holding hands and kissing under an umbrella in the rain.

She looked really happy. Bloody hell, this was a mistake. I shouldn't have come here. Grabbing my drink and clutch, I stood in a rush. Before I took a step, the sound of clapping had me rooted to my spot.

Enter my brother and his gorgeous girlfriend, also known as the woman of the hour.

Stuck, that was my current position. Next, Charlotte breezed into the room and I only hoped I could maintain my composure long enough to talk to her about Fashion Week and her latest collection because I totally missed *all* the shows. I was otherwise occupied and too fucking busy pining away for a man that apparently just wanted me to live in his house while he was out doing fuck knows what. I downed the rest of my drink and before I knew it another glass appeared in front of me. That's when I remembered she'd put me on the guest list for her show.

*Oh, Jesus. She just saw me.*

Bloody hell.

*What the fuck is wrong with me?*

That was the million dollar question.

She approached looking elegant in her curve-hugging, blood-red dress with her blonde hair swept into a classic chignon. "Ella, how are you?" She kissed both my cheeks.

"I'm doing well, thank you. And you?"

"Exhausted, but it's all in a day's work, right?"

I nodded and sipped some liquid courage.

She waved to someone across the room. "Keep smiling," she whispered. "When I hand you an invitation to attend my show for fashion week, I expect you to fucking be there. I could have opened a lot of doors for you, Ella. I trust you won't make the same mistake twice?"

*Fuck. Fuck. Charlotte Ricchetti hates me.*

All the sweat from my body just seeped through my glittering gold dress. "I . . . I'm terribly sorry, Charlotte. I will do my best next time to RSVP. I swear I didn't mean to blow off your show."

"Do better than your best. This is a tough business and New York City is not for the faint of heart." She hugged me, but I was scared there was a knife about to be plunged into my gut. Suddenly, I felt like Robb Stark at the Red Wedding.

*Is this party over yet?*

After we played with sparklers on the outdoor patio, I walked out to the main dining room and took a seat on a bench. I scrolled through my phone's contact list and my finger hovered over his name. Tears welled in my eyes, between Charlotte's not so subtle threat and seeing my brother in love and so blissfully happy, it was all too much. This was my breaking point. I sucked in a breath to hold the waterworks at bay, but the tears cascaded down my cheeks.

People gathered around the bar ordering more drinks. I swiped the tears away, and busied myself with a magazine someone left behind.

I flipped the pages and my eyes landed on a picture of Grady James wearing his polo attire. *Oh God.* The Stars and Stripes Polo Challenge.

My hand shook as I flipped to the next page. Several photos staggered the centerfold, including one of Alex and me standing at the bar chatting. I stared at the picture and my fingers traced over his face.

Tears spilled onto paper as I tore out the page. I shoved it into my clutch and then swiped my cheeks.

"Hey, Ella," Holliday said as she took a seat on the velvet bench beside me. "You okay?"

Besides the fact that your sister was a huge bitch to me and I missed the man I loved more than anything? *I'm fine.*

"Oh, I'm fine," I said, plastering a saccharine smile on my face. "It's a work problem I need to fix, but it can wait until Monday."

"Are you sure that's all it is?" She tilted her head and smiled.

"I'm positive." I gave her a quick hug.

"Okay. Well, if you need to talk, you call me anytime."

"Thank you. I hope you had a lovely birthday, Holliday. Will you excuse me?"

I didn't give her a chance to reply, with my phone in my hand, I rushed down the hallway and then pushed open the door to the ladies' room. My chest tightened and I was having trouble catching my breath.

I splashed some water on my face and used a paper towel to wipe away my smudged mascara. My lips were puffy, too, and there were red splotches all over my neck. I dropped into one of the vanity chairs, and took a few deep breaths. It wasn't until I heard echoes of laughter outside the door that I realized fourteen minutes had gone by.

*Me: I'm ready to leave.*

*Marcus: Okay, I'll pull around to the side entrance.*

*Me: Thanks, and I need to stop for a huge bottle of vodka.*

*Marcus: No need. I had the hotel staff stock the bar in your suite with all the essentials.*

*Me: You're the best. Does this mean you will actually have a drink with me tonight?*

*Marcus: Sure, why not. Pulling out of the garage, now.*

After I pulled myself together, I plodded down the stairwell. I decided that I was going to get Marcus tanked tonight and then pump him for information about Alex. The crisp fall air swirled around me as I pushed open the door. There was no sign of the Range Rover, only a town car idling by the curb. I tried to pull the exit door back open, but of course, it had locked behind me. Turning around, I let out a frustrated groan. That's when I felt a hand wrapping around my neck and everything went black.

# Chapter Thirty-Five

## Ella

The blaring sound of a horn awakened me. There was a sharp pain at the back of my head, which only intensified when the horn sounded again. Opening my eyes, sunlight from the windows spilled across the wooden floor. The smell of mold and fish nauseated me and my stomach lurched.

Blinking against the light, my eyes took in a wide space and I found myself lying on a wrought iron bed. I studied the pea-green and yellow paint chipped walls, as my fingers picked at the edge of the brown comforter underneath me.

Six wooden chairs with colorful cushions surrounded a large rectangular table that sat opposite the bed. Situated on an ornate woven rug were a black leather chair and a small coffee table. The décor was modest, fresh sunflowers sat in a plastic vase on the floor and red roses brightened up the table.

The decorator had a varied sense of style.

*Where in the bloody hell am I?*

Despite the fact that I was confused and scared, I knew I needed to catalog as many details to memory that I could. I shuffled quietly across the floor, noting that I was still wearing the dress I'd worn to Holliday's birthday party.

"Oh fuck," I gasped as I peered out the small window.

Water surrounded the place, which explained the fish smell. Beyond that was a stone walkway lined with a few trees and a lamp post.

*Could I be somewhere in The Harbour?*

I spun around looking for a clock or my phone. My next thought was to find my clutch and my shoes.

After a few passes around the room without any luck finding my things, I ran towards the door. My heart pounded in my chest. Twisting and shaking the knob violently was of no use.

I was trapped and I could not remember how I got here. My mouth felt like cotton and my head throbbed with ache.

The pressure on my bladder was annoying and hurt like hell. Is there a toilet here? I trotted across the room, doing my best to not piss down my leg. Grasping at the window's handle, I tried lifting. It wouldn't budge. I slammed my hand on the glass, it was fucking painted shut. They all were.

"Help! Someone help me!" I pounded on the glass, screaming at the top my lungs for someone to help me.

In my fit of rage, I studied the drop from the balcony. If I managed to pop out the glass, I could jump and swim to the embankment.

When the urge to pee intensified, I scrambled past the kitchen towards the darkened hallway. I turned the corner and found a set of stairs. Moving with caution, I walked down the narrow steps. To my surprise, the first floor smelled brand new. The scent reminded me of Alex's home. My fingers smoothed down the white walls.

Gorgeous glass doors showcased the boat dock and garage area. I tugged on the handles—locked. Of course.

Oars, fishing poles, and life preservers were staggered across the wall. A large first aid kit was bolted to the wall above a long wooden bench. I was wasting time.

Okay, pee and then escape.

I slipped into the washroom, and the sound of a motor paralyzed me with fear. My stomach growled and echoed off the walls.

*Pee faster, Ella.*

I finished in the bathroom and raced up the stairs. Adrenaline spiked in my veins. I darted into the small kitchen area pulling open the wooden drawers and cabinets. No knives, no sharp objects anywhere. I saw nothing that I could use to defend myself against the psycho who was holding me inside this dungeon on water.

I jumped on the bed and held my breath anxiously waiting for my captor to appear. With each sound of a foot connecting with a wooden step, my heart rate kicked up and I fought the urge to scream.

"Hello, Ella, glad to see that you're finally awake."

At the sound of his voice, I shot up off the bed. "Charlie, what the fuck is the meaning of this?" I screamed, as my hands balled into fists at my side.

He dropped the bags onto the counter and then marched towards me. When he stood too close to me for comfort, his eyes met mine and panic swept through me.

"The meaning of this is business. We have unfinished business."

My hand connected with his cheek. He let out a haughty laugh and then backhanded me. I fell onto the bed. He grasped my arm and pulled me up to my feet. "Bitch, you're about to learn a very valuable lesson."

Rage set my blood on fire, mustering all I could, I hurled my body forward and darted towards the stairs. Charlie caught me by the waist and tossed me onto the bed. The mattress dipped and terror sparked inside me.

*Please, do not let this man force himself on me.*

Reaching his hand out, he smoothed his palm up my thigh. I flinched at the contact of his calloused thick fingers grazing along my skin.

*Do I slap his hand away or will that anger him again? Jesus Christ.*

Tears stung my eyes, but I would not cry in front of this man. I swallowed every emotion, and even though all the inconceivable things I thought he might do to me was fresh on the surface, I resolved not to falter.

Charlie pulled me from the bed, I struggled against his hold. He heaved me onto one of the wooden chairs.

"Does it make you feel all big and tough tossing me around?"

"You don't know when to shut up, do you?"

My head snapped to the side, and my eye felt like it would explode. Fire blazed across my cheek and everything went blurry. I managed to bite my tongue in the process of his connecting with my cheek.

"Your mouth has always been the problem."

The taste of copper was bitter on my tongue. "You can hit me all you want, Charlie, but it won't make you feel better."

Huffing out a laugh, he stormed into the kitchen and pulled something from one of the bags. "You see this?" He waved an object wrapped in plastic through the air. "This is my golden ticket, Lovie."

I couldn't really see what he held in his hands. "Did you shake down a pre-teen for a Wonka bar?"

He prowled towards me, striking me once more. The plastic cut my chin, blood dripped onto my dress. Charlie grasped the back of my head. "See, this is a burner phone. We're going to call your boyfriend and your brother and I'm going to exchange your sweet ass for some cold hard cash. And once I have the money, I'm out of here."

Sickness swirled inside me, and I struggled to breathe. "In addition to kidnapping . . . you want to add extortion to your list of crimes? The only place you'll be going is jail."

Narrowing his eyes, he grabbed me by the back of the head, pulling my hair. I cried out in pain. "Charlie, you're hurting me!"

He released the hold he had on me and then tramped back across the hardwood to the tiny kitchen. The sounds of Charlie mumbling and rustling paper was all I heard. I wanted to know what he was doing. It was hard to see through the small space between the hanging cabinets and counter.

"The pictures I sent to your shop, I really thought that would have sent your bloke over the edge and I would get my payday. Lucky for him no media outlet gave a shit about photos from a fight at a polo match. So he got to keep his money."

Light coupled with darkness swirled into a hazy shade of grey. It didn't help matters that I was light-headed. My legs trembled, as I tried to stand. I took in a deep breath to shake the dizziness.

"Kidnapping you is a much better idea. I'll get a payout from your rich bloke and your rich brother. It's a win-win for me. Now I just have to decide what you're worth to them."

I crept towards the kitchen. It was odd how his words became softer with each step I took. A sharp jab made contact with my skin and pain screamed through my body. Warmth slid over me and I floated off onto a soft cloud. My eyes closed and through the darkness, a light appeared, it was Alex.

*Alex.*

I struggled to keep my focus on him. "Alex, come back to me."

# Chapter Thirty-Six

## Alex

Nothing on this Earth could have prepared me for the news about Ella's kidnapping. On top of that, Marcus was seriously injured and lying in a hospital. Around two o'clock on Sunday afternoon, the hotel staff discovered that Ella had not checked out of her room. In between watching the Lions game and helping Ethan close up the lake house, I hadn't bothered checking my messages. Otherwise, I would have been here sooner. My brother worked his magic waking every employee of Everett Sterling Aviation in the early morning hours in order to get me on a flight to New York.

*No bodies matching Ella's description have been found.* Dean's words grated on my soul like nails on a chalkboard. Where was she?

As I stood in the doorway, the scene around me unfolded in slow motion. The din of multiple conversations carried throughout the room. Dozens of people were bent over laptops or on the phone. It was as if I stepped back in time to the command center for an Elite Eight mission briefing. A base of operations had been set up at The Addison, one of the most famous buildings in New York City and residence of Ronan and Holliday. When Dean had called me about Ella's disappearance, he'd informed me of the set up. My hands shook, fear and anger shot through my veins. I needed to focus. We were going to find Ella. I was going to find her and bring her home, and whoever did this to her was going to pay a very fucking high price.

"Alex, good, you're here," Dean called out, motioning me to the large conference table. With my bags still in tow, I walked through the mass of people taking in every detail that surrounded me.

"Celia, please take Mr. Robertsen's bags to the apartment on the thirtieth floor."

"Right away, Mr. Winters."

I raked my hands through my hair. "What's the situation, Dean?"

"Not much has changed since we spoke last. We had an eyewitness confirm the black town car at Lorenzo's Saturday night, and we have video footage of the same car in the parking garage just before Ella disappeared."

"Any change with Marcus?"

"I'm sorry," he replied, shaking his head. "No word yet, he's still in surgery."

Earlier Dean had told me a van came out of nowhere and crashed into the Range Rover sending Marcus head-on into a cement pillar. That was all according to the parking attendant on duty. The hospital couldn't give us much information since none of us were his immediate family.

Everything around us came to a grinding halt at the sound of Holliday's raised voice.

"You said *what* to her?" Holliday screeched from across the room. "I understand that you can be a mega bitch at times, Charlotte, but don't you ever speak to Ella that way again."

"I wasn't thinking." Charlotte wiped the tears from her eyes and smoothed her blonde hair behind her ears. "Jesus, what if we never see . . ."

"Don't you say it—don't even *think* it." Her tone was warning.

Dean held up his hands. "Anyone that isn't directly related to Ronan, Holliday or Ella or connected to them in a personal capacity, take a lunch break. And, yes, I realize that we've already had lunch, but I need this room cleared. Phones on and we'll text you when we need you back here. Thank you."

The noise of shuffling feet didn't mask the whispers and grumblings as the room thinned. *Good man.* That was exactly how I would have handled the situation. When the dust settled, it was only Ronan, Holliday, Charlotte, Lucan, Blake, Grady, and the eldest Connolly sibling, Molly—I recognized her from her picture—left standing. And then there was Liam Frost, the man who recommended me to his buddy for the job to protect Ella. *He must think the worst of me.*

Tension rolled into the room, casting a heavy shadow over all of us. All I could do was stand back and let this scenario play out.

"What the hell did you say to my sister, Charlotte?" Ronan roared, when the door to the suite closed.

"I was pissed that she blew off my Fashion Week event, I might have told her, in a not so friendly way, to never do that again."

"Over fucking fashion week, are you serious?" Holliday

threw her hands in the air.

Ronan's hands balled into fists. "Goddamnit, you can hurl insults at me all you want, but don't you ever talk down to my sisters *ever*. You got me, Princess?"

Charlotte glared at Ronan. "Don't fucking call me that."

Lucan stood, and grasped his wife's arm. "Charlotte, la mia bella, you need to take a breath."

"Ronan," Molly began, taking a step forward. "Calm down, I am sure she didn't mean anything by it, besides we both know Ella can be a bit flakey."

"Flakey?" Ronan repeated, glowering at his sister. "Honestly, do you even hear the drivel spilling out of your mouth? Our little sister is missing and her bodyguard is lying in a motherfucking hospital bed. Yeah, I'm certain her former 'flakey' behavior got her kidnapped." Ronan walked away shaking his head and Molly quickly followed.

Silence fell over the room, and all I could think about was the movie *Summer School* when Chainsaw screamed before taking the exam, "*Tension breaker, had to be done.*"

Charlotte turned to her sister. "It is just me or does his brogue get thicker when he's emotional?"

Holliday let out a small giggle. "Sometimes, when we're fucking, I can't understand him at all."

Liam and Blake exchanged smirks. Grady coughed out a laugh, and Holliday flipped him off. My shoulders sagged with relief and I was grateful for the humor dispelling the tense situation. Everyone was on edge and the lack of sleep didn't help. I should order some comfort food, and then everyone could fall into a nice deep sleep while I get to work on finding Ella.

"If I may." I cleared my throat. "I know Ella and Marcus pretty well. I think they'd laugh with us, and I have a feeling they know we're thinking of them. We will find Ella and bring her home safe."

"Oh really, pretty boy," Ronan said, approaching me slowly. "Is that so? You know my sister well enough, so well that you up and left your job and now you're back here acting as if you give a shit."

"You think because I left that means I don't give a shit about Ella? You can't be serious."

Dean stepped between the two of us. "Alex, *now* would be the time to tell him."

My eyes went wide, and I felt the urge to punch Dean. My fingers curled against my palms, I wanted to pop Ronan in the mouth, too, but I knew his reaction wasn't about me. His sister was out there, fuck knows where, and he needed someone to be *his* punching bag.

His eyes narrowed. "Tell me what?"

This was not the ideal time or place to let Ronan know I was in love with his sister. My eyes darted from Dean to Ronan and that's when I noticed the peanut gallery had formed a semi-circle around the three of us.

"Hold on a minute," Grady said, stepping forward.

I shook my head. "Don't, man."

Grady held up his hands in mock surrender.

*Fuck.*

I could tell that Ronan was a fairly well-built guy. A runner most likely and he probably lifted the occasional weight to maintain muscle mass. However, being an inch taller, not to discount that I easily had twenty pounds on him, add in all the years of combat training, in the event that he decided to take a swing at me, I was fairly confident I could defend myself. If I was being honest, though, and I had learned someone that I hired to keep my sister safe was actually screwing her—on second thought, *yeah* I'd definitely kick my ass.

"Look, Ronan," I croaked out. "This wasn't how I . . . how *we* planned on telling . . ."

"Oh my God," Holliday gasped.

In that moment, I swore my balls jumped right up and into my throat. I felt like Chandler on the episode of *Friends* when Ross found out about him and Monica. Only I was pretty sure Ronan wasn't going to be too pleased. I'd been watching way too much Netflix over the last two months.

"Oh, *come* on," Ronan shouted, shaking his head. "You've got to be fucking kidding me." He ran his hands through his hair and it looked as if he'd been electrocuted, which was fitting since this news obviously came as a shock.

*Shit.* Yep, I was going to have to move to Yemen.

"You're screwing around with my sister?"

"It's not like that."

"Oh, so what is it like, because I am certainly not paying you to sleep with my little sister."

"Actually, you're not paying him at all," Dean pointed out.

Ronan shot him a confused look.

"Alex came to me a while back and requested the money from his paychecks be split between two charities."

His gaze shifted to me. "Is that so?"

I straightened my shoulders. "It is. And we're not just messing around. I love Ella and she loves me."

Ronan ran a hand over his jaw. He looked back and forth between Dean and me. It was hard to get a read on him, but his body language discerned he was a little ticked off.

Liam cleared his throat. "Guys, the clock's ticking to find Ella. Why don't you table this for now and hold your tribal council later."

I knew I liked the Welshman. He was right, we were wasting precious time, and we still had no clues as to Ella's whereabouts. We harnessed our emotions and opted to focus on the task at hand—finding Ella. I rolled up my sleeves and looked over all the data in front of me.

Lucan swiped his phone, I heard him instructing someone to order catering from Kitchen Provance. Two women wearing brightly colored dresses breezed through the doors carrying multiple coffees, making a beeline for Charlotte.

"What's everyone working on?" I asked, powering up my laptop.

Celia appeared at the table. "Your room keys, Mr. Robertsen."

"Thanks."

"At this point, we're searching social media and the news blogs for any information that could pertain to Ella," Dean replied, handing me a coffee. "Mostly, I think the family is grateful to be together."

"What about Ella's parents? Are they being told anything?"

"The Connollys are in KwaZulu-Natal, South Africa on some private game reserve. They are relatively unreachable, but Ronan and Molly don't want to reach out unless they absolutely need too."

"I would have advised the same thing." I scrubbed my hands down my face. "And the cops. Why don't they have anything for us?"

"The cops are doing all they can. I have personal contacts at the NYPD and the Bureau. My buddy, Rhodes, is keeping me fully in the loop. We'll be notified the second they hear any chatter."

My gut twisted with overwhelming worry. "We should be out there doing more." I pointed towards the windows.

"I know you're frustrated, but we don't have anything solid to go on, yet."

"I don't think I can sit here and drink coffee, knowing that Ella is out there somewhere possibly hurt and scared." My fingers laced together. I could count on one hand the number of times in my life where I'd felt completely helpless, this was one of those times. I scoured through my emails, hoping Patrick had sent me something I could work with regarding Ella. Nothing from Patrick. This was agonizing. My fingers flew across my phone as I typed a message to Patrick.

*Me: I need any information on Charlie McNeil's whereabouts in the last twenty-four hours.*

*Patrick: You got it.*

The list of potential suspects was growing longer by the hour. Everyone was guilty until proven innocent. My mind opened files on everyone Ella had come in contact with since her arrival. I'd ruled out the creep who suggested Ella pay her rent in sexual favors. I also omitted Mark Daniels. He was safe only because the team was on their way to the World Series. I even scratched my contractor, Gary, off the list. That may have been a stretch adding him, but when I brought Ella to my home, his longer than necessary stare was aptly noted.

There was only one person who stood out and *he* was at the top of the list. It couldn't be McNeil. I didn't want to think it was him. If only for Ella's sake, I didn't want to pull at that thread and open those old wounds again. The media would have a field day drudging up all that shit from her past and splashing it all over the tabloids. I refused to let her be put through that again.

Two cups of coffee and twenty eliminated suspects later, the food arrived. No one seemed to want to eat and I was climbing the walls. I stared out the window, admiring the city skyline, going over all my moments with Ella. Did she know I was going out of my mind with worry? No, there was a good chance I was the last person she figured gave a shit about her. Just like Ronan said.

Dean joined me at the window. "There's plenty of food."

"I'm not hungry," I lied.

"They say never give advice during a crisis, only assistance. So, I'm not going to tell you to eat. I'm sure that you're going nuts right now, but I assure you that the police are doing everything they can to find Ella."

"They need to do more. *We* need to do more."

"And you need to trust in the Intelligence Unit." He took a bite of his pastrami sandwich.

I cocked a brow. "Is that what you were doing where Derek Saunders was concerned? Trusting in the law?"

He swallowed. "That's a fair point. Do what you need to and I'll do all I can to help you."

We walked to the door. "I want to go back to Lorenzo's and the parking garage. I'm going to see if I can't get a look at that security camera or talk to the guard."

"Bring her back home to her family."

I nodded. "I will. Count on that."

# Chapter Thirty-Seven

## Alex

The parking garage attendant was useless. The white van hit the black Range Rover he said over and over, along with the fact that he was the one who called 911. As far as I knew, the police had turned up zip. I hadn't heard from Patrick in over an hour. When I last spoke to him, he still had no information on McNeil.

I walked along the sidewalk near the side entrance of Lorenzo's. Leaves tumbled across the concrete in my path. The urge to crush them under my boots was strong. I studied every point of direction as I stood at the curb where the town car was spotted.

"Give me a sign, come on," I murmured.

A couple stood staring up at a building across the street as I approached the side door. They were talking about the architecture of the structure. Once they left, my fingertips trailed along the warm steel, and then curled around the handle.

She stood in this very spot. My fists slammed against the glass.

"Ella," I breathed.

Expelling a harsh breath, I kicked a rock across the pavement. A man with a camera stood across the street. When his gaze met mine, he bolted.

I darted across the street. "Hey man, stop!"

Anger and frustration coursed through my veins. We rounded a corner down an alleyway and rage spurred me forward. The smell of garbage and stale beer was enough to make me gag. He tripped and crashed into a row of beer kegs. I grabbed his hoodie and then slammed him against the brick wall.

I studied his face, as he struggled against my hold. This guy was at the polo match with McNeil. "Where the fuck is Ella Connolly?"

"Hey, man, watch my camera. This is an expensive piece of equipment."

"*Man*, I don't give a fuck about your camera," I snarled. "Where's my girlfriend?"

"She . . . she's . . . if I tell you, will you leave me out of it?" His voice shook with every word he uttered.

"Tell me where she is, motherfucker, and I'll think about it," I growled, and struck a swift blow to his stomach.

On a long groan, he doubled over in pain. "That fucking hurt." He gasped for a breath. "If I tell you, you've got to promise me that you won't turn me in to the cops."

I gripped his collar tight, hauling him upright against the bricks. "I make no promises and just so you know, I can do this all afternoon. I suggest you start talking or the next hit will be to your face."

"Okay, okay!" He held up his shaking hands. "She's upstate in Canandaigua. Charlie rented a boat house up there on the lake a few weeks back."

"You got an address?"

"Yeah, it's in my phone. Charlie, he . . . uh, plans to call you and her brother, the movie star. He's going to ask the two of you for money."

My fingers uncoiled and I let go of the hold I had on him. As he sagged against the wall, he pulled his phone out of his jacket. He tapped the device to life and handed it to me. "Here, that's the address."

I snatched the phone from his hands and typed the address into the notes app on my phone.

"Man, are you going to tell the cops about me?"

I squared up to him, and my fist collided with his jaw. His head bobbed back against the bricks. "If anything happens to Ella, you won't need to worry about the police, asshole." Blood from his lip dripped onto his hoodie. I grabbed his face, angling it towards me. "I'm your worst nightmare."

He dropped to the ground like bag of cement, crushing his camera in the process. Before I left, I snapped a photo of his ID then flung it at his chest and walked away.

"John Kemp, I'd start praying," I mumbled under my breath.

I flagged down a cab a few blocks up from Lorenzo's, and then instructed the driver to drop me at The Addison. As I crossed the lobby to the bank of elevators, I pulled out my phone and called the private line to Everett Sterling Aviation.

"Connie, I need a plane today, the sooner the better. It's a very urgent need."

"I'm sorry, Mr. Robertsen, it looks as if Mr. Everett and Mr. Sterling have chartered both of the company jets. Let me check the other flights, hold please."

While I waited for Connie to come back on the line, I sent Dean a text message.

*Me: I got a tip on Ella's whereabouts. We need to talk privately. Where should we meet?*

*Dean: Good work. Meet you at your Addison apartment. We can formulate a plan of action.*

"Mr. Robertsen, the closest plane I have to you is going to arrive in Boston tonight at seven thirty-four. Will that work for you?"

I shook my head, scratching my scalp. "No, no it won't. Is there nothing else?"

"Let me check again, sir."

I hung on the line and waited. Two elevators had come and gone. I hoofed up the stairs and crossed the mezzanine level just as Connie came back on the line and told me none of the E&S planes were coming to Manhattan, the elevator dinged.

I thanked her for her help and stepped into the empty car. *Fuck, looks like I'm driving.*

An hour later, I was sailing down the highway on my way upstate. In between briefing Dean and mapping a route to Canandaigua, Celia had arranged for a car. At the sight of a police car in the median, I pumped the brakes. I hadn't realized I was speeding, but I needed to get to my girl. My Ella.

My cell rang and I swiped the screen. "Talk to me, Dean."

"We just received the ransom request from McNeil. He's asking for five million."

Drawing in a breath, my hand slapped against the steering wheel. "Greedy little fucker isn't he?"

"Alex, there's more."

My chest shook, and I feared the worst. Charlie was stupid, he was really fucking stupid, but he needed the money.

"Ronan was able to talk to Ella, she said she was fine, but he sent photos and it was visible he has beaten her up pretty good."

"I'll kill him!" I roared. "I will fucking kill him."

"Alex, you've got to calm down. What's your ETA?"

"I'm still four hours away. *Fuck!*" My hands gripped the wheel until my knuckles were white. "Fuck, fuck, fuck!"

Silence passed between us, and all I heard was the sound of blood rushing in my ears. Taking deep breaths, I managed to calm down.

"Call the authorities. We can't wait, tell them to go in."

"I'll call you when they have Ella and McNeil is in custody."

Saying nothing, I killed the call. My foot pressed the gas and I wanted to break every speed limit to get to her, but all I could do was *wait.*

*Wait* to see Ella. I would have to wait to hold her. Wait to wrap my arms around her and tell her that I loved her.

*Wait* to get my hands on Charlie for putting his on her.

Charlie McNeil had made a very grave mistake.

# Chapter Thirty-Eight

## Ella

Tears dripped onto the white cotton tee that Charlie so *nicely* bought for me, along with a pair of black leggings. My beautiful gold dress lay rumpled on the floor, stained in blood and vomit. I'd eaten a slice of bread, only because I was starving, and it didn't end well.

I told myself I wouldn't cry, but Charlie had left and I allowed myself a few tears. They weren't for me. Instead, they were for my brother and sister. It was a relief to hear their voices, but my gut twisted with ache that I'd put them through such worry.

During the short phone call earlier, Molly had told me not to worry. I heard the pain in her voice. I told her I was fine, though I doubt she believed me after seeing the photos Charlie sent. Ronan said only four words, *I love you, Lolly.* Charlie ended the call before I could respond.

Before the call, I'd been allowed to brush my teeth, shower, and wash my hair under supervision, which was both frightening and humiliating. He angled the camera so that the sunlight washed over me and I was sure he was doing it to purposely disguise the bruises he'd decorated my skin with over the last few days.

Days, hours—I couldn't recall how long I'd been here.

The only time stamp I had was that I'd washed my hair on Saturday afternoon, before the party. Two days, that was the most I could let it go before I need to wash it again. So according to my earlier limp and greasy hair, I thought that today might be Monday. It was so stupid. I didn't know what I was supposed to think about being locked in this place.

My head was spinning and I was so tired. Charlie had asked for five million dollars. He expected that payment for my safe return. *Jesus.*

My fingers twisted the ends of my hair. How would Ronan know where to find me? Charlie had five burner phones. He ditched the one from earlier, busting it to pieces and then scattering them into the water. He joked about how he'd be feeding me to the fishes if the money didn't come through.

The blare of a steam engine startled me, sending my pulse thumping.

*I'm entirely too jumpy.*

Charlie had been so nice to give me a lesson on the Canandaigua Lady, the Mississippi style paddle wheel boat that served as a reminder of the old steamboats. Steamboats were the primary mode of transportation here until roads were built.

All that stupid information told me that I was nowhere near The Harbour. I was nowhere close to Manhattan either, and I was even farther away from Alex.

*Alex.*

I wondered if he'd been in the room with Molly and Ronan at the time of the call. Had Alex heard my voice? Swiping away the tears, I dreamed about indoor picnics with ice cream, baseball games and dancing on the beach under the stars.

With a heavy sigh, I slammed my fists to the comforter. I jerked at the zip-tie wrapped around my ankle. The plastic dug into my skin, but thankfully not enough to cut. It was unnecessary, and I hadn't given Charlie any reason to think I would run. I mean honestly, there was no way to get out of here that I could find.

"Help me! Can anyone hear me?" I bellowed at the top of my lungs.

Why did I even bother? No one was around to hear my cries and pleas for help. I peeled another strip of green paint off the wall. Why couldn't Charlie have left me a magazine or even a book to read whilst he was out. There wasn't even a television or radio in this place. Modern amenities, I was expecting too much. This was not The York Hotel.

To entertain myself, I began re-playing scenes from *Friends* in my mind. Nabila and I started binge watching the sitcom as soon as it became available on Netflix. We'd spent an entire weekend in our pajamas watching seasons five and six and debating which season had the funnier moments. I lobbied for five because of the episode where everyone found out about Monica and Chandler. The sexual showdown between Chandler and Phoebe, seriously hands down was the fucking funniest thing I'd ever seen. Not to mention all the great one-liners.

*"Maybe, I'll dance for you."*

*"You look good."*

And my favorite quote of all time from Phoebe, *"They*

*don't know that we know they know we know.*"

At this point, I was crying and laughing, I pressed a fist to my mouth to calm down. Silence surrounded me and then I swore I'd heard a clicking noise.

The door cracked open and snapped on its hinges. Light spread into every corner of the space, casting glittering rays of dust beams through the air.

"Holy fuck!" I screamed, while an army of men trampled across the floor shouting commands. My screams intertwined with a litany of broken curses as I watched the scene unfolding before me.

"*Entry clear.*" A booming voice called out.

"*Hallway clear.*"

My mouth hung open and my fingers gripped at the bedding beneath me. The bed shook and rattled against the wall. Darkness swirled with lightness and my stomach flipped.

"*Go, go, go.*"

It was hard to tell who was speaking to whom in the flurry of activity. At the sound of glass shattering, I instinctively buried my face into the pillows. My chest shook as my heart pounded fiercely.

"All clear here, boss."

My leg jerked and this time the zip tie cut into my skin. The rush of blood slid down my ankle dripping onto the ugly brown colored comforter.

"Ouch, *dammit*," I groaned into the pillow.

"Miss," a deep voice called to me. "Ella Connolly?" the voice asked over the stomping of boots against the hardwood.

I looked up to see a man with dark hair and bright blue eyes staring back at me. "Miss Connolly, can you hear me? Are you okay?"

Nodding, I swallowed and gasp, "Yeah, well, no actually,

my ankle hurts." I pointed to the zip tie that bound me to the bed's iron frame.

He smiled. "Ah, let me fix that for you." He pulled out a knife and with one swift movement I was freed from the bed.

"Thanks, uhhh, *Sir*?" I stumbled over the words, feeling my cheeks heating.

"Agent Rhodes," he replied with a wide smile.

"Thank you, Agent Rhodes." I swung my legs off the bed and then massaged my thigh and down my leg trying to circulate some blood flow.

"Let's get you out of here and get that piece of plastic removed properly. Do you think you can walk?"

"I think so." I hobbled and Agent Rhodes offered his arm to help me. Once outside, the chill of the air wrapped around me and I inhaled a deep breath. The paramedics rushed towards us.

"She has a zip tie on her ankle," he informed. "It needs to be cut off immediately."

Men and women in various uniforms raced up and down the pier. My eyes took in the row of houses on both sides of me, not a single resident in sight.

"All done, miss."

"Hmm." My eyes met the male paramedic's. He waved the bloodstained plastic in the air, and it finally registered to my brain that my ankle wasn't throbbing with biting pain. A pair of fingernail clippers was all it took to snap through the plastic. His fingers swept across my skin applying ointment and then he covered the cut on my ankle with a bandage.

"Miss, we should get you to the hospital. You really should have someone look at those cuts and bruises on your face."

"Oh, okay," I said, pushing my hair away from my face.

Agent Rhodes approached. "I'll drive Miss Connolly

to the hospital. Detectives Marshall and Seelen have some questions."

The paramedics exchanged glances while packing up their gear. No words needed, it was clear that Rhodes was in charge and his word was the only thing that mattered. Shivers twirled up and down my spine and I wrapped my arms around my body. Agent Rhodes took notice, because the next thing I knew, he was draping his blue FBI jacket around my shoulders. I pulled it tight as I continued walking along the pier towards the parking lot.

My teeth began to chatter with every step I took. "My *feet* . . . feet are freezing."

"I'll get you some socks, I promise," he said, and ushered me into the back of a black SUV.

Doctor Baker angled my face towards the light, studying my bruises. "All of these should heal with time. Nothing is fractured, which is a very good thing."

"Nurse Shaw will be in with a rape kit in a few moments."

My brows knitted together, and I shook my head. "No." I swallowed hard. "I wasn't raped."

He stood and then tossed his gloves into the bin. "You're sure?"

Feeling the shock run through my veins, I could only stare at him. "Yes, I'm quite positive that I was *not* sexually assaulted."

Giving me a small smile, he nodded and then left the room. My face burned and my heart skipped a beat. I thought about how lucky I'd been that Charlie had not forced himself on me. The worst damage he'd done was slap me around and those bruises would go away.

I sat there, going over everything in my mind. One minute I was thinking about how much I missed Alex and the next I was a miserable mess leaving Holliday's party. Oh, Marcus, he was probably out of his mind with worry that I wasn't waiting for him. Sighing, I buried my face in my hands.

Maybe some television would help. After all, laughter is the best medicine. I started to scroll through the channels, and just my luck, I landed on an episode of *Two Broke Girls*. I loved Max and Caroline.

*Knock, knock.*

"Miss Connolly," Agent Rhodes greeted me, carrying a dark colored bag. "Sorry to disturb you."

"Oh, hi," I said, pulling myself up the bed, and then muting the program. "What are you doing here?" I didn't think I would be seeing him again. He'd been kind enough to sit with me while I answered the detective's questions earlier.

"Well, miss," he began, approaching the foot of the bed. "The team swept the boat house and found some items that we believe belong to you."

Nodding, I extended my hands taking the bag from him. "Thank you." I dug into the bag, sifting through the items. It was all there—dress, shoes, clutch, and phone. "Have you found Charlie yet?"

He ran a hand through his dark hair. "Not yet." As Agent Rhodes said the words, my stomach dropped.

"He won't get far. There's a manhunt underway and every available officer is out there looking for him." He pointed to the window. "Miss Connolly, I assure you that we will find him and he will be prosecuted to the fullest extent of the law."

"Good." My fingers rubbed over the bruises on my face, and a violent shiver moved through me. "That's good."

"I need to be on my way, so I'll leave you to rest."

"Thanks again for everything."

"No need for thanks, just doing my job, miss." He turned, and then made his way towards the door.

"Oh, Agent Rhodes," I called after him.

He lifted his head and turned back to face me. "Yes."

"Has my family been contacted? I haven't had a chance to call them yet."

"They know that you are safe and here at Memorial. It's my understanding that a gentleman is on his way to pick you up."

Once he left, I shifted in the bed and my head fell back against the pillows. Needing to shut my mind down, I turned off the television. Shadows decorated the walls of my room. The sky was painted with beautiful shades of pinks and oranges, just like the night of Holliday's party. The night Charlie . . . I couldn't think about that anymore. It was over.

I drifted in and out of sleep. Outside the wind howled and whipped against the glass—every noise kept me awake. I wasn't sure if I managed to get any rest.

Expelling a deep breath, I tossed over to face the hallway. A pair of black shoes stood on the pink tile. My eyes lifted to see Alex standing in the doorway, his face twisted in pain.

Tears cascaded down my cheeks. "*Alex,*" I breathed his name like a prayer. "It's about bloody time."

# Chapter Thirty-Nine

## Alex

I stepped further into the room, and the faint light from the windows washed over Ella's face. At the sight of her bandaged chin, bruised lip and cheek, anger and hatred boiled inside me, but the relief that she was safe doused the flames that raged.

"Ella," I whispered, my heart throbbed in pain. "Are you okay?"

She pulled herself up the bed. "I'm much better now that you're here."

I wrapped my arms around her, holding her tight. "I'm not hurting you, am I?"

She started to shake, her body vibrating with laughter. "No, the only way you could hurt me is if you let go."

It was good to hear her voice, and her laugh.

"At some point I might need to, but for tonight I'll play

by the rules."

"Good. I need you in this bed with me."

After tossing my leather jacket onto the chair in the corner, I kicked off my shoes and then snuggled into the bed. I cuddled her close, and she rested her head on my chest. I kissed her forehead, stroking my hand up and down her back.

"I've missed you," I breathed. "I am a stupid, stupid man, Ella. Can you ever forgive me?"

"I know that we have a lot to discuss," she said, lifting her head to look at me. "But the thing I want more than anything in this world is to hold the man I love while I sleep."

"You still love me?" I asked my voice barely audible.

She broke out into a smile, and tears welled in her blue eyes. "I never stopped."

Fuck, I missed those eyes. So much emotion flowed behind them and I knew without question she belonged to me.

*We belong to one another.*

"I think I belonged to you, before I even met you," she whispered.

"What?" I stared at her in confusion.

"You said that out loud, well, you whispered it out loud."

I bent my lips to hers, kissing her gently. "I love you, Ella."

Her head fell against my chest and I hugged her tighter. Having her in my arms, her skin against mine, feeling her steady even breathing, I realized Ella was my whole world and I was never letting her go.

As soon as the pilot said we'd reached our cruising altitude, Ella jumped onto my lap. Her lips landed on mine.

"Ella, your lip." The brutal force of the kiss had me worried about that cut.

"I don't give a fuck about my lip. I *need* you." She cupped my face in her hands, crushing her lips to mine once more.

"What's gotten into you?"

She arched an eyebrow, her blue eyes dazzled. "Let's talk about you getting inside of me, instead."

"Are you sure?"

Ella pushed to her feet and I followed. Her hands went to the hem of the sweater I bought for her, tugging it over her head. Before she was able to be discharged, I made a quick trip into town and purchased Ella some clothes. I didn't want her to be in those shitty rags that Charlie had her dressed in. More importantly, I didn't want any reminders of him around her.

I clicked the call button. "Joni, please make sure that Miss Connolly and I aren't disturbed for the next hour."

"Yes, Mr. Robertsen."

Her blonde hair spilled over her shoulders and she ran her fingers through the ends.

"You're so fucking sexy." I reached out and tangled my hands in her hair, yanking her towards me.

*Shit.* Was I being too rough? Would that remind her of what she'd just been through?

"Alex, I know what you're thinking," she said, gripping the edge of my t-shirt. "What he did to me *that* was assault. What you're . . . *we're* doing is pure pleasure. He doesn't get to have that control over me."

"Understood." I moved my hand to the back of her neck, pulling her mouth to mine. I kissed her hard, thrusting my tongue against hers.

Her hands flew to my jeans, popping the button and they dropped, pooling at my feet before I had a chance to take off my shoes.

"Impatient much?" I smirked.

She took a step back. Her fingers dug into the waistband of her pants. She called them lounge pants. I thought they were just leggings. She discussed, at length, the differences between leggings, loungewear and yoga pants over breakfast. As we drove to the airport, Ella asked me to add a note on my phone reminding her to look into French lingerie for the store.

All the little things just reminded me of how much I missed her quirky sense of humor and her ability to transition from topic to topic without skipping a beat.

She stood before me in a strapless bra and cotton panties. Fuck, she was beautiful. "That's new," I remarked, pointing to the ink that marked the upper part of her thigh.

*l'amour sans crainte*

"What does it say?"

"It says love fearlessly, in French."

As if this woman couldn't get any goddamn sexier, she'd gone out and inked herself.

"Speaking of new, you have more facial hair than I remember," she remarked, tugging at the thick hair covering my cheek.

"Get naked, Ella," I said, stripping out of my t-shirt. "Naked *now*, talk later."

My hand worked my cock as I watched her reveal her amazing tits. She twisted her nipples, hardening them to perfect peaks. She turned away from me and shimmied out of her panties, giving me a full view of her sensational ass attached to those killer stems. It had been so long, I almost didn't know where to start with her.

"Absolutely stunning," I said, as she sauntered closer to me.

"Let me help you with that." She grasped my cock with two hands, pumping me with long slow strokes.

Leaning forward, I brushed her long hair over her shoulder, feathering kisses along her creamy skin. I lifted my hands to her face, pressing my lips to hers, pouring weeks' worth of frustration, misery, worry, and passion into one kiss. Ella understood what I was conveying, because her hands left my cock and roped around my back, pulling me closer.

I kissed down her throat, across her collarbone, licking a line down the valley between her breasts before taking her nipple into my mouth. I nipped and sucked her along her skin, kissing as much of her body that I could.

"Alex," she sighed, her nails digging into my shoulders.

"I've missed hearing my name on your lips."

I lifted her against my body and walked us over to the bar, where I pinned her against the counter. Her eyes were wild with anticipation. I dropped to my knees and then pressed my lips to her tattoo. My tongue traced over the beautiful scripted ink as my hands palmed her ass.

"Spread your legs."

Her nails dug into my scalp with a sharp bite as she widened her stance. The scent of her arousal washed over me, drawing my attention to her glistening slit. I dragged my tongue through her wet heat and she let out a soft whimper when my tongue lashed against her clit.

"Oh, there *you* are," she moaned.

"I'm right here." I smiled against her skin and slipped two fingers inside her. A full body shiver rolled through her and she cried out my name.

"You're so fucking beautiful."

I twisted my fingers inside of her, pushing against all the right spots while her fingers tugged and pulled at my hair.

Pleas and whispers alternated with breathy moans as I thrusted deeper. Ella shifted her hips as I licked and lapped up her slickness. I devoured her, teasing, tasting and taking everything I could. The spasms hit her body quickly and as she shook from the pleasure, her thighs brushed against my beard.

"Alex, my God," she gasped, as my tongue swirled against her clit drawing out her orgasm. Withdrawing my fingers, I glanced up seeing her flushed and her head lolling from side to side.

"I'm not done with you, sweetheart," I growled, gripping her hips and spinning her around. Her palms slapped against the marble tabletop. With one hand pressed against the base of her spine, I angled my cock and shoved into her with one smooth motion.

"Ahh, yes," she moaned, pushing back against me. The sensation was almost too much to take. Cupping her breasts, my mouth mapped a trail between her shoulder blades. We started slow and increased our thrusts, finding the perfect rhythm.

"Alex, more Alex," she begged. "More of *you*."

She had no idea what she was saying, well *maybe* she did. How right she was though. I wanted more of this, the two of us together. No more running away. No more worrying about guilt. I was letting that shit go.

"Harder, oh, please," she rasped.

Waves of my orgasm stirred at the base of my spine. One of my hands clasped over hers and I sank deeper into her, groaning at the feel of her pussy squeezing my dick. Driving my hips harder, her legs trembled and I knew she was close.

"Ella, you feel so fucking good, let go."

She drew her free hand around to the back of my neck, whispering, "I love you, Alex."

My eyes screwed shut as I pumped into her with everything I had. Lust drove me and ecstasy lit up every cell in my body. Her walls tightened around me and my orgasm shot up through my balls. We climaxed together. *Fuck.*

"That was incredible."

"I missed you," I said, trailing kisses along her back.

She turned around to face me. "I missed being just Alex and Ella."

My lips found Ella's and her hands writhed in my hair as she melted into me. She was beautiful and perfect and all mine.

"Me too."

# Chapter Forty

## Ella

It seemed that the only communicating Alex and I had been doing since leaving Canandaigua was of the physical nature. When we arrived home, Alex scooped me up and carried me straight to the shower. Without missing a beat, he stripped off our clothes and then fucked me against the cool tiles as the steam curled around us. The only time we left the bedroom was to eat dinner and then we ended up screwing each other mindless on the floor in the living room.

It was without question that Alex and I were very good at speaking the language that required no words. However, I wanted us to be better at actually talking to one another. I thought we were pretty decent at that part of our relationship. In fact, we were probably better than most, but something was flawed in that capacity and we had some tightening up to do.

The afternoon had quickly faded to evening. Instead of

sweating balls and begging Alex to crank up the air-conditioning, we lay in bed staring at a roaring fire in early October. I snuggled into his side, and he dropped a kiss to the top of my head. His hand massaged slow circles against my hip and tangled my legs with his. I don't think he'd stopped touching me once since yesterday.

"You're really sticking to the rule of not letting go of me."

He shifted his body so that we were lying face to face. "Some rules should be followed."

Our lips met for a long slow kiss, which escalated into a tangle of tongues and his fingers teasing my nipples. Every part of him was hard and his hazel eyes widened the moment I flipped the tables and straddled him.

"Sex can wait, we have things to discuss."

"How about we talk while you're riding my dick?" His hands were on my ass pulling me closer to his erection.

"Behave," I warned slapping his hands way. "And I'll consider it."

His hands smoothed up and down my arms. "Okay, I promise."

"First of all, I noticed Marcus wasn't home. The Range Rover isn't here either."

His face fell and he turned to look out the window. "*Ella*," he sighed heavily. "There's no easy way to tell you this. He's in the hospital."

My hands flew to my mouth. "What happened?"

Alex took me in his arms, pulling me beside him. "There was an accident the night you were taken."

Poor Marcus, my heart climbed into my throat. I listened as Alex explained that a van had crashed into Marcus while he was driving. He went on to tell me that Marcus wasn't wearing a seat belt at the time of the accident. The rest of the words played on repeat . . . concussion . . . internal bleeding . . . surgery.

I stared at Alex and couldn't help but cry. "I refuse to be anything but positive."

His thumb swiped away the tears. "Staying positive is a very good idea. Speaking of positive, things at La Vienne Rose are going well."

Alex was so very kind to change the subject. Knowing there was nothing he could do for his longtime friend lying in a hospital bed had to be total agony for him.

"Charlotte and Holliday stopped by to let Mary-Ellen know what had happened and she agreed to not alert the staff. Ronan and Dean went to great lengths to keep the media out of all of this. Your parents . . ."

"Oh my God, my parents." I closed my eyes. "They must be worried sick."

Alex's fingers tugged at my chin, forcing me to look at him. "They don't know anything. Ronan and Molly thought it was better that way. Also, your parents are in South Africa on some remote game preserve. They're currently unreachable."

I blew out a deep breath, trying to absorb all this information. Marcus being hurt and in hospital weighed heavily on my mind. He just had to be okay. Gathering my hair in my hands, I twisted the strands tossing them over one shoulder.

My teeth grazed over my bottom lip. "How did you know where to find me?"

His hands locked behind his head. "Well, that's an interesting story. Honestly, I felt helpless sitting around at The Addison. I needed to go back to where he took you." He swallowed down his emotion and continued, "I had to do more."

I smiled, taking his hand in mine. "You felt something calling you there didn't you?"

He nodded and went on to tell me about the command center Ronan and Molly had set up and all the people that stopped by to help and aid in finding me. My heart was bursting, overflowing with gratitude.

"After the parking garage was a bust, I went to Lorenzo's. Across the street, I noticed a man with a camera around his neck. When he saw me, he bolted and I ran after him. Turns out he was one of the guys that was with Charlie at the polo match and he gave me all the information I needed to find you." He swallowed hard, scrubbed his hands down his face. "I don't know what I would have done if I'd lost you Ella."

I brought my hand to his cheek. "You knew how to find me. I am here because of you."

Grasping my hand, he peppered my knuckles with kisses. Oh, how I loved this man.

"Speaking of cameras, here's a bizarre story for you. Nabila and I went to an end of summer party at Castle Hill and some guy asked if he could take our picture, thinking we were fashion models. Clearly it was a very bad pickup line."

Alex cocked a brow. "Did you get a look at him?"

"No, I didn't."

Alex stood up, and crossed the room giving me a fine view of his beautiful ass. He grabbed his phone, and his fingers swiped across the screen. "I'm texting you a picture of a guy named John Kemp. Can you send it to Nabila?"

I picked up my phone and glanced at the screen. Despite the fact that I had two very lengthy conversations with both of my siblings before leaving hospital, they had each texted several messages over the course of the afternoon. I quickly constructed a group message, letting them know that I was still doing well and that I would check in with them both soon.

When I pulled up the photo Alex sent, I recognized the

man's face. I sent the message to Nabila. It was one o'clock in the morning in London. It was a toss-up between Nabila sleeping or out clubbing with Finn.

"Okay, now that we have those crucial matters out of the way. How about we get back to more intimate matters?" He waggled his brows and grasped my calves avoiding my injured ankle, pulling me to the middle of the bed. The mattress dipped when Alex climbed on and settled between my thighs.

"We still need to talk about why you were gone for so long."

His chin dropped to his chest. "I'm sorry, Ella. I shouldn't have left you alone." He lifted his head, his hazel eyes fixated on mine. "I should have stayed and worked it out. Actually, I should have worked through my guilt and grief years ago."

My chest tightened hearing the regret in his voice.

"My sister says that I run away from emotion. She made a very good argument that it's my first instinct. Apparently, it's a pattern."

Given what Alex had told me about how he'd come to here to The Harbour after his affair with Amanda and then leaving after the mishap with the van that put me in hospital, I could see that being the issue.

"I'm inclined to agree with your sister."

He smirked, trailing his fingers down my thighs and over my knees. "You know what else Amy told me, and I hope that you'll agree."

"Tell me."

"She told me that you and I were destined to meet. I never really thought much of destiny and fate before. I think her psychic told her that, but who knows."

My brows arched, at this information. "Your sister has a psychic?"

"Yeah, she also practices Buddhism, but don't tell my Catholic mother." His fingers stroked higher, eventually skimming across my abs.

I nodded. "I won't tell a soul, but I think that I'd really like to meet your family."

"I think that's fair, considering I've met half of yours. You should know that I had to come clean to your brother about the two of us."

I rolled up on to my elbows. "So, everyone knows about us?"

"Yep and I'm officially retiring as your bodyguard."

I frowned and shifted up on my hands. "Really? But what will you do now?"

He gripped the back of my neck pulling me closer. "I had a lot of time to think while I was in Michigan, and so much more over the past forty some odd hours. Remember I told you that I was thinking about expanding Robertsen Security to Manhattan?"

"Mhmmm."

"For the first time in my life, instead of running away from something, I'm running towards something—someone. I had a reason for coming here, it might not have been clear back then but it is now, it was you, Ella. It's always been you." He lips brushed over mine, and my hands tangled around his neck.

The kiss was long and slow and wonderfully warm. His beautiful words rippled around me and unraveled an avalanche of emotions slamming into every part of me.

Alex snaked his arm around my waist, guiding me back onto the mattress. His mouth dipped to the hollow of my throat, his body vibrating with tension.

Alex and I were two strangers who met on a sidewalk in

Manhattan unaware that we were bound to one another in a surprising, yet, significant capacity. We walked away, not knowing each other's name, in fact I still didn't know Alex's middle name.

"Hey, what's your middle name?"

A smirk pulled at the corner of Alex's mouth, his hazel eyes sparkled with amusement. "William."

Eyes wide, I stared in disbelief. "No way."

"Yes way, now can I get back to the matter of seducing you?" he asked, before wrapping his mouth around my nipple.

"Oh, yes, *please* do continue."

# Chapter Forty-One

## Alex

Walking into the police station, a cool chill settled in my spine. It had been three weeks since Ella had returned home and every day those memories drifted farther from our lives. Dean had called me an hour ago to let me know the authorities finally captured Charlie McNeil. Apparently, he'd seduced a female college student and she took him to her parent's lake house near Ithaca where he'd been hiding out.

Since the kidnapping, Ella had woken up a few times in the middle of the night sweating and panicked from nightmares. Tonight, however, I was sure that she'd sleep peacefully knowing that Charlie had been arrested and was going away for a long time. Her nightmares varied from being kidnapped and beaten to having Charlie dumping her over the side of a boat into the ocean. I hated that for her, because the water was my calm, and I didn't want it to be a source of fear for her. But I'd put the house on the market in a second if she asked me too.

With Dean's help, Ronan and I were going to do everything we could to make sure Ella didn't have to face the bastard in court.

Turns out that John Kemp was, in fact, the guy Nabila had talked to at Castle Hill that night. Charlie had him stalking Ella, apparently that was the night they planned to take her, but things obviously went awry.

More good news, Marcus was doing great. Since he was healing quickly and begging me to come back to work, our docs cleared him to return to light duty. I told him to take another week and then we'd talk. He agreed, although I could sense there was much reluctance.

"Alex, good to see you." Agent Jake Rhodes approached extending his hand to mine. "He's been asking for you."

"I shouldn't give him the satisfaction." My fists balled at my side.

"Totally your call," he replied. "Five minutes seems like a fair amount of time to give him some friendly advice."

I ran a hand over the stubble of my jaw. Yeah, the beard had to go. Ella complained that it hid my face. I had other theories that involved rashes and scratch marks on her breasts and thighs. Truth be told, I was glad she asked me to shave if off.

I blew out a harsh breath. "Yeah, okay, I'll see him."

The metal door clanked shut, and my eyes met Charlie's. He sat in a plastic chair with his hands bound to the table in chains. My jaw ticked as I took as seat across from him.

"Glad to see you could make it, mate." A single brow rose, and he leaned back in the chair.

"I can't say the same, *mate*."

"How's Ella? Did those nasty bruises heal?"

He was taunting me and I wasn't going to give him the satisfaction of knowing he'd pissed me off.

"I should have fucked her sweet little cunt when she was in my bed."

When he spoke *those words* all I saw was red. I stood and my hands flew across the table, grabbing him by the collar of his orange jumpsuit bringing him inches from my face. "You listen to me, motherfucker," I snarled. "It's over. You deserve everything that's fucking coming to you." I heaved him back onto the chair. As I walked backwards, the smug smile remained imprinted on his face.

When my back hit the door, I tapped twice. "Have a nice life locked away, rotting behind these bars, asshole."

The door opened and I walked out into the hallway. Agent Rhodes gave me a nod as I walked past the front desk. As I turned the corner, I came face to face with Ronan.

"Hey, man, what are you doing here?"

He crossed his arms over his chest. "Did you think you were the only one having a one-on-one with McNeil?"

A harsh laugh rumbled from my chest, and I ran a hand through my hair. "I guess I did, yeah."

He squared up to me and I steeled my spine. This guy wouldn't deck me in a police station would he? Ronan didn't strike me as a hot head. In fact, he reminded me of someone with a calm demeanor. However, the man was a protector. I'd been privy to the details of the Derek Saunders situation. He'd gone to great lengths to make sure Holliday was safe and I supposed he would do the same for his sisters and his daughters.

But, this is a guy who knows I've had my hands all over his baby sister, and I'm sure he can see it all over my face that

I've fucked her six ways to Sunday. If he needed to clock me for that, I understood. It's probably fair to say that I would do the same where Amy was concerned.

He slapped a hand to my shoulder. "In times of crisis, I've always believed a man shows his true character. You're a class act, Alex. Thank you for helping bring Ella home safely."

My brows rose. Relief washed over me. Not only do I get to keep my balls, but I didn't have to move to Yemen.

"I'd do anything for Ella. You have my word; I'll always keep her safe."

The grip he had on my shoulder tightened and he held my gaze with steady authority. "Good. Don't give me a reason to think otherwise."

Standing a bit taller, I nodded. "I assure you that I won't."

A small smile tugged the corners of his mouth as he walked away. I didn't think Ronan and I would be calling each other bros anytime soon, but it was clear we had come to an understanding.

Outside, the smell of wet leaves stewed with exhaust fumes hung heavy in the air. Across the parking lot young kids exited a school bus. They formed two lines, as instructed by their teacher. I smiled and then jumped into my newly restored Range Rover. As I exited the parking lot, I thought about the day when my own kids may take a field trip to the police station to talk to real every day heroes.

*Slow down, Alex. Take it all in stride.*

The sound of bells rang out. From my seated position at the counter, I saw a sexy blonde appear. *My* sexy blonde sashaying towards me as her ponytail flipped from side to side.

"Hey, babe," she said, taking a seat beside me.

In the fifteen seconds it took her to walk from the door to the bar, I'd thought of half a dozen ways I'd convince her to skip this afternoon's coffee date in favor of going home and getting naked.

"Well, hello to you." I leaned in, and pressed a kiss to her cherry red lips.

"What have you been up to today?"

She shrugged out of her coat and then set her purse on the empty barstool beside her. "Well, this morning I stopped by La Vienne Rose and checked in the shipment. Called the London store and talked to Bianca about the winter trunk show. I am positively beaming that sales are up six percent over last year. I am thinking about giving her a raise."

A small plate with a gluten-free cranberry orange muffin appeared before us along with a large tea and black coffee.

"I took the liberty of ordering for you."

"Yum, my favorite," she said, her blue eyes sparkled. "Oh, I need you to mark next Saturday on your calendar. We're going to Charlotte's boutique opening."

I eyed her over the lip of my mug. "Yes, dear."

She focused on the muffin in front of her, first peeling back the paper and then pinching off a tiny piece. "What have you been up to today?"

"Well, I drove into the city and stopped by the police station."

Her head snapped to look at me. "Tell me more."

This is how it was with us *now*, straightforward and to the point. We agreed not to sugar coat anything. Ella admitted she loved the way I expressed myself when I had talked to her about my affair with Amanda. Real. Raw. Honest. Apparently, we were going for nonchalant on all important matters. I had a feeling that would change in time.

My thumb stoked over her knee. "They arrested Charlie and I had a little chat with him."

She swallowed hard, and bobbed her head. "Thank God they caught him. I'm sure that went over well."

"Let's just say he's remorseful of his actions," I lied. It was a tiny fib, but I couldn't stomach telling Ella what he actually said about her.

"Right," she drawled out, pinching off a piece of bread. "I'm sure he made some snide comment about my tits or my ass or my lady bits and you told him to fuck right off. Did I get the gist?"

I laughed. "Damn, you're good."

Sometimes I forgot just how thick-skinned Ella could be, on top of being intelligent and sweet. She was impossibly beautiful, funny, my favorite running buddy, and I was in love with her. All of her.

"I also ran into your brother."

Her face scrunched up. "Ooooh, and how'd that go?"

"My cock and balls are still attached, and he didn't threaten to kill me for defiling you all these months."

She leaned closer whispering in my ear, "That is good news for me because *I* am quite fond of your cock and balls."

God, I loved her dirty mind. There was no way in hell I was letting her go. We'd been lucky enough to find each other. There was no mistaking that what we had was a real love.

"Oh, Tinley Atkinson stopped by the store today looking for me."

"Who is Tinley Atkinson?" I shrugged, before taking drink of my coffee.

She rolled her eyes. "Oh, sweet Alex, she lives like ten houses down from you. She's dating Matthew Barber, the guy who plays the super hero dude in all those comic book movies."

I shook my head. I honestly had no clue.

"Not important." She waved her hands in front of me. "She asked me to dress her for this upcoming television interview she has and I am *so* excited. *And* I'm having cocktails with her and Holliday next month. Apparently, there's this fashion event called a Sip n' Shop the first Saturday in December."

I slapped a fifty down on the counter, and stood. "Ella, let's go."

Her eyes narrowed. "But I haven't finished my sweets or tea."

The server placed a giant pink box in front of us. "I got an order of muffins to go. Now, grab your tea. We're outta here."

She scowled at me, and scooped up her things. "You're so bossy."

I leaned in, and whispered in her hair. "Home. Bed. Fucking you, now."

She grasped my hand and led the way towards the exit. *That's my girl.*

# Chapter Forty-Two

## Ella

"So where did you two meet, anyway?" my brother asked, unfolding his napkin.

"Outside O'Brien's. It's an Irish Pub not far from The York Hotel, actually," I answered, pointing at my brother and Holliday.

They exchanged glances and laughed.

My brother slapped his palm against the table. "Holy hell, *now*, I have to fucking buy the place."

My brows knitted together. "What?"

"Ronan and I had one of our first dates there," Holliday replied, smiling and then kissed my brother's cheek. "He's been thinking of buying it ever since."

"It's true," he admitted, lifting a shoulder. "Now, what should we order?"

Despite my best efforts to say peace out from Charlotte's

boutique opening, we'd been roped into a late lunch. Truth be told, it was long overdue.

"I hear the Thai curried duck is excellent," I said over my menu.

Ronan and Alex looked at each other. "Burgers and fries."

On the way to the restaurant, Alex and I tried to come up with varied excuses to bail, but we knew none of them would work. It seemed we'd found a mutual love of cancelling plans at the last minute. Was it so wrong that we just wanted to go home and binge-watch *Chicago Fire*? We started watching *Chicago PD* and then we realized the characters crossed over from time to time, so we then became obsessed with catching up on *Chicago Fire*.

Although secretly, I thought it was entirely possible that we were still living in fear. When I started to notice this pattern, I remembered Alex's words "live fearlessly." I decided we would no longer be homebodies. One evening by the fire, we'd spent time making up a travel bucket list. In addition to Michigan, Alex wanted to take me to Napa Valley. Apparently, his friend Ethan's family had a winery there. I wanted to take him to a yoga retreat in the Dalmatian Islands. It didn't take much convincing, all I had to do was show him the boat that would sail us around the various ports in Croatia. I also think the opportunity for paddle boarding was rather appealing.

"Oh *my* God," Holliday chirped, and swiped the screen of her phone.

"What is it?" I asked, before taking a drink of my dirty martini.

She clutched the phone to her chest. "Okay, I have a huge secret, but I am bursting to tell someone. I've been biting my tongue all day."

Alex eyed her. "Well, if it's a secret maybe it should stay

a secret."

She waved him off. "Kill joy. You're no fun."

Ronan eyed her and shook his head. "Holliday, *no*."

Bless his heart, that wasn't going to keep her from spilling the juicy details to me. I was glad that I would be staying in the States permanently, because I was so happy to be getting to know Holliday and I loved having my brother so close.

I cocked and eyebrow. "Dish, girl."

Her face twisted up and she whisper screamed, "Grady James and Heather Young went to Vegas and got married. He's sent me a photo this morning, and now they're off to Belize for their honeymoon."

"No," I gasped and my mouth hung open in stunned silence.

Holliday shoved her phone at me and I saw the picture, proof positive these two had in fact tied the knot. "How long do you think it will last?"

I shrugged. "Millions of women across the world just had their hopes and dreams go up and flames. And you," I said, lifting my glass towards Ronan. "*You,* my brother, dodged a bullet. Heather is such a twat."

Holliday nearly choked on her mimosa. "I love your sister," she coughed out.

Ronan scowled at me. Alex just shook his head and took another sip of whiskey and then inquired about the purchase of the bar. I had a feeling Alex wanted in on that real-estate investment. Time would tell.

Our waitress approached with a huge smile. "Ready to order?"

The rest of our lunch was uneventful, but we had a lovely time.

Bonding over business led Ronan and Alex into topics surrounding baseball stats and country music. It was the oddest thing, but I was pretty positive that they were going to become good friends.

The sky changed from a peaceful shade of blue to a wondrous grey. Alex turned into the driveway and I swore I saw a snowflake skate across the windshield. I kept my focus on the glass and sure enough a flurry of heavy wet flakes appeared.

"First snow of the season," Alex pointed out as he parked the Range Rover.

"It's beautiful," I remarked, stepping out into the cold.

He rounded the front of the Range Rover with his hands in his pockets. "You're beautiful."

Unsure of how long we stood there admiring nature in all her beauty and catching snowflakes on our tongues, I felt a deep chill in my bones. My teeth chattered and Alex wrapped his arms around me from behind. I felt my insides melting despite the cold wind howling around us.

Alex punched in the security code from his phone as we skipped up the back steps. I opened the door and we tumbled inside. Alex stood before me, his hair wet from the snow and his hazel eyes shimmering with flecks of gold. He took my breath away. His arms banded around my waist and my body pressed against his.

He took my mouth in an urgent kiss and I pulled him closer seeking warmth. Unbuttoning Alex's coat, I tossed it onto the bench in the mudroom before removing my own. We stripped out of our wet clothes and I begged Alex to warm me up in the hottest part of the house he could think of.

With a flick of his wrist, his phone had lit up the living room fireplace. He grabbed my face and kissed me, his warmth radiating through my entire body.

"How did you know?"

Alex's teeth scraped across my earlobe and his fingers tangled in my hair. "How did I know you wanted me to fuck you in front of a roaring fire?"

"Naughty." I smacked his chest, his muscles flexed under my touch.

He picked me up and hauled me over his shoulder to the living room. When we were situated on the carpet, his hands massaged up my thighs and everything in me started to coil and tighten. My hands found their way over his shoulders and I guided him over me.

His head dipped to kiss me and his lips were everywhere—my lips, my cheeks, my throat, eventually making their way to my breasts where he sucked and licked until I was begging him to fuck me.

"I want you, Alex. I need to feel you inside of me."

His teeth grazed over my nipple. My arms wrapped around his neck, a gentle coaxing on my part to get him to give me what I wanted.

He pushed into me, rolling his hips, filling me completely. Moans of pleasure and seductive gasps for more accompanied the smooth slow strokes.

"You feel so good." My voice was breathy, my pulse racing.

Intensity flared in his eyes. He worked his hips and my fingernails dug into his waist.

"You're so perfect, *this* is perfect," he murmured.

I shifted my hips, stretching wide, he slid all the way in making me arch and cry out.

"I'm so deep inside you," he whispered darkly.

Tingles radiated and I could feel the deep ache of my orgasm taking hold. The muscles in his neck and shoulders pulled tight. I smoothed my hands up his back, crushing my lips to his, thrusting my tongue into his mouth.

He increased his rhythm knowing I was on the brink. "Get there, sweetheart," he rasped seductively, as he thrust up into me. "I'm close and I need you with me."

I churned my hips beneath him, chasing the orgasm that was so very close. His hips worked a magnificent speed that had me nearly combusting. He drew his thumb to my clit and wonderful waves of pleasure ripped through me. I let out a breathless cry followed by his name, "*Alex*."

And then he was right there going over the edge with me. On a groan, he fell on top of me, and then rolled to nestle beside me. We clung to each other, gasping for breath.

"You look so beautiful, all pink and flushed." His hand came up to the base of my neck. "I love you."

"I love you, thanks for making me all pink and flushed." I curled into him and we fell asleep tangled together. It was perfect and magical, and somehow I knew that it would always be like this with the two of us.

# Chapter Forty-Three

## Ella

***Several Months Later***

I lifted my head at the smell of warm cinnamon tickling my senses. Alex stood in the doorway of my office looking sexy as hell, wearing a blue t-shirt tucked underneath his leather jacket. My eyes admired his long muscular legs, his taut torso, and those brilliant hazel eyes, which never failed to say "come fuck me." He wasn't even naked, yet I had very dirty thoughts swirling through my mind.

*Holy hell, I'm one lucky girl.*

"What are you doing here?" I asked, glancing at the clock. It was half past eight, and I'd yet to finish number crunching the weekly sales report. Additionally, I had the open-to-buy plan that needed my attention along with a fashion edit for *One Park Avenue Magazine*. I was blown away when they'd asked me to guest edit for their March issue—next to the September issue, this was their second largest fashion edition.

"I just wanted to check on you, I know you've been working hard, tidying up loose ends before we leave."

"Aww, you're very sweet, but Tiffany and I have that covered. You don't need to worry about that."

"I sent Tiffany home, she has a boyfriend and it's her senior year, let her enjoy the last week of her winter beak."

"Damn, you're so nice."

He shrugged and pressed a kiss to my lips. "I can't help it, but you should know I did it for purely selfish reasons. So really, I'm not *that* nice."

I smiled. "Whatever you say, handsome."

After taking a sip of my coffee, I flipped off the music and closed down my laptop. The last few months had been amazing. Both of my stores had increased sales earnings by nearly twenty percent combined. Even though her store was not far from mine, Charlotte asked if I would carry some pieces from her collection. She'd apologized for her bad behavior at Holliday's birthday party and I accepted. She wasn't wrong in her actions, her timing sucked. We had a good conversation. Besides, we'd be family soon enough.

I pulled the report that I printed up from the copier. "When does our flight leave for Park City tomorrow morning?"

Ronan had been invited to attend The Sundance Film Festival as one of the judges. So he invited Alex and me to come as well. He and Heather Young were going to debut the trailer for their movie, *A Thousand Words,* at the Connolly Campaign Fundraising Dinner.

Alex eyed me over his cup. "Ten o'clock. Ronan called this afternoon and finalized the flight itinerary. He mentioned that Van Wyk is hosting a welcome party tomorrow night."

"Yeah, Holliday called earlier and said the same thing." I stood up and moved to the file cabinet, tucking away the latest sales figures. "She wanted that grey wrap sweater, the one with the zippers. I packed it along with a few other pieces that will be perfect for the snowy weather."

"You girls and your clothes," he mocked, shaking his head. "Your plan to squeeze me out of our closet is nearly complete."

"Why don't you just build me a bigger one?" I asked, shoving my laptop into my bag and hauling it up onto my shoulder.

"I'll get right on that with all the free time I have."

Alex had very little free time these days. He'd taken himself out of fieldwork completely and was perfectly happy being the boss. Tucked away in his office, he spent his days tracking logistics, monitoring intelligence and, because he could, he took on the occasional celebrity scandal. Patrick moved to Manhattan to run the New York office and Marcus was head commander in Grand Rapids. On top of all of that, he'd gone into business with my brother and they purchased O'Brien's Irish Pub. It was quite a coincidence that it held such special meaning for both my brother and me.

We drove into the city once a week because Alex agreed to see a therapist a few times a month to work through any guilt or fear issues that may still linger. I was so proud of him. He would get back to his neutral soon enough.

I rounded the corner of my desk and breezed to the stock room where I turned out all the lights and the sound system. My work could wait until the morning, or at the very least when I was on the jet. The only thing left to do was set the alarm and the security panel was near the front of the shop.

"Oh." I bumped his shoulder with mine. "Did I tell you that Tinley and Matthew invited us to a party at his house in Aspen after the festival?"

"What kind of party?" he asked, before tossing his empty coffee cup into the trash bin.

I shrugged. "She said it was an intimate affair, cocktail party, I assume."

He blew out a breath. "I'm going to need an assistant to help me keep track of my social life."

I laughed. "That's part of my job. I can help with all things pertaining to parties."

"Says the *former* party girl."

"Touché, but we can't spend all our time watching TV and hiding out."

"I like having you all to myself," he sighed, hitching his arms around my waist. "See, I am selfish."

"Live fearlessly," I reminded him, before pressing a kiss to his lips. "Also, love me fearlessly."

One night after dinner, I explained to Alex the meaning behind my tattoo, even during the darkest part of our relationship, I loved him and he loved me. I believed we could be together, loving one another without anyone or anything holding us back.

Fuck the rules. Fuck our rules. *God, we were so dumb.*

"Not a problem there."

"Good, let's get out of here."

After I locked my office, we walked down the hallway hand in hand. Life was good. Actually, it was better than good it was literally amazing. We spent Christmas with his family in Grosse Point and then we rang in the New Year lying on a beach in St. Barts. It was hard to imagine what my life was like before I met Alex. Our life was turning into one adventure after another and there was no one I'd rather be on that journey with.

On our way to the door, I stopped to pick up a scarf that

had fallen onto the floor.

Stepping behind me, where his hands fell to my hips, he whispered, "I had a dream that started this way once."

"Interesting . . . me bent over a table folding clothes?" I turned to face him. "Are you sure that wasn't you watching me doing the laundry?"

His lips grazed over mine, but he didn't kiss me. "Hand me that scarf and I'll show you." The heat of his voice matched the fire in his intense gaze.

Intrigued, I handed him the scarf. He led me across the sales floor to one of the columns in front of the dressing rooms. A smirked pulled at the corner of Alex's lips.

"Strip."

I arched a brow. "What now?"

"Come on, be a good girl and indulge me."

"Oh, so we do this sort of thing now," I said, gesturing from the column to the silk fabric he held in his hands.

He shook his head. "We do *not* have to do any sort of thing."

Still my curiosity got the better of me. "Perhaps I've had this dream once or twice myself."

Truth be told, I'd had a few dreams about being tied up, my nightmares had morphed into my fantasies. Maybe I was a little twisted.

"Really?" He cocked a brow and a smug smile crossed his face.

My lips twisted up. "I can practically hear your cock hardening at my admission."

"I love it when you talk dirty."

"Perhaps I need to have my head shrunk. I should make an appointment with your therapist."

"Don't knock it until you try it."

Without delay, I wiggled out of my jeans and tossed my blouse aside. Soon we were both naked in middle of my store. Thank God, the lights were out. Otherwise, everyone on Harbour Drive was going to get a sex show.

*Hmm, Amsterdam.*

He compelled me forward, bringing my hands around either side of the column. "Am I hurting you?"

"No," I answered truthfully feeling my nipples harden as they brushed against the cool concrete.

"Do you trust me?" he asked, wrapping the silk around my wrists, making a double knot.

"Absolutely."

Alex hadn't even touched me yet and I was already on fire for him. He moved to stand behind me. His fingertips whispered down my back, leaving hot trails of fire pricking every inch of my skin. The cold concrete was almost a welcome relief.

"Hello, gorgeous." The warmth of his breath fanned against my cheek, sending a delicious shiver down my spine.

"*Alex*." His name came out in a low moan. I rocked my body against his, feeling his cock against the swell of my ass. His hands drifted up my ribcage, cupping each breast and massaging in slow circles.

My head fell back against his shoulder. Nuzzling my hair out of the way, he kissed his way up my throat. His cock ground against my ass. I was so hot, I thought I might combust.

"I've been thinking about you all day. Did you know that?"

Aroused I trembled at his question. "Yes . . . I know."

I was incredibly wet, I felt the moisture pooling between my thighs.

With a quick thrust, he was inside me, rolling his hips

against me. Not being able to touch him was torture, even though I couldn't see him, I felt him, he was there touching me. Alex was everywhere—bound to me, not because of some silken fabric, or a paycheck for that matter, but because we lived inside each other. What we didn't know was that the stars definitely had a plan for us, and we were connected in a much bigger way.

"Give me everything, *Ella*."

The deep spasms of my orgasm rippled, lighting up every nerve in my body. His fingers dug into my skin as he picked up the pace. Driving his hips harder, I knew I was close, when my legs trembled and knocked against the pillar.

"Yes . . . Yes . . . More." My mind was foggy lost in a haze of lust.

"I want it all," he growled. "Fuck, you feel so good."

My walls constricted around him and I dove, plunging into a sea of ecstasy. He came with a quiet roar as his lips kissed between my shoulder blades. A litany of curses groaned into my skin.

"How about Amsterdam?"

"Did you say aftershocks?" I was mindless, the tremors continuing their relentless assault.

Naked and beautiful, he stood in front of me, a lazy grin attached to his lips. "I said, how about Amsterdam?"

"Oh, okay?"

"You used your out loud voice, again." He loosened the silk from my arms. "By the way, put this on my account." Alex pushed me back, gently massaging my arms. He brushed the hair away from my face and dipped his lips to mine, kissing me softly and slowly. I melted into him.

"Dinner?" he asked, his hands stroking up my back.

"In Amsterdam?"

He laughed. "You're adorable, I need to tie you up more often. Quick, what's my name?"

"William, was it?"

"Yeah, Kate, once upon a time, for *one* amazing night." He smirked, pulling his jeans up and over his hips.

"Wow, we've come full circle from role playing to bondage."

He pulled his shirt over his head. "That was hardly bondage."

"Kiss me, Alex."

"Oh," he prompted, as the pads of his thumbs stroked my cheeks. "So you do remember my name?"

"I could *never* forget your name."

# Epilogue

## Alex

*One Year and A Few Months Later*

"You have a son," Vince stated proudly, slapping my shoulder. "Congratulations, brother."

"He's just beautiful, Alex," Amanda said with a bright smile. Their daughter, Leandra, had just turned two not long ago.

"Thank you, we couldn't be happier," I said, placing him back into his bassinet.

Ethan stepped into the room with Nabila on his heels.

"It's almost time, buddy. You ready?" he asked, his hands digging into my shoulders.

"Oh, my little godson is positively adorable," Nabila cooed, adjusting Will's blanket.

Smiling, I motioned towards our nanny. "Rosie, could you take William up to the nursery?"

She nodded and then scooped him up into her arms. Rosie was so good with him. It was hard to believe he was already five months old. Vince and Amanda exited the house and joined the other guests on the beach.

"How's my girl?" I asked, standing in front of the mirror adjusting my tie.

"Ella's good. She can't wait to marry you."

"Excellent news," I said, clasping my hands together. "E, here's the deal. I need to get married. My bride and I have a plane to catch soon, and I'm very eager to celebrate properly."

"Well, I can't control the sun, buddy. You're the one who wanted to get married at dusk on a beach in June."

"Ahem, actually, Ethan, that isn't entirely accurate." At the sound of Ella's sweet voice, I covered my eyes.

"Ella, you know it's bad luck for us to see one another before the ceremony."

"Could you guys give us a moment? I need to speak to Alex."

The sound of heels clacking against the wood floor made my heart stutter in my chest. The blood rushed to my ears, and suddenly I felt faint.

*Quit being a pussy, Alex, and man up.*

"Sweetheart," I called over my shoulder. "If you are having second thoughts, now would be the time to tell me. I mean, it's totally okay. My mother is a little pissed at me that we aren't getting married in a church, but I know she'll get over it. Amy is going to tell her she's a Buddhist to take the pressure off us today."

Her hands came up to mine and then she pushed them away from my eyes, which I still kept screwed shut tight.

"Alex, look at me please."

I slowly peeled my eyes open. My jaw hit the floor. She was breathtaking, a vision in ivory, and that fiery red color slicked on her lips made my dick half hard. Half of her blonde hair was tied back with some loose pieces framing her face and long waves cascaded over her shoulders.

*Jesus Christ.*

The dress she was wearing hugged her in all the right places and showed off the fullness of her tits. Post baby, Ella was even more gorgeous. When I asked her to marry me, she was five months pregnant. She said no and then downed half a carton of ice cream. Later that evening, I found her crying in the shower mumbling about being bloated and ugly. I stripped out of my clothes and joined her, I kissed her everywhere and I didn't stop. I told her how much I loved her and that to me, she was the most beautiful woman in the world. Then we had the most amazing sex in the shower. Apparently, pregnancy sex was crazy hot.

*Who knew?*

In between shower sex and restocking the freezer with her favorite ice cream flavors, she agreed to marry me. I stared at the sparkling diamond on her left hand. Ronan set me up with his ring guy, Tomas, and I had the perfect ring designed—a four carat French Pave Halo diamond set in platinum. Her wedding band was a circle of shining diamonds. Combing two things she loved: the French style and classic details.

My fingers teased under the thin strap of her dress, brushing across the new ink above her breast. Roman numerals for the date we met, giving me a new reason to remember.

She dipped her head to meet my eyes. She was saying something, but it might as well have been in French because I was too busy admiring every inch of her body to hear anything.

"Babe, you look stunning," I said, sliding my hand over her stomach. I explored all the ways I would get her out of this dress. Short of ripping it, there was only one way that made logical sense, a zipper that started at the small of her back.

*Piece of cake.*

"Thank you, so do you," she said, running her hands up and over my chest. "This suit is incredible, the tailoring alone." Her eyes continued gazing over every inch of my dark blue suit.

My fingers tugged under her chin. "What's going on?"

She looked up at me, those bright blue eyes piercing my soul. "I don't think I can do it. It's all too much."

My arms wrapped around her waist, and I breathed in her flowery scent. "Okay, let's runaway and get married. I'll give Ethan the keys to our house and he and Nabila can take care of everything."

She shook her head, pounding a fist to my chest. "*Fuck*, I love you."

I swept her hair off her shoulder and then pressed a kiss to her golden skin. "I love you, too. Let me grab the keys to the Mercedes and the bags from the bedroom and then we can make like trees and leave."

"Babe, no, we have guests."

My lips brushed over the skin below her ear, and I felt my worry vanishing just like afternoon sun. Our guests were most likely sweating their balls off, so I needed to hurry this conversation along.

"So, you're going to marry me today?"

"Maybe, but I'm not going to be standing up there alone."

"No," I said, looking into her eyes. "Nabila, Tinley and Holliday will all be right behind you. And I'll be standing across from you."

She laughed. "Alex, babe, I'm pregnant—again."

"Holy shit, are you serious?"

She nodded and said, "Eight weeks. You must have some kind of mutated super sperm or something."

My arms wrapped around her, and I lifted her up off the

floor. "You have made me very happy."

"And you've given me more than I ever dreamed possible. The moment I laid my eyes on you, my whole world changed."

"So how about changing my world today and allow me to become your husband."

"Would it be possible to get some ice cream after the ceremony?"

I dropped a kiss to her forehead. "You can have all thirty-one flavors if you want."

I scooped up my bride, forgoing the tradition of having her father walk her down the aisle. The guy would have to forgive me. My reasons were twofold. One: We gave our son the middle name Carrick, aptly named after Ella's dad. Two: He already walked Molly down the aisle. Bonus: Ella and I were giving him another grandchild.

How mad could he be?

I carried her past the pool, across the lawn and up to the dune overlooking the ocean. I couldn't wait to marry this woman. Ella's father shot us a confused look and walked down the steps to stand by his family.

"We're pregnant!" Ella giggled raising her fist in the air. "Now marry me, Alex Robertsen, so we can go have sex!"

Ronan and his father narrowed their eyes at me.

*Shit. Maybe I should re-think Yemen.*

THE END

Books by Christy Pastore

THE WEEKENDS SERIES
*Fifteen Weekends*

THE SCRIPTED SERIES
*unScripted*
*Perfectly Scripted*

Be sure to sign up for my newsletter for the latest news on releases, sales, and other updates.

# Acknowledgements

When readers messaged me and asked for more from Alex it left me stunned. Alex was a secondary player in *Fifteen Weekends,* but his mystery and charm captivated readers and they fell in love with him. I was left with no choice but to write *his* story. After flipping through my notes and the small character bio I had created for him, it became quite clear that Alex's story began years before his tangled affair with Amanda. Alex had a lot to say, and so did Ella. I loved my time with both of these characters and giving them their Happily Ever After. Thank you for reading *Bound to Me.*

Special Thanks to my hubby Kevin who travelled with me to author signing after author signing supporting me in every aspect of my writing journey this past year. I am very lucky to have you aboard this train of epic awesomeness even when someone gets riled up about phone chargers. Without your love and support, I would be even crazier than I already am. I know that is hard to imagine. To sum up, it is without question, that you can handle a fuck-ton of crazy.

Next, I have to mention My Editor, Missy Borucki aka "The Comma Wrangler" Thank you so very much for your guidance, encouragement and for making the editing journey, dare I say, FUN?! Believe in miracles, fourth times a charm.

Robin Bateman, loads of thanks to you and your red pen for making sure that this book was perfectly polished. Perhaps one day I shall write a character just for you. Of course he will be the lumbersexual version of Tom Hardy. Also, if we happen to be in Chicago together ever, we MUST hit up Giordano's.

Kylie, Jeananna and the Give Me Books Promotions

Team, for the amazing cover reveal and launch. I very much enjoyed working with all of you.

Sara Eirew, thank you for the most unbelievably gorgeous cover. I am in awe of your talent as a photographer and a designer. This cover perfectly captures the overall feel of *Bound to Me*.

The reason the inside of this book looks absolutely beautiful is all thanks to Stacey Blake at Champagne Formats. Thank you so very much.

Andrea Joan, Thank you for loving Alex enough to help me envision his story with Ella. #LobstersForever

Kelly, where would I be without our morning conference calls . . . excuse me morning ops meetings? It's all fun and games until someone gets a screw, can't reach ones coffee, or nearly gets kicked out of Marriot. Iowa will never be the same. Your support and your invaluable feedback are more appreciated than you will ever know. And thank you for just making me fucking laugh and remember to take things day by day. To sum up: You look good.

Christina Manis Westrich, you came into my life like a beautiful shining light. This past year you have helped me in a bigger way than you will ever realize. It truly is the small things that make a really big difference. Thank you for being you. I love your face.

Rachel Blaufeld and Fabiola Francisco, seriously, I don't know what I would do without you both in my life. Thank you for the marathon support sessions via messenger or sometimes when a phone call is warranted. #SoapyThighsForLife

Jennifer Naumann, I adore you, and I am so freaking happy that we met last year. You're always there on the other end of the line listening, offering support or giving me a good laugh. Thank you for your friendship.

I'm lucky enough to have some special friends in my life – Alison aka Beatrice, Amy Kelly, Cori, Megan, Millie, Michelle Rodriguez, Patti, Susie, Melissa, and Kelly aka #FuckinJenny. This a mixed bag of things that kept me sane whilst writing this book, and it was all because of each of you—cocktails, game night, epic conversations with meme's, filling me in on the happenings of The Young and The Restless, drunk texts, hate watching The Bachelor, Bachelorette and Bachelor in Paradise (all with color commentary), vodka, cocktails by the pool, cocktails at the Fubar Lounge, more memes, Snap Chats during Game of Thrones and general debauchery.

Thank you to Josh Galloway for answering all the medical questions and talking out solid scenarios with me. You are now on speed dial.

Will Shouse, thank you for allowing me to pick your brain with all my questions. Your knowledge gave legitimacy to the characters in this book with a military past. Many thanks for your service to the United States.

To my Author Friends who inspire me and continue to believe in me—Alyson Reynolds, Ann Serafini, Anna Bendewald, Ashley Erin, BJ Harvey, Kate Canterbary, KI Lynn, Pawnie Santana, Stacey Lynn, and Skyla Madi. When I have a question no matter how big or small it's nice to have your words of wisdom and straight talk. I feel very lucky to have all of you in my life.

Each day, I am in awe of the incredible bloggers who work tirelessly to spread the word and love of our books to this community. From the bottom of my heart, thank you to those of you who took a chance on me, my misunderstood, bold heroines, and each one of my heroes—my swoony gentlemen with a naughty side.

# About the Author

Christy Pastore lives in the Midwest with her husband, two lovable dogs and their crazy cool cat. She has a Bachelor's Degree in Textiles, Apparel and Merchandising and Marketing. Writing has always been a part of her life. Her first writing gig was for a celebrity entertainment website. Later she went on to create her own blogazine and media company combining her love of writing with fashion and marketing.

When's she not writing flirty and dirty books or updating her celebrity fashion blog, she loves shopping online, binge watching her favorite shows and daydreaming.

She believes books, especially love stories are an escape from the real world.

A few of Christy's favorite things:
Bold Heroine's – Swoony Hero's with a Naughty Side— Guilty Pleasure Reads and TV Shows – Designer Handbags – Men In Suits – Black and White Photos— Sexy Accents— Snow— Pinterest – Twitter – Instagram— Wine— Champagne— Soy Latte's – Gummi Bears— Gourmet Grilled Cheese Sandwiches – Pickles—Popcorn— Sparkling Water— Eye Cream— Pedicures— Traveling— 80's Music— Musicals— Movie Trailers – Celebrity Red Carpet Interviews – Award Shows – Making Lists.

Please connect with me on:
www.christypastore-author.com
Facebook: www.facebook.com/ChristyPastoreAuthor
Twitter: twitter.com/christypastore
Send her an email: info@christypastore-author.com

51731568R00190

Made in the USA
San Bernardino, CA
30 July 2017